1

JESS

Ding!

> AUTO-TEXT ALERT:
>
> Your delivery has been left at your front door.
> Enjoy!

Excited, I hop out of the shower, singing along to "MMMBop" by Hanson.

I don't want to leave my delivery out in the hall too long. Either it'll get cold, or someone will walk by and snatch it, which sadly, has happened before.

Not on my watch.

The thought alone is enough to light a fire under my ass. Honestly, if that's the worst thing that happens today, then I'm doing better than great.

Opening the front door, I inhale the fresh air drifting into my apartment. May's warmth has replaced the chill of winter, and spring has firmly taken hold. My favorite season.

With a bounce in my step, I leave my apartment to pick up my order. It has been placed a few steps away, and excitedly, I twirl toward it. A considerable breeze blows through the open balcony doors, and I realize what's going to happen a second before it does.

The front door slams behind me.

Happiness turns to panic. I jiggle the handle and swear under my breath.

Locked. *Of course.*

"Well, shit."

I weigh my options. Here I am in my towel, yogurt-cucumber mask on my face, locked out of my apartment with a bag of food. The super-intendent is several floors down, but I don't want to take the elevator in my towel with no shoes—because, gross. Besides, he's been giving me the creeps, especially with the way he stares at my boobs. Nope, I'm good.

I have two neighbors down the hall: Lottie and Antoine. But they left for Paris in the early morning and won't be back any time soon.

Then I remember that someone just moved into the apartment next door and a brilliant idea comes to mind. Our balconies aren't too far apart. I can get back into my apartment from theirs.

Since the apartment has been empty for a long time, I'm dying to know as to who they are. Lottie caught sight of a man moving in, and upon my return from my trip to Scottsdale, she cautioned me that he's a *very* unfriendly character. Apparently, he didn't even bother with a simple "Hi" and instead, seemed to communicate through growls. Classic Lottie, with her flair for exaggeration. He's likely the regular friendly guy next door—poor Lottie just caught him in the midst of moving in.

After making sure the corner of my towel's tucked in, I knock on the door. "Hello?"

THE CEO ENEMY

JOLIE DAY

The CEO Enemy; Jolie Day

info@joliedayauthor.com

Cover Design: ARP Book Covers

ISBN: 9798328398770

For all the girls who dare to say no to the man in charge—this one's for you.

I know someone is home because I can hear the TV news. There's some movement, but it doesn't seem like they're coming to answer.

After a few seconds, I knock again, only louder this time.

"Hello? Anyone home? I need help!" I knock repeatedly. The door opens a second later. "Hi, there, sorry to bother y—*whoa*."

I can't believe I said that out loud, but I'm not even a little embarrassed about it.

He towers over me. *The* hottest man I've ever seen in my damn life.

This man is *at least* six foot one, rippling muscles, thick dark hair, chiseled jaw (under that thick weekend stubble), bright-green eyes piercing into my soul...and not a damn stitch of clothing on. Yeah. He's standing there completely naked. And here I am thinking that me in my small-ish pink towel, wearing nothing underneath, is weird. My eyes keep straying south—they have a mind of their own. I can't help but catch more than just a glimpse of the view below the horizon.

Yep. There's his dick.

Believe me, I'm as surprised as anyone else here. Even in its "relaxed" state, it's long and thick. Or is he half-hard? Because the size is quite impressive. Easily eight inches. Maybe nine. I'm staring...and disbelieving...and staring...until I realize what I'm doing and quickly avert my gaze back to his face.

My new neighbor looks alarmed, mad even, as if he's rushed to the door without bothering to dress.

His plump lips turn down in a frown as he stares at my face and the thick yogurt mask I slathered on this morning.

"What is it? What's wrong?" he demands, eyes narrowed.

Crap. Why am I here again?

Right, I'm locked out. "Um, sorry to bother you, but, um, I locked myself out of my apartment," I say, gesturing toward my door and the blueberry pancakes I ordered. As I speak, I realize how difficult it is to have a regular conversation when you've just caught an eyeful of all *that*.

"Well," he huffs, "unless you slipped a spare key under my door when I wasn't looking, then I'm not sure how I can help you." He arches an angry-looking brow.

"Er...do you maybe want to put clothes on?"

"I'd rather close the door if you don't actually need help," he grumbles, already in the process of swinging it shut.

"Wait! Please don't! I really do need your help."

I manage to keep my gaze trained on his, mind still reeling. He's a stranger who's incredibly pissed off that I'm bothering him. I better be quick. Also, my pancakes are getting cold, so I really need to get back inside my place.

"So, Ms. Lockout Queen, do you need me to call the super or something?" he asks, scrutinizing me the whole time.

What a jerk. "No, thanks." *Mr. Grumpy King*, I think, but I don't say it. "Actually, our balconies are right next to each other. I was wondering if you would let me in so I could climb over."

"No."

I blink a few times. "I'm sorry?"

"I said no."

"It will only take a second." A glop of yogurt starts to slowly slide down my forehead. Oh no, not now, please not now! I silently plead with it to stick to my eyebrow. *He won't let me in if I start dripping yogurt everywhere.*

"It doesn't matter."

All right. I understand that I barged into this grump's morning while he was obviously indisposed, and he has every right to be annoyed that this random chick yelled that she needed help, then ogled his manberries. That's on me for panicking and not keeping my eyes firmly locked on his face. However, he doesn't have to be an absolute *chumphead* about it. Lottie had understated this guy's irritability. I crown him the Emperor Extraordinaire of Grumps, the undisputed grumpiness monarch.

"Look, I'm sorry we started off on the wrong foot," I say, trying to take the high road, while casually flicking at my eyebrow, ensuring the gooey disaster stays put. I'm not going to get anywhere with this guy if he's pissed off at me. I gesture to his nakedness and then to my towel. "Clearly, neither of us had our 'social batteries' charged for this early-morning rendezvous. But I promise, it really will only take a second for me to hop over to my place. Then I'll leave you alone."

He gives me a stern look. "Climbing between balconies is reckless and unsafe."

"I'll be fine."

"And if you're not? I'm not going to be held responsible if something happens to you."

"Fine," I say, attempting to keep the exasperation from my tone. "If I promise not to sue you if I get hurt, then will you let me in?"

He studies me for a moment, and it's hard to get a read on him. His expression holds nothing but annoyance, though I'm hopeful I've gotten through to him, considering he hasn't slammed the door in my face yet. I offer him a bright smile.

There's a moment's pause before he mutters something under his breath and steps to the side. "Fine. Come in."

Thank God! I want to do a little happy dance, but well, I'm trying not to lose my towel.

Before entering his apartment, I grab my food delivery and give my towel an extra little tuck for good measure. As soon as I take that first step inside, *plop* goes the yogurt—not this again, and *OMG*—I catch it just in time. Then, discreetly as possible, I wipe it on my towel. I don't think he noticed.

Crisis averted... for now. I'm in!

The place looks minimalistic. Sleek. Somehow bachelor-esque with all the black furniture and monochrome artwork. I spot a black helmet. He rides a motorcycle? Hot!

At once, I realize he was exercising. I notice his treadmill and weights near the balcony, and there's a pile of workout clothes on the floor. He must have been on his way to the shower when I knocked. I should have known he works out. With that body, it's safe to say he's not the "lounge around all day" type.

"Just a second," he mutters, storming down the hall, and that's when I catch a glimpse of his other side, and oh, boy, it's just as appealing as the first. I'm pretty sure I could bounce a quarter off his ass if I had the chance.

Awkwardly, I stay put, switching my weight from one foot to the other, playing with the paper bag in my hands. He returns wearing a simple pair of black boxer briefs. They cover his assets, but honestly, the outline still makes quite the statement.

"The balcony is this way." He motions with his inked arm for me to follow him.

Dear God, his back is rippling with muscles, something I missed when checking him out below the waist. How does someone get that well defined? I don't have the energy for exercise—unbelievable, I know.

I tear my gaze away to focus. When did I become so easily distracted by a man? True, it's been a while since I've had any action, but I didn't think it had been long enough for my knees to just go all wobbly in the presence of a tall, chiseled, tattooed, but let's not forget, rather chilly... let's be clear: masterpiece of grouchiness.

Once we step outside, reality slaps me in the face, and I wince. Crap. The balconies are a little farther apart than I originally thought. Not ridiculously far, only a couple of feet. The distance is still manageable. However, it does make this whole thing a tad riskier. Setting my bag of pancakes down, I move to the edge to get a closer look, trying to figure out what my best move might be.

"We're really high up," my neighbor says. "You know what, I'm going to call the super."

"Nonono, absolutely not necessary. I got this. Easy-peasy. Just...stay there in case I slip or something."

"I thought you said you could handle this?" He sounds even more irritated than before.

I glance back at him to find he hasn't followed me out onto the balcony. He stands in the doorway, tattooed arms crossed, that frown still etched in place. Geez, doesn't this guy have any other facial expressions?

"I can," I tell him. "Doesn't mean I'm immune to the effects of gravity. It might be easier if you come out and spot me. Just in case."

He shakes his head, a protest clearly on his tongue. When he notices that I'm already maneuvering my right foot over the railing, he quietly steps out and moves closer to me. "I got you."

The weight in his voice gives me a warm feeling. My heart flutters as he draws near. Deep down, I know that if anything were to happen, he would have my back. At least in this crazy endeavor. With those muscles, he'd definitely be ready to snap me back up!

But let's be real here. I can already sense it. This is shaping up to be the most awkward moment of my life.

As I carefully maneuver my other leg over the railing, I try to keep my breathing even and focus on *him*, the grim culmination in front of me, in an attempt to avoid looking down. I stand on the other side of the railing, gripping the metal so tight my knuckles turn white.

"Talk to me," my neighbor says.

At the sound of his deep, but surprisingly calming voice, I take a slow breath. "Okay..."

"Now, come back. Careful there. Don't think about the height."

Instantly, I have the urge to look down, and I have to fight it. "Easier said than done."

"Hey, look at me."

I lift my gaze to meet his green eyes. I have never seen eyes with such an enchanting shade reminiscent of lush pine trees, and it takes my thoughts away from my precarious situation. I could easily lose myself in the depths of them...

"You got this," he says. "Slowly. No need to rush."

Nodding, I take another deep breath, tearing my gaze away from the most distracting male specimen I've ever encountered. I figure it will be *hard* to pay attention to what I'm doing if I'm ogling him. Rotating, I face my balcony, and I'm slapped with a gust of wind that nearly sends me flying. The shriek that escapes is foreign to me, practically enough to make me backtrack and say, "Screw it." The last thing I want to do is go *splat*, almost naked, on a Manhattan sidewalk.

No. Thank. You.

"Whoa there," he says, grabbing me like his life depends on it. "Come back. Now."

I can't suppress a surprised squeak, my heart fluttering at the unexpected closeness. "Whoa, buddy, I barely know you," I tease.

But after a moment's pause, with his strong arms enveloping me from behind, I think I'm good.

I can't stop now.

I'm almost there.

It'll be way easier to follow through instead of turning back at this point. Cautiously, I stick my foot out until I feel the ledge. I find it easily and, in one smooth movement, I step over and grab my railing. Dear God, if anybody were to look up, they'd be treated to a firsthand view of what not to wear on a balcony.

Phewwww.

My adrenaline is through the roof. I'm proud of myself as I straddle the railing. Almost there.

Ufff. Thank goodness.

When I glance back at my neighbor, he still has that serious expression he's been sporting since he opened the door. But I notice his shoulders slump and some of the tension leaves his body.

"See?" I say with a grin, lifting my other leg over. "Ha! Piece of cake. Told ya!" I shrug, waving it off like I've been doing this all day, every day.

"Call me Lockout Queen by day, and Balcony Spider-Woman by night," I joke.

I'm too focused on my triumph to notice that my towel has become loose. The next thing I know, I'm standing on my balcony all right, with my towel on the floor and *everything* on display for a complete stranger. Yes. I'm talking tits and delicate lady bits, officially making their debut. A balcony drop and a towel flop! Way to keep things interesting, life.

Seriously, though: piece of cake, *my ass.*

My neighbor's eyebrows shoot up.

For the first time since we've met, that surly exterior cracks. His face maintains its stern expression, but there's a subtle uptick at the corner of his mouth. "Yeah, I can see a piece of something," he rumbles, rubbing the stubble along his jaw.

Blushing? Check.

Unforgettable? Yep.

Embarrassment? Absolutely nailed it.

"Well, at least we're even now," I say, picking the darn towel up and hurriedly clutching it to my chest. My cheeks are hot with embarrassment, but I try not to make a big deal of it. There is no need to make this moment any more memorable than necessary. Also, thank goodness I shaved this morning.

"Can you hand me my pancakes?" I ask, because: priorities.

The serious expression is back—so quickly that I think I might have imagined the other look. He picks up the bag of food and moves toward me. There's a pause before he reaches across the gap to hand me the pancakes.

"You know," he says, "you could've left the food in front of your door and circled back to it."

Yeah, and risked locking myself out again? But I don't say that. "Thanks," I say politely. "Nice meeting you."

"I don't know about nice," he grumbles. "We'll say it's been *eye-opening.*"

Desperate to end this interaction and figuring I have wasted enough of this guy's time, I hurry back into my apartment (kinda angling sideways to spare him from any accidental ass exposure). I'm shaking, but I'm not entirely sure it's from the little Spider-Woman stunt I just pulled.

It isn't until I close the balcony doors behind me that I realize I didn't even get his name.

Nothing like walking in on a naked man and then accidentally flashing him without even knowing who the hell he is.

He looks like a Gideon. Or a Roderick. No, wait, he could be a Damian. In no way is he a Peter (you know, as in Peter Parker, the civilian identity of my ultimate hero Spider-Man—the always-friendly neighborhood guardian).

From his cage, Pippin squawks and flaps his wings. Sometimes, he's such a little grump, too, and that's honestly one of the many things I love about him. But right now, it seems as if he's laughing his ass off, having watched the whole thing. His cage is right by my balcony so he can look out when I'm away. Double-checking the balcony doors are closed, I walk over and open it, putting my hand in so the rescue parakeet can hop onto my finger. Sometimes he nips it, but not this time. Oh, no. This time, he happily complies, and I pull him out.

Petting him instantly puts me at ease. I'm good. Everything's fine. I made it back inside safely. *He* will forget this happened. Just like me. Pippin lets me stroke his head a few times before half-flying, half-hopping onto my shoulder. His wings are partially clipped and still in the process of growing back out, which means he can't go far. It's the only reason I let him roam free at times.

When I got him, the woman from the rescue pet shelter, Rose, had warned me that he hadn't warmed up to anyone. He just needed time. As surly as he can be, he can also be a sweetie. Not many people think birds can be as loving as cats or dogs. I know better.

"You are not going to believe what I've been just through," I tell him. "I met a guy grumpier than you."

2

SEAN

*T*hat was *not* how I expected my morning to go.

I didn't expect to be interrupted. I had already torn off my sweaty clothes on my way to the shower after my daily intense exercise routine when someone started banging on my apartment door. Normally, I would have ignored it. But when a frantic voice from the hall asked for help, I reacted before I could throw some clothes back on.

I don't know why I let her in.

After all, I only moved in a week or so prior, and the last thing I needed was my neighbor falling from my apartment.

Clearly, she was either overconfident or batshit crazy, although her big blue eyes gave me no indication of that. She had to be, to think climbing from one balcony to the other was the best course of action for her predicament. I nearly had a heart attack when she did. Thankfully, it went smoothly. However, it didn't silence the swearing spree echoing in my thoughts. It would've been much safer and smarter to let me call the damn superintendent of the building. Then again, if I had, I wouldn't have caught an eyeful of her naked body. I knew the towel was going to fall the second before it did. A true gentleman might have averted his gaze, but I needed to keep my eyes on her for safety's sake. So, I was met with smooth skin dusted with freckles, full tits, curved hips, and a shaved pussy.

Overall, not a bad visual to have first thing in the morning.

However, she isn't my type.

In fact, she's everything I dislike in a woman. Bubbly. Chatty. Way too enthusiastic, almost unsettlingly so, and more importantly, full of stupid ideas.

Me, I don't waste time on foolish or illogical concepts. I have way too much on my plate. There isn't room in my life for anything aside from work. Least of all a woman who won't give me a moment of rest with her endless stream of nonsense. When things inevitably fell apart, which I know they would, based on my track record, living next to her would be hell.

She has the looks, but when it comes to smarts—not so much.

A quick check of the time has me swearing. It's 7:14 a.m.

I have to shower, shave, and get ready for the day. Getting naked again, I jump in the shower, relaxing as my aching muscles respond to the hot water. My mind hasn't quite let go of that dropped towel. My dick twitches with interest, and without thinking twice, I reach down to touch myself.

I'm no stranger to getting off after a good exercise. Normally, it's my preferred choice of cardio when I'm sleeping with someone. If I'm single, I have no qualms about taking care of it myself. Today is one of those days. The only difference is, I don't take too long to come up with a visual. I can imagine how soft her skin would be under my hands, how it would feel to squeeze those hips after I yank her into the shower with me.

Steadying myself with one hand on the wall, the other tightens around my dick. I think of that body, wet and soapy as she rubs against mine. Her soft nipples, resting on top of perfectly full, taut curves, would pucker into firm peaks under my glancing touch, begging me to suck on them. I'd let my tongue brush from one to the other, and then slide down, spreading her smooth pussy lips to taste her sweet cunt. How easy it would be to pick her up, to pin her to the wall while I fucked her.

Well, maybe not her specifically but probably someone with a similar body. My mouth would latch onto that pale throat, and I'd kiss and suck until I marked her, claimed her.

I don't hold back my groan when I come hard, the water cascading down my body to carry away the evidence of my release. A calmness settles over me as I catch my breath.

Beep-beep!

My phone alarm sounds from the other side of the shower curtain, and I quickly wash myself and get out.

My neighbor has thrown off my morning routine, and I wasted precious time. Now I have to hurry to dress for work. If she had interrupted any other morning, I probably wouldn't be so fucking annoyed. My phone has been going off with texts and emails from the various managers, sending me their daily reports and updates. Nothing major requires my immediate attention, except one thing.

I have an important meeting in about half an hour, and I will not let the incident make me late. I didn't take Blackwood Holdings Inc. to billion-dollar status by dragging my feet. And I'm not going to let a too-cheerful neighbor derail my morning.

No matter how many hotels or motels I buy, I still love the process. I see things in a way no one else does. I know that I can take any drowning business and turn it around. I have done it hundreds of times before, and I will keep doing it as long as I enjoy the work.

However, the current hotel chain I have set my sights on will be a challenge. It has changed hands multiple times since its construction, with varying results.

The first time I visited the New York property, I immediately saw the potential. I knew it could be bigger and better. And I knew exactly how to make that happen. I convinced the owner, Norman Whitman, that I could take over his shares and make something of them. He had been reluctant, at first. I told him we would only make things better, and when I made him one final offer he couldn't refuse, he agreed to sell.

He has a co-owner who still owns the other shares, but she won't be a problem.

I'm not one to have a partner.

Things are hectic enough with the board of directors of Blackwood. Doesn't matter, I'm not concerned. I like a challenge. My closing rate for sales is nearly one hundred percent, and no matter what that co-owner throws at me, I know I can convince her to sell me her half. I've already convinced Norman. Once he signs, there won't be anything she can do to change it. Even if she protests, the ink will already be dry. She'll have to deal with the board just like I do.

If she doesn't like it? Tough. She can sell to me and leave.

With that in mind, I forget about my neighbor and finish getting ready to meet Norman. It will be a stimulating one, that's for sure. Legal has already drawn up the final sales papers.

It's a now-or-never deal.

All that is left is to sign on the dotted line.

3

JESS

*a*h, it feels nice being back in New York after two weeks of taking care of my elderly aunt Bernice in Scottsdale, Arizona.

I co-own a small chain of hotels.

The Westerlyn Hotels. Short: WH.

They are a small chain comprised of four hotels spread throughout the East Coast. Nowadays, I work out of the New York City branch.

My fellow co-owner is a kind older man named Norman Whitman. Five years ago, he sold me an equal share of the hotels, establishing a 50-50 ownership split, in the hope I'd assist him in restoring them back to their former glory. A significant advantage of equal ownership lies in its inherent fairness. Norman and I are in this together, equally committed to making this business a success.

Luckily, we're always on the same page, so deadlocks are not a concern for us.

Dropping my life savings into the failing hotel chain drew plenty of "you're crazy" comments. Let me tell you, the journey to my dream wasn't all sunshine, pancakes, and cute parakeets. But, as we near the quarter's end, the hotel is on a streak with two back-to-back profitable runs—nothing flashy, but hey, a win is a win, especially in these challenging times.

My first stop is the main lobby.

Construction crews finished right on schedule and walking through the bright, remodeled entrance makes my heart swell. They have brought the original mahogany woodwork back to its past magnificence, and the wood grain tile floors have been polished to perfection. I can see my reflection as I walk across them past the tulips that grace the room and contribute to the inviting atmosphere. All the old lobby furniture has been replaced with new fresher items, without sacrificing comfort, and the walls on the left and right are filled with local artwork, depicting iconic New York City scenes. However, the central piece for the lobby is still pending. I attempted to secure tickets for a charity auction where my favorite native New York artist is set to reveal her latest undisclosed artwork, but unfortunately, they were all sold out. When my aunt called for assistance, everything else had to take a back seat.

"Good morning, Ms. Summers, how lovely to have you back," the front desk manager, Emma Simpson, says with a bright smile, and gets up to give me a hug over the counter. She's in her late fifties, originally from England, and had been working at the hotel long before Norman or I took over.

"It looks great in here," I say, my eyes sweeping across the room. "That crew did an amazing job."

"They really did," Emma agrees. "I'm so relieved I won't need to direct guests around the ongoing construction any more. It looks like we're finished with the room renovations now, is that right?"

"Most of them. We're still planning a few finishing touches on the suites. And deciding on the main art piece for the lobby. How are we looking?"

Emma's smile grows wider. "Reservations just snapped up the last available room, which means we're fully booked for the rest of the month."

Excitedly, I knock on the counter. "That's what I like to hear. Have you seen Norman?"

"He's not in yet, Ms. Summers."

Hmm, that's somewhat unusual. On weekdays, he typically arrives first. "All right, thanks."

I leave the lobby and head for Operations.

W hen I arrive, the crowd of housekeepers is already dispersing to go about their business.

I poke my head into the big office and smile. "Good morning, Pauline!"

Pauline Kent, Director of Housekeeping and certified best friend since childhood, looks up from her computer. "Have I told you how annoyingly cheerful you can be in the mornings?" she quips in her low, deadpan voice, only the subtlest hint of a smirk gracing her lips.

"You're only saying that because you're jealous."

"I'm saying that because it's true." She gets up to wrap one arm around me in a hug, pressing her big motherly bosom into me.

"You look like you need this," I say, handing her the holder with her cinnamon latte with oat milk, plucking out my iced French vanilla with a shot of espresso.

"Glad to have you back, Jess. How's your aunt's leg?"

"Thanks, doing much better," I say, propping myself on the edge of the desk. "Did you hear the great news?"

Pauline takes a sip of her latte and leans back in her chair. "Yup. Sold out for the month." She lifts her hand for a high-five, which I happily grant. "I'm proud of you. Don't get me wrong, Mr. Whitman is a sweetheart, but he would still be running around like a chicken with his head cut off if you hadn't swooped in."

I smirk and reach over to playfully flick her nose. "I'm going to remember you said that any time you want to mention how crazy you thought I was for buying into these hotels."

"Oh, you were absolutely batshit to do what you did. Especially after what happened with Mr. Asshole Ex."

"Ugh, don't ruin my good mood by mentioning *him*. Besides, I have something much better we can talk about."

Pauline arches an eyebrow with interest. "Oh? Do tell."

"I met my new neighbor."

"How did that go?"

How did that go? That mental image of his body pops into my head, and there's a little twinge of "Ooh-la-la!" in my gut. I do a quick glance out the door to make sure none of the other employees are hanging around before I update her with a quick summary of this morning's events, throwing in a detailed account of the, ahem, unexpected nudity I stumbled upon (while conveniently omitting any mention of the glory *he* witnessed). When I finish my story, Pauline looks upset.

"Oh, my God," she says, shaking her head in disbelief. "What the hell were you thinking climbing balconies like Spider-Woman? You're lucky you didn't fall to your death."

"Agree, not my finest moment. At least I got a nice eyeful."

We continue our in-depth analysis of his "assets." It's possible that the term "perfect" slips into the conversation at some point.

"*Damn*." She eventually sighs. "That's a shame on the personality. The gorgeous ones usually are a pain in the ass."

I take a sip of my French vanilla coffee. "Well, ain't that the truth."

By the time I get to my office, Norman is in. My and Norman's assistant, Sarah, gets up to greet me with a big hello and warm hug before she returns to her phone call.

"Hey, Norm, look who's back," I say with a smile, entering his office. "Glorious day, isn't it?"

Norman looks up at me, and instantly I know something is off. Any other day, he'd cheekily return my smile and ask me how I'm doing, how my travel went, and if Aunt Bernice couldn't have managed without me. I'd chuckle, in light of the hilarious tale of her "broken leg" that turned out to be nothing more than a sprained ankle. She's quite the dramatic character, that's for sure.

This time, he smiles, but it doesn't reach his eyes. He doesn't even wear one of his signature silly ties. That's a first. "Morning, Jess. Glad you're back."

"Everything okay?"

Norman is quiet for a moment before he stands from his desk. "Let's walk."

Worried, I take a long sip of my coffee as I follow him out of the office. Norman usually only asks to walk when there's something on his mind. Even though I'm concerned, I try not to get anxious. We're doing well. All properties are finally generating profits, and as far as I know, renovations have stayed within budget.

"What do you think about the renovations so far?" I ask, trying to keep things light. "The crew did an amazing job."

"The hotel is beautiful, it's inviting, and the lobby is flooded with sunlight. I never thought I would get to see it all restored." His voice is tight, and I notice he's trying to avoid eye contact.

"Norman, what's wrong?" I ask. "I can tell something is up. You know you can tell me anything."

"I know, Jess. I just know you're not going to like what I have to say."

My stomach churns, and I have to take another sip of cold coffee to steady my nerves. "Just come out and say it. Whatever it is, I can take it."

Norman sighs and finally looks at me. "I sold my shares of the hotels."

I nearly trip over my own feet.

Stopping in the dead center of the hall, I stare at Norman, unblinking. He couldn't have possibly said what I think I heard.

"Please tell me you're joking," I say.

"I'm not."

I stand there, unable to wrap my head around this information.

I can tell by the look on his face that he's one hundred percent serious. Not that he's one to make a joke in poor taste, but still. This *cannot* be happening. After everything we've been through together and all the hard work we've put into the place, I can't believe that he up and sold his half of the properties, especially without telling me about it first.

Then it hits me: He didn't have to.

In the early days, when Norman and I teamed up to start our partnership, we hammered out an agreement that gave either of us the green light to sell our fifty percent ownership stake in the hotel chain without needing other partner's consent—as long as we found a buyer who met specific qualifications, like financial stability and industry experience. Back then, it actually was *me* who suggested it, appreciating the idea of an easy exit strategy. This way, if, for any reason, I didn't enjoy working alongside Norman or, more crucially, if he turned out to be as unscrupulous as the man I once loved, I'd have a perfect escape route in place.

The irony of it all! Never in a million years did I anticipate that Norman would be the one considering a departure.

"Norman, I was only gone for two weeks! Why didn't I know this was happening?" I demand, puzzled. "Are you in some sort of extreme midlife crisis?"

"I suppose I am." Norman puts a comforting arm around me, rubbing my shoulder. "Jess, I'm old," he says, the wrinkles of his face somehow becoming more prominent under the new light fixtures. Or maybe I'm finally realizing that he truly isn't the youngest anymore. "I have been doing this for decades. I'm ready to retire, have been for a long time. I never thought this day would come. To be honest, if it wasn't for you and all your hard work, I wouldn't have even considered it."

My heart goes out to him. But that doesn't stop me from also feeling upset. "Then why didn't you sell all your shares to *me*?" I ask. "I would have happily bought you out."

"Jess, you don't have the money, and taking on debts is out of the question. And before you say anything, you've already poured so much of your heart and soul into these hotels. If you took on all this by yourself, you'd be burned out by the time you're forty. I couldn't do that to you."

As the reality of the situation starts to sink in, I can barely keep my growing distress from seeping into my voice. "That's a sacrifice I'm willing to make, and it's my choice, Norman! I don't like the idea of some rando suddenly coming in and trying to change things."

"I was concerned about that as well. The 'rando coming in' will serve as a co-owner and adviser, rather than assuming a managerial role. He will give you guidance—nothing more, nothing less. Trust that I wouldn't have gone through with the sale if I wasn't completely sure it would be in the hotels' best interest."

"Norman—"

He cuts me off by putting his hands on my shoulders and staring directly into my eyes. "I know you can handle this place on your own," he says. "Me selling to someone else has nothing to do with questioning your abilities. I mean this in the best way possible. Now that we're in the green, I sold to someone else for your own good. All right?"

For my own good? Who is he to decide what's good for me?

"Did you already sign the papers?" I ask.

"Yes. About half an hour ago. I was presented with a 'take it or leave it' deal."

Dammit. Observing a profit in both the current and upcoming quarters, Norman saw the chance to negotiate the optimal offer for his exit. It's a fundamental principle of economics that the value of a thriving and profitable business increases significantly when considering a sale. It's likely why he had gotten an interesting offer in the first place. "Who did you sell it to?"

Norman hesitates.

"Is that a secret too?" I push.

"You'll meet the new owner soon enough," he finally says. "Tomorrow, in fact. Now, before you say anything else, he's a CEO, an accomplished figure in the hotel industry, a billionaire mogul, with a track record of turning struggling properties into extraordinary successes. In fact, his success in the field is unparalleled—nobody does it better than him. He'll be good for this place, and for you—"

"Who is it?" I interrupt him.

"Mr. Blackwood of Blackwood Holdings Inc."

Blackwood? I gulp. I've certainly heard of Blackwood—everyone in the hotel business knows that Blackwood Holdings Inc. is a colossal conglomerate holding "Blackwood Hotels & Resorts" under its umbrella. However, I've never had the privilege of meeting the company's mighty chief executive. They label him as cold, calculating, and ruthless.

But one should never take rumors at face value. These same allegations had once swirled around Norman, and we all know how that turned out—he's a secret softie who showers his wife with handwritten love notes. Perhaps the new mystery CEO has a hidden fondness for kittens and cries during romantic comedies.

"The meeting with Mr. Blackwood is scheduled for tomorrow at 11:30 a.m.," he says.

Swallowing past the lump in my throat, I sigh heavily, grappling with the desperate reality of it all.

To be fair, a small part of me *does* understand why he brought someone else on board. If I'm completely honest, it makes perfect sense. Taking on all the responsibility of managing the hotels would be a monumental task (not to mention the added challenge of incurring debt), and although I don't doubt that I would have crushed it, it definitely would have taken over my entire life. Norman has a wife and kids —kids he freely admits he wasn't around for as much as he would have liked. I would like to have a family someday. And running the chain on my own wouldn't leave room for anything else.

Anyway. What's done is done.

"I understand," I tell him, trying a weak smile. "And I really am happy that you're finally retiring. I'm going to miss you."

"I'm going to miss you too, kid." He gives me a brief hug before he pulls away and straightens his tweed jacket. "Come on, let's do our morning walk-around, and I'll brief you on what you'll need to handle for a while until you re-delegate the tasks. But first..." He reaches into his jacket and pulls out a big envelope, his eyes glinting with mischief, "...here's a little something for you."

"What is it?" I ask.

"A ticket to the charity auction next month."

My eyes widen in surprise. "But they were sold out! And the prices are through the roof!"

He chuckles. "Well, someone cancelled, and I may have sweet-talked my way in. Perks of persistence, you know?"

I pull the thick burgundy ticket out of the envelope in disbelief, and choke up. My fingers run over the intricate smooth finish. Its opulence is overwhelming. The words "Grand Hospitality Affair" are elegantly embossed with gold metallic accents. Norman must have invested a substantial six-figure amount for the high-profile auction.

"Enjoy, I know you've always wanted to go."

I'm over the moon, and the idea of attending alone doesn't bother me in the slightest. "Norman. You shouldn't have—"

"Think of it as an investment in the right art piece for the lobby... *and* a small gesture to mend any lingering grievances between us. So you keep me in good memories."

My shoulders drop. "Well, I suppose that's a pretty clever move," I tease.

He brings me into a fatherly hug. While Norman's news has thrown me for a loop, it's hard to stay mad at him, and I'm determined to look on the bright side.

Change is good.

It's a normal part of life.

Change shouldn't be feared.

Maybe the new owner won't be so bad. At least it won't be me training a newbie with zero experience. I'll be working with a peer who understands. Perhaps he can offer valuable insights. Maybe I can learn a thing or two from Mr. Billionaire Mogul.

These positive thoughts get me through the rest of the day and help me look forward to our meeting.

Everything is going to turn out perfectly fine.

4

SEAN

*D*one and done.

Deal closed. Papers have been signed.

The meeting with Norman Whitman went off without a hitch.

I'm on a roll.

The board has been on my ass about closing the deal, and I'll be glad when they can focus on other matters. Securing the other half of the Westerlyn Hotels is our top priority, and I have full confidence that we'll achieve it. However, my father, Douglas Blackwood, the board's head, isn't exactly known for his patience. My relationship with him is strained at best. He's always been more of a boss than a father, even before I started working alongside him.

Right on time, I stride into the headquarters of Blackwood Holdings Inc., a towering high-tech construction of gleaming steel and tinted glass. With our many hotel and resort properties spread across the East Coast, we set up shop in New York City because it made sense. Our first hotel was in the city. Understanding the power of NYC connections is fundamental in my line of work. Our company is proud to be located in one of the city's leading high-rises, with the executive offices on top.

When I walk into my office on the polished granite floor, my personal assistant, Jasmine Williams, smiles up at me. She's in her late fifties, always impeccably dressed, and her black hair is neatly tied up in a tight bun. Sometimes she acts more like a mother than an assistant, fussing over me and making sure I actually take my breaks and have something for lunch. But I let her get away with it because she's a good worker.

"Good morning, Mr. Blackwood," she says. "There are several messages in your inbox. The paperwork for the Westerlyn Hotels has been filed with Legal, and everything is set for the transition to Blackwood. Oh, and your meeting with the board is in one hour."

"Good. Anything else I need to know?"

"Mr. O'Malley is back from his business trip."

"Let him know I'm in. Otherwise, hold my calls."

"You got it."

I go into my office and close the door behind me. Outside, the sun is bright, and my view of the city stretches for miles with the cloudless sky. I ignore it, more interested in the steaming coffee cup on my desk. Some of the black liquid is downed in one gulp. I settle in my chair and pull over my work tablet to review some documents. These are the same papers I meticulously reviewed before signing off on the Westerlyn Hotels acquisition, but now, with the ink dry and the deal sealed, I revisit some of the financial reports and the property's history.

Tomorrow, I'm headed to the hotel to meet the co-owner. While I've found that ninety-nine percent of partners who initially refuse to sell change their minds once they glimpse those zeros on the check, there's no harm in fine-tuning my pitch and preparing for the next phase.

About half an hour later, my office phone rings. "What?"

My assistant's voice comes through. "Mr. O'Malley is here."

"Let him in."

"Of course, sir."

Knock-Knock. Knock-Knock.

The door of my office opens, and Connor O'Malley walks in. A tall, buff guy born and raised in Ireland, Connor looks like he would be more at home in a garage or as a nightclub bouncer rather than in an office. Because of that, a lot of people tend to underestimate him. He's one of the slickest, smartest sales associates I've had on my staff. My closest buddy for at least a decade, he's one of the few people in my immediate circle who I trust completely. I know that if I ask him to do something, he'll get it done and get it done right.

"The meeting went grand. I've got those eejits eatin' out of me hand," he says in his Irish accent, his tone a mix of triumph and amusement, as he makes a jerking-off motion. With a sly grin, he plops onto the chair across from my desk. "Them seaside cabins in northern Providence are a sure thing. Sky's the limit from here! How's Westerlyn?"

"Whitman's signed and sealed. Have the paperwork right here."

"Grand job! Delighted the auld fella didn't give ya any trouble."

"Nah, I didn't expect him to. He's been ready to retire for eons. Told me how excited his wife is to spend her days on her own island off Bali."

"What about the co-owner?"

"What about her? She can either get on board or sell."

"*Exactly.* If she starts givin' us grief, she can cop on or jog on."

I shrug, pushing the paperwork aside and picking up my coffee again. "I'm prepared to handle anything she throws my way. From what I've gathered, her experience and negotiation skills pale in comparison to Norman Whitman's. Once we extend an offer, she'll be reaching for the nearest pen and saying *sold*!"

"You know what this calls for, don't ya?" Connor grins wider, leaning back in his chair. "Pints. Tonight."

I make a face. "I'm not in the mood."

"Oh, come on! You're never in the mood."

"And yet, you always drag me along."

"Because you're no craic anymore, Sean. If I didn't drag you out every now and then, you'd waste your life away workin' and sulkin'. And sure what kind of friend would I be if I let that happen to ya?"

He has a point. I consider his offer as I sip the rest of my coffee. "I'll think about it," I say. "It depends on how my board meeting goes."

Connor makes a face. "I forgot about that. It'll be good to get your auld lad off your back about this deal."

"You said it, not me."

"Speaking of retirin' dinosaurs, I don't get why he's still hangin' in there. We both know you've been doin' most of his work for years."

"The pitfalls of working with your father."

"And all the more reason for you to come out tonight. I won't be takin' no for an answer."

"I'll let you know."

Connor sighs and shakes his head. He knows me well enough to not keep pushing. "Fine. Text me when you decide. I'll be in my office."

I don't bother to reply.

As he leaves, I shift my focus to my computer. I have a few minutes before the meeting and want to review my notes. Numerous prospective clients have come in over the last few business days, and part of my job is to filter through the mess and assign hot leads to my staff. The larger we grow, the easier we can negotiate. Blackwood Hotels & Resorts is one of the largest privately owned hotel chains on the East Coast. Recent acquisitions and publicity have catapulted us into the public eye, and if we're not being sought out to sell to and cash out, we're doing the seeking. Like Norman.

It's my primary goal to have our name rival Hilton—and Rutherford Plaza Hotels. With my leadership, I can see that becoming a reality within the next five years.

It could be sooner if my father would give me the reins.

Even after steering the company from millions to billions over the past decade as CEO, I still need board approval for major decisions. With my father as Chairman of the Board of Directors, clashes are inevitable. While the board members have a say, they typically defer to him, given his founder status. It's damn frustrating, but that's just how it goes in our corporate landscape.

I walk into the conference room to find him already there. He sits at the head of the table, his white hair meticulously groomed, papers placed around him.

"Morning," I say, taking the seat at the opposite end of the table. I only have my phone and my tablet, and I put both on the table, suppressing the urge to lament the unnecessary waste of good trees.

One of the first things I did when I stepped into his shoes as CEO was go paperless. It felt like waving goodbye to the dark ages. Despite the millions we've saved and the streamlined work processes, my dad, Douglas "Boomer" Blackwood, seems to be oblivious to the benefits.

"Did you get the signature?" my father asks, not bothering to look up.

"He signed the contract this morning."

"And the co-owner?"

"Not going to be a problem," I say. "When we meet tomorrow, I'll be able to convince her to sell. She doesn't have much experience and will no doubt be drowning very soon."

Dad finally tears his gaze away from his forest of paperwork only to fix me with a hard stare. "So, you're telling me that you *haven't* closed the deal then?"

"That's not what I said. I just told you the deal is done. Weren't you listening?"

"Oh, I was listening. And what I heard was that you're only half-done. Buying out one of the partners doesn't mean the deal is done."

I pin him with a glare. "It's only a question of when, not if. We've done takeovers like this many times before. Some partners sell right away, others hold out, hoping for a better deal. But in the end, they always come around." The moment she catches sight of the figure we've handed Norman, she'll be keen to negotiate until we find common ground, and from there, it'll all be smooth sailing. "I'm not worried."

"You should be." Dad gets to his feet and starts to pace. "Do you know how I became as successful as I am today?"

"Well, you've certainly kept that story under wraps," I quip, hinting at the countless times he's shared it before.

Dad pauses, facing the expansive windows that only the upscale rooms in the building have. He glares at me over his shoulder. "Save your witty comments for your clients, Sean. They didn't amuse me when you were a teenager, and they don't amuse me now." He gazes out the window once more. "I started this company from nothing. Poured my heart and soul into it…"

I tune him out after that.

True, my father founded and ran a good company. However, it came with a cost: the cost of any kind of relationship with his only child.

"…and I made it what it is today," he finishes his speech.

I bark out a laugh. "That was ten years ago. We've acquired well over a dozen new properties in the last two years alone, and we're on track for our most profitable year in this company's history," I bite out. "Brush me and my accomplishments off all you want. The numbers speak for themselves."

My father waves his hand dismissively. "Well, son, I'm pretty sure you wouldn't be where you are today without my guidance," he says, taking his seat again. "Your track record aside, this deal of yours won't officially be considered done until you've bought out *both* partners."

Silence and tension settle between us. We've been this way ever since my mother passed away when I was thirteen. It's like we're stuck in this perpetual standoff, unable to bridge the gap that her absence left behind.

A few minutes later, the conference room door opens, and the board members start to trickle in. After giving the update on my deal, the other board members parrot my father's sentiments. Predictable as ever. They're waiting for the complete buyout before breaking out the champagne. As always, I'm all geared up to silence the skeptics.

5

SEAN

"Ow, what the fuck?" I ask, glaring at my soon-to-be *ex*-friend. "That fucking hurt, dick-bag."

"Don't make it obvious," Connor says, staring straight ahead as if he didn't just kick me under the table. "But look at your wan with the brown hair at the bar... she keeps lookin' over at ya."

Intrigued, I casually glance over my shoulder to find a pair of big eyes staring right at me. They belong to a brunette in her thirties, who's sitting alone, wearing a long black dress that hugs her curves and reveals a sliver of a silky-smooth leg through the high slit. Her hair is tied up in a twist, leaving her neck bare except for a delicate gold chain. I have a faint sense of recognition, but in the dim light of the room, it's hard to make out the finer details.

Still, I can see enough to know, that yeah, she's gorgeous.

"Are you goin' over there, or what?" Connor asks, swirling the contents of his glass as we sit in our favorite booth at Swayze's, toward the back. "Because if you don't, I will."

There's definitely something familiar about her, yet I can't quite put my finger on it. She reminds me of someone.

I consider it and almost decline. After all, the day hasn't been that great, and my mood hasn't exactly improved yet. Throughout the rest of the afternoon, I had to deal with my father's phone calls and voicemails as he attempted to dish "advice" on how to proceed. As if I haven't overseen hundreds of takeovers in the past. I did my best to ignore him, and when five o'clock rolled around, I was out the door quicker than normal.

That being said, I'm not in the habit of making foolish decisions, and disregarding the attention of a beautiful woman who's showing interest would clearly be unwise. I need to blow off steam, and what better way to do that than with her?

I pick up my steaming coffee cup and throw Connor a look. "Don't wait up," I say, getting to my feet.

"Oh, don't worry about me. Plenty 'round here to keep me distracted."

He's caught the eye of a blonde woman on the other side of the room and is in an intense staring contest. Leaving him to it, I keep my gaze on the bar as I cross the room toward my prey. Both stools on either side of my target are empty. She sips from one of those brightly colored cocktails, the ones that come with a piece of fruit or garnish on the rim. When I get close enough to finally make out some details, I notice a smattering of freckles across the bridge of her nose and the top of her shoulders. Her blue eyes have a bit of a glaze to them, which leads me to believe she isn't nursing her first drink.

"Is this seat taken?" I ask, motioning to one of the stools.

"Classic pickup line. A lot better than the newer ones I've heard over the last two hours." Her voice is as smooth as her skin looks, and it draws me in.

It also triggers that feeling again. The feeling that she reminds me of someone. I take the seat, placing my half-finished cup of coffee on the bar top.

"You seem familiar to me," I say. "Have we met?"

For a moment, there's a flash of emotion in her eyes. Her lips press into a thin line, and she looks away, shaking her head as she picks up her drink. "Wow. Talk about a dagger to the heart. Well, not heart. Ego is more like it."

Ah, shit. I *do* know her from somewhere.

Have I slept with her?

No.

Since I haven't done much dating lately, and she doesn't look like any of my previous flings, I conclude I at least haven't chatted her up before. Studying her closely, I take in the lines of her face and the features I can now examine more closely.

"Since I don't remember hearing your voice filled with ecstasy," I say, "I'm going to conclude we haven't had sex."

She laughs, a deep full laugh that I enjoy. "No, nothing like that," she insists. "Although, maybe picture me without the dress and in a pink towel..."

It hits me like a freight train.

Holy *shit*.

It's my neighbor from this morning.

How the hell did I not notice it before? Then again, my last view of her was of those freckled tits and soft pink nipples in the morning sunlight, so I had been slightly distracted.

"I didn't recognize you with your mask off—and your clothes on," I say, stunned by her transformation. Damn, she cleans up well.

She snorts in amusement and shakes her head. "Yeah, clearly, which is more than a little offensive. Wearing a yogurt face mask shouldn't exactly make me unidentifiable."

"True, but can you blame me? We only met once for like, what, ten minutes."

"And yet, *surprisingly*, I remembered your face, even beneath that stubble, and despite the fact that I also saw you naked."

"I'm sure it wasn't my face you thought about the moment you saw me sitting over there."

Redness blooms across her cheeks, and she rolls her eyes. "Rude and smug. You really are the full package, aren't you?"

"You've seen it, you would know."

She smirks as she picks up her drink and polishes it off in one long gulp. She waves to the bartender for another. I shrug out of my suit jacket and drape it over the empty stool next to me. She's gotten my attention, and I'm settling in for an interesting conversation.

"Celebrating or on the rebound?" I ask.

"Neither...umm, I mean, well, something like that. Just need a little pick-me-up." She gives me a sweeping once-over. "What about you?"

"Blowing off steam after work with my buddy."

She glances off to the side, and when I look, I find Connor chatting up the skinny blonde he'd set his sights on a few minutes earlier. She's nice looking, sure, but I prefer natural tits.

She grins. "Seems he's looking to blow off steam with someone else."

"But hey, I don't blame him," I say. "Clearly, she's got more curves than me."

She laughs, all vibrant. "But not more than me."

"You certainly have a point there," I say.

I like this back and forth, this banter. She's quick with her words and doesn't seem afraid to say what's on her mind. Not to mention, I catch her biting her bottom lip when she picks up her new drink. It adds a captivating charm to her.

"It was bold of you to come over." She takes another sip of her cocktail.

"Well, you know, they say luck favors the bold."

"And...how's that luck of yours panning out?" she asks, her smile hinting at the promise of an interesting evening ahead.

"I don't know, you tell me."

"I haven't decided yet," she declares.

My phone starts to vibrate, and I take it out of my pocket to glance at the screen. When I realize it's work, I bite back a grunt of annoyance.

"Well, while you decide, I need to answer this," I say, getting to my feet. I leave my coffee and jacket so she doesn't think I'm trying to bail. "I'll be back."

She takes a sip and motions for me to go ahead.

I step away to the restroom area where it's a bit quieter, and answer the phone with a sharp, "Yes?"

"Hi, Mr. Blackwood, I'm sorry to bother you." On the other end, my PA, Jasmine, sounds nervous. I know if she's calling, it's important because I've been clear with my staff about reaching out after my work hours.

"It's fine, Jasmine. What's going on?"

She's learned that another—undisclosed—company has expressed interest in acquiring a stake in Westerlyn, and she wants to ensure I have the information in case I decide to respond and possibly up my offer tomorrow. Apparently, word about my purchase of half the shares has spread like wildfire, fueling the eagerness of competitors to throw a wrench into my future plans. I've faced similar situations before.

Definitely not something that really constitutes an emergency phone call, but there's no use dragging out the conversation. There's a woman waiting for me at the bar.

After instructing her to investigate the identity of the interested party, I end the call.

The second I turn around, I almost collide with said woman.

"I've decided." She beams at me, all happy, swirling her almost-empty cocktail glass.

Raising my eyebrow and noting how close she's standing, I lean my shoulder against the wall. "Oh, yeah? What did you decide?"

My neighbor steps closer.

She slides her hand into my hair and goes up on her tippy toes, likely going for a kiss. Well, trying to go for a kiss. The moment her lips are about to meet mine, she slips and her tits crash into me.

She's tipsier than I first anticipated.

The nameless brunette giggles and gives me *that* look.

Part of me isn't surprised that she's so brave, audacious even. I mean, this girl's out here balcony-hopping like it's a sport.

But, when it comes to post-work fun, I have two principles.

I don't drink, and I don't fuck intoxicated girls.

A glass or two is fine, but my neighbor may have indulged a bit too much. She isn't entirely inebriated, but she's definitely pushing the boundaries of what I consider an acceptable limit.

I wrap my arm around her waist, steadying her. Plucking the glass from her hand and placing it on a surface next to us, I give her a firm look, my body temperature rising. I'm just about to make my grand exit, suggesting to her that she's not in the state to make sound decisions, when I feel more of those curves. My dick hardens, pressing into her thigh as she grinds her hips against mine. Next thing I know, she pushes me so my back hits the restroom door, and she reaches behind me for the handle.

Life's too short for goodbyes, I decide.

I won't go *there* with her. But an orgasm won't hurt anyone.

We stumble in, and she locks the door behind us. As I wrestle for control, she pulls up her tight dress so I can slip my hand underneath while she grabs at my shirt. My palms skim along those smooth thighs, and all I can think about is burying myself between them. With my mouth, with my fingers, doesn't matter which one. I plan to do both.

My fingers skim her panties, and I smirk when I feel her arousal. Damn. I've barely touched her and she's already wet. Granted, I'm harder than steel. But we'll get to me. Right now, I want to lose myself in her, needing the distraction.

I slide my hand under the thin fabric, and she gasps, her eyes the color of a deep blue ocean. They flutter closed, and her head falls back against the door, leaving her neck bare and begging for my mouth. I immediately latch onto it, sucking and kissing while my fingers glide through her heat. She's soft and wet and warm, everything I could want and more. Immediately, her thighs clamp around my wrist, keeping my hand locked in place. My thumb swipes over her clit, making her knees buckle, and she moans. The reaction is so fucking hot that it makes me do it again.

My other hand cradles her jaw, trapping her between me and the door.

All she can do is stand there moaning and writhing. My thumb strokes her cheek until she turns her head, wrapping her lips around it, sucking provocatively and making me think of her mouth around something else. I bet her lips would look perfect around my cock. The image of her on her knees, looking up at me with those blue eyes as I thrust into her mouth is a goddamn glorious visual.

Everything about her is drawing me in. She's soft and supple. Her sweet, fruity perfume hangs around me like a cloud, making me dizzy. Having her shuddering in my arms is intoxicating. It's overpowering and makes everything else fade into the background. Fuck, it's been too long.

I love making a woman whimper with only a few swipes of my fingers. It's fucking delicious.

But there's something about my neighbor that's different. I can't put my finger on it (no pun intended). Maybe it's because I've seen her naked and know what's hiding under that dress. Or maybe it's because she had a bite to her voice a little while ago. She'd been upset I hadn't remembered her, and yet, she's here with me, her hips rocking along with my hand.

I need to taste her.

Grabbing the sides of her lace panties, I drag them down as I lower myself onto my knees. Yeah, I like the thought of her being in this position—bare, wet, and eager for my cock—but the urge to taste her is greater. She's looking down at me with the most heated gaze as I slide her soaked panties into my pocket. Her pupils are wide, pink lips swollen.

I throw her a wink, rumbling, "Lift your dress up and out of the way."

She promptly follows my order, and I spread her legs. With the tip of my tongue, I give her swollen clit a teasing flick. It's a move meant to provoke, and considering the way she gasps, I know it's worked.

I do it again, and again, keeping my touch light.

Each time, her hips shoot forward, seeking, begging for more. That's when I grant her her wish. I press my mouth to her mound, and her eyes flutter closed.

The moment my tongue swipes through her folds, she stretches against the door with a loud moan.

"Oohhh..."

Her hands bury themselves in my hair, making me softly bite into her heated flesh.

Everything I felt with my hand I can feel with my mouth, though it's better because now I can taste her. She's like strawberries and cream, a delightful treat at the end of a fucking busy day.

It's my turn to close my eyes and lose myself in the experience. I nudge her legs farther apart, giving myself better access to what I want most. I push my tongue into her sweet cunt, grunting as her walls flutter around it.

I think of doing this back at my place, how she'd look spread out on my bed, panting and begging for more. My dick is pressed to my zipper, impatient to feel the tight heat of her.

"More, please, more," she mewls, hips rocking back and forth like they did when my fingers were inside her. "I'm on birth control."

My mouth is too preoccupied to reply, though I can't help enjoying how needy and desperate she is. She's going to make a fantastic lay. I can tell.

But not tonight.

Tonight is just foreplay. With that thought, my lips close around her sensitive nub, sucking in her clit, and her gasp turns into a long-drawn-out moan when I slide my fingers inside her again.

It doesn't take her very long after that. Within seconds, she's grinding hard against my mouth and hand, tugging on my hair as she tries to let me know what's about to happen. I'm ready for it.

She lets out a cry. When her body locks into place, thighs clamping down on my ears, I tease her sensitive clit, eagerly working her through her climax.

She slumps back and lets me go.

I only draw away because my cell vibrates in my back pocket. With determination, I silence the devil on my shoulder, urging me to take her hard and fast, and make her realize that while I may not have recognized her face, she's never going to forget mine.

When I stand, I gently smooth her dress, which is bunched around her waist, down over her hips, ending the show.

"What...*no,* please."

She begins undoing my belt, and my phone starts to buzz—again.

Shit.

"Ignore it," she urges, her lips going for my throat.

She attempts to yank me into a filthy kiss, but I stop her. Given the insistent phone call, I know it can only be a work-related emergency, and I don't have time for explanations. I reach down and stop her, gently pushing her hands away.

"Can't." Reaching into my pocket, I draw out my phone and notice that it's a call from Connor.

"I'm sure I can persuade you."

The thing is, she absolutely could, if circumstances were different. What little we've done together is enough for me to want more. I'm tempted to accept her offer. But dealing with the wrath of a tipsy lady who, in her sober moment, recognizes that I'm not prepared to commit is a precarious storm I'm not sure I'm ready to step into.

"Any other time, sweetheart, I'd be all about it. But I have to take this. You take a moment to freshen up, and I'll drive you home."

Without waiting for a response, I push past her and out the door.

"How much did she have?" I ask the bartender.

"Two Strawberry Starlet cocktails."

Only two? Clearly she's not used to alcohol. I grab my jacket and throw down money for our drinks. With that handled, I step out to call Connor. "Hey, what's wrong?"

"Nuthin'. Just lettin' you know I've headed out with the blonde from the bar. That pretty pussy is about to eat me dick up to me balls. Thought you'd like to know."

"That's it? That's why you fucking called? Send a message next time."

"Wanted to deliver the visual myself since you fucked off without me anyway. Where'd you end up?"

"Good night, Connor." I end the call without another word.

Dick.

6

JESS

*W*hat the hell just happened?

I stand in the bathroom, rocking my dress with no undies—but with a surplus of irritation. Trying to get my breathing under control, my body is still tingling with the aftershocks of my orgasm. The throbbing between my legs reminds me that we were only getting started. One second, I have Mr. Neighbor's fantastic mouth on me, and the next, he's gone.

What...the actual—? Who does *that*? *Rude.*

My opinion of him continues to decrease the more we interact.

Hurriedly, I pull myself together, wanting to go after him and give him a piece of my mind. Again. But when I finally manage to make it back to the main bar area, his suit jacket is gone and he's nowhere in sight.

The bartender looks up at me when I approach.

I sit down with a huff, fishing out a few bills to pay my tab.

"Your friend covered what you've drunk already," he says.

Some apology.

"He's...not my friend. Nope. He's my...neighbor," I explain, sliding the cash over. "Ke-eep it as...a tip. I can buy...my own drinks." It comes out in more of a slur than I intended. Oops-y.

"Your neighbor said he's going to fetch the car and wait for you outside."

I'm filled with a storm of emotions I can't even begin to navigate. On the one hand, oh, my God, was that the hottest thing that's ever happened to me. On the other, he really just left me there to make a phone call. Every time I think I'm warming up to the guy, he does something else to remind me what an utter jerk he is.

I shouldn't ride home with him.

I should get an Uber.

When I get up from the barstool, I feel wobbly. Really wobbly. That cocktail must have been stronger than I thought. I haven't had a sip in ages, and all of a sudden, it's hitting me like a freight train. I guess I'm just out of practice.

In my defense: a rough day at work, which somehow triggered memories of my ex, and *bam*, those thoughts practically begged for a glass of bubbly (or three. Or four?).

I insist on paying my bill. I still have *some* dignity.

Just when I stumble out of the bar, two firm hands grab me.

Sitting inside a comfy limousine, I close my eyes.

I'll only sleep for a minute.

Or two.

Or.

A few moments later, I open my eyes.

And blink.

And blink.

"Let go," I hear him grumble.

"Ooo-kay," I chirp, and reluctantly, I let go of these beautiful steel-hard shoulders of this gorgeous specimen of a man. Wait. Was he carrying me? What's his name again? How strong he is, because I'm not a lightweight—no, sir, not this one. Where am I? Definitely not in the huge limousine anymore. How good he smells. Woody. Intoxicating. Dominant. Nothing like my ex. This one, he smells like a *real* man.

"No good night kiss?" I ask him, looking up into his eyes from my lying position. It's comfy. Those long eyelashes on him! He has beautiful eyes. Brown. Or green. Or are they blue? It's too dark to tell.

"Not tonight," he grumbles.

"K."

Next time I open my eyes, it's still night. I'm lying on a couch, snuggled under a blanket. Where the hell am I? My head hurts, and I'm thirsty. When I hear the rustle of wings nearby (Pippin), I know I'm on *my* couch. Thank goodness. I can barely recollect my grumpy neighbor hoisting me over his shoulder, but once we were on our floor, he made it his personal mission to help me find my key (which, I swear, had decided to play hide-and-seek in the depths of my purse), and then he unceremoniously *plunked* me down on this very couch.

It's all a bit of a tipsy blur, to be honest.

I look up. It's 3:13 a.m.

Did we have...sex? No. We didn't.

I sit up.

And blink.

There's a glass of water and Tylenol on the coffee table. How thoughtful of him. It was a small, yet unmistakable act of heroism on his part. I feel instantly better when I gulp it all down.

But I still have no clue when it comes to his name.

Perhaps he *is* a Peter.

Once inside my bedroom, I strip, take my makeup off, and fall face-first onto my pillow.

It's only then that the throbbing returns, and I squeeze my thighs together in an attempt to make it stop. Yeah, that doesn't work. Having someone else touch me for the first time in forever, it's like my body has come out of hibernation and is desperate for more. Still on my stomach, I raise my hips and place my hand between my legs, shuddering at how sensitive I am.

With the memories of his hand and mouth, I moan into my pillow, my fingers immediately coated with my wetness. It's not the same. His were rougher and thicker than mine, and I have to use two right off the bat to feel the stretch one of his provided.

I picture him there with me, pressed against my back and pinning me to the bed as he gets me off. I wish those lips were on my neck, sucking and nibbling like he had been earlier. Demanding, challenging, relentless. God, that buff body would feel so damn good right now. The idea of being completely at his mercy has me more turned on than any other fantasy ever has or could.

When I come, my moans are muffled by the pillow.

It's not nearly as mind-shattering as I was hoping, but it gets the job done. I'm left shaky and sweaty, yet still frustrated. Not sexually, at least. Emotionally. Who the hell is this guy who acts like a dick when I first meet him, then saunters up to me at *my* bar, bats those piercing eyes and has me with my panties down minutes later? A voice in my head interjects, reminding me that *I* was the one who cornered *him*, so I reluctantly take on a bit of responsibility. Meanwhile, another voice wonders if he's still in possession of my panties.

You'd think after the hell I've gone through I'd be better at choosing men.

Spoiler alert: not quite.

Chalking it up to being horny and vulnerable, I sleepily bundle myself in my comforter.

The combination of a long day, a splash of alcohol, and the dwindling endorphins from a steamy hookup knock me out faster than you can say "lights out."

· · ·

A ll things considered, I wake up in a relatively good mood. Apparently having several orgasms really puts a pep in your step. Even though I have to meet with my new co-owner, I'm trying to be positive.

Last night's experience was certainly enjoyable. I'm still not thrilled that Mr. Neighbor immediately ditched me but, hey, what am I going to do? I'm not about to simp and pine over someone I barely know.

It'd been a great way to alleviate some of this tension. My only regret is—despite everything—not having had a chance to repay the favor. He clearly needs it. He's got that grumpy look on his face. I wonder what his "O" face looks like. I'm sure I can coax *that* look out of him.

Don't think about him, I tell myself as I jump in the shower.

I need all my wits about me to face this new owner.

Pippin sees me coming out of the room dressed and starts shrieking in his cage, like he does every morning when I leave for work. Chuckling, I go over and reach through to stroke his feathered head.

"I know, I know, you don't want me to go," I tell him. "But I swear I'll let you fly around when I get home. I can't risk being late this morning. And as soon as the shelter gets another parakeet, you'll have a friend."

He nips my finger a little harder than normal, letting me know he's not happy. I roll my eyes affectionately, drop a couple of treats through the bars, and make sure the curtains are open so the little guy has a good view outside.

O n my way down the hall, I pause to look at my neighbor's door. Too bad there's no nameplate.

I stand there, wondering if I should knock.

It feels like the right thing to do.

You know, at some point, I need to ask for my panties back. Something like, "Hey there, new neighbor, so the panties you borrowed and mysteriously stashed in your pocket—any chance of a return?" Yeah. It's bound to be awkward (and hilarious at the same time).

With a mix of curiosity and temptation, I'm tempted to rap on his door like I did the day before, wondering if he'll answer naked again. Imagine his face if I gave him a cheerful good morning "Hello," with that line above, just to throw him off. Or better yet, start with a surprise kiss! On his lips! Oh, the suspense would be unbearable.

However, it's early, and I don't hear any noise inside, so I assume he's still sleeping.

Besides, we had a sweaty hookup in the back of a bar. It doesn't mean I'm about to start throwing myself at his feet. He's good but not *that* good.

Maybe next time.

I like to start my day bright and early, getting to work ahead of the game so I can do my usual rounds and ensure everything is in top-notch condition—today is no exception. Late yesterday afternoon, we broke the news to the staff about Norman's retirement, and their reactions were like mine. He's been such an integral, comforting presence, he's going to be missed. Now that the news has sunk in, I notice they are worried about what a new owner could mean. I do my best to remain positive in front of them. They know they can trust me, and no matter what the new guy tries to do, I'm still the co-owner, and I still have a say.

No one is going to come into *my* hotel and shake things up without my say-so.

"The new guy is stopping by this morning, right?" Pauline asks when I stop by her office.

I nod, keeping a smile on my face and glancing at my watch. "Yup. That's right. Norman is introducing us in about three hours."

Pauline digs through folders. "I'm surprised you're so cheerful," she says. "I thought you'd be in crisis mode."

I shrug, leaning against the doorframe as she puts a folder down and collapses onto her chair.

"I thought about it a lot last night," I tell her, "and I'm trying to stay on the positive side of things. Going in with a negative attitude is only going to make things harder. I don't want that."

"You're always looking on the bright side. That's one of the things I admire about you. *But also* one of the things that annoys the crap out of me," she teases. "You make it look so easy."

"It helps that I had some fun last night."

Pauline's eyebrows shoot up, and she does a double take, as if I've just confessed to bungee jumping off a skyscraper for kicks (nope, I'm brave, but not that brave). She spins in her chair to give me her full attention. "What kind of fun?" she asks.

I lower my voice. "The half-naked kind."

"Only half-naked?"

"There wasn't time for anything else." I shrug. "We weren't exactly in a private space."

"Where and with who?"

"I ran into my new neighbor at Swayze's."

Her eyes go wide. "No way! You mean the one you saw naked? The grumpy perfection whose balcony you climbed?"

"Yup, that's the one."

"It's about time," she says dryly. "I'm proud of you."

I laugh at her calling me out. "Thanks. I'm proud of myself too," I admit. "We didn't get to do too much, but what we did do was fun."

Honestly, my mind is still all over the place thanks to the nameless man who made me orgasm harder than I ever thought possible.

"You should stop by his apartment on the way home for an encore."

"Oh, I will," I say, keeping the conversation playful.

Behind me, I hear footsteps approach and I opt to move on, not keen on diving into my personal orgasm statistics in front of other employees.

Pauline hears them too. "To be continued," she says in a hushed tone.

S miling to myself, I leave her to her work while I finish my rounds. Even though I'm anxious about my meeting, I keep the lingering tension at bay and head to my office to finish my coffee and prepare.

Norman didn't say I needed to prep or review anything. He was clear the meeting will be a way to provide formal introductions. Everything is expected to operate business as usual until me and the new co-owner can sit down and talk things out face to face.

That doesn't deter me from dedicating the remaining time to analyzing our recent occupancy rates, assessing our financial performance, and reviewing our staff's training and performance records. I have to ensure I'm well prepared to demonstrate my expertise in the hotel industry. Of course, Norman already handed over all the numbers, but hey, a little extra preparation never hurt anyone, right?

In the back of my mind, I have my suspicions that they're going to try to buy me out.

I might as well be facing an enigma, for all I know. All I have is Norman's vague take on Blackwood—but when it comes to billionaires, they all seem to follow the same playbook, don't they? They swoop in and snatch up privately owned businesses—like our hotels—only to transform them into those cookie-cutter versions that seem to sprout up everywhere.

No, thank you.

I don't want that for us. The WH properties are individually designed to reflect the distinctive characteristics of their respective locations. Norman and I dedicated ourselves to creating the ambiance of a bed and breakfast, but on a grander scale. Our loyal patrons frequently express their fondness for the welcoming, personalized atmosphere.

No matter how much money that "so-called" hotel super mogul

offers, I won't sell. No, sir. I'm not going to let them buy me off, bully, or intimidate me.

They bought the hotels knowing I would come with them.

They'll have to deal if they don't like me.

It's not like they can fire me either.

I'm an owner with just as much say.

My phone buzzes, and Sarah lets me know it's almost 10:00 a.m. Time for the meeting. Taking a deep breath, I remind myself that I've got this.

I can handle any rich guy in a suit.

7

JESS

I keep my back straight and my head high like the queen I am as I walk toward the conference room, smiling confidently at the staff and guests I pass.

However, the moment I walk through the door of the conference room, my metaphorical crown drops to my feet with a *thunk*.

I stop dead in my tracks, my smile faltering.

I blink.

No.

Wait, what?

This can't be happening. I must be hallucinating.

What's *he* doing here? I want to ask him, but I just stare at my hallucination.

To my absolute horror, my neighbor, the one I haven't been able to stop obsessing about, the one whose nine-inch dick I had seen and who made me come harder than I ever have in my life, is sitting at the conference table next to Norman.

This can't be right. He can't be here. Because if he's here, that means...

Oh, *no*. Nonono.

He didn't recognize me last night, and for a brief moment, I pray he doesn't recognize me again. It's possible. First time: yogurt-cucumber mask, second time: dramatic nighttime makeup, now: pale as death, with burning hot cheeks.

Unfortunately, my uncanny resemblance to the Boogeyman himself doesn't work in my favor.

When he looks in my eyes, it's clear he knows *exactly* who I am. The glimpse of recognition lasts exactly for a millisecond, then he reveals nothing. His expression is composed, perfectly concealing what he's thinking.

Now *that's* composure.

My face starts to grow hotter, and I know I must be brighter than red. Curse my pale skin. His poker face is gold standard. Mine? More like a neon sign.

Norman stands from his seat and moves around the table as I approach them. "Jess, there you are! This is the new co-owner, Mr. Sean Blackwood, CEO of Blackwood Hotels & Resorts," he says. "Mr. Black-wood, this is Jessica Summers."

We shake hands.

So much for Peter.

He's a Sean.

"Although," Norman says, "judging by your reaction, I take it you two know each other already?"

I won't go as far as to say we *know* each other.

We've seen each other naked and made out at a bar while he rubbed my clit. Oh, God. My new co-owner rubbed my clit. He didn't just touch me, he ate me out.

And now we have to work together.

Closely.

Every day.

The universe has a sick sense of humor.

Never in a million years did I think my Spider-Man was *him*. Him, of all people. My cold, unfriendly next-door neighbor. He's about as far from a neighborhood guardian as you can get! In fact, he's the type to terrify trick-or-treaters rather than hand out candy!

"We've run into each other once or twice," Sean says. "It's nice to officially meet you, Ms. Summers." There's a hardness in his expression that is more rigid than what he's presented so far. The way he glares at me, it's anything *but* nice to officially meet.

Also, what did he say? "Run into each other?" Is that what he's calling it? And what's with the roughness of his voice? What the hell did I ever do to him?

He clearly doesn't get laid enough. (Which is not my fault.)

"You as well," I say, trying—and failing—to sound equally cold. At least I remember my manners. "I apologize for my initial astonishment. Your presence caught me off guard."

Norman offers me a seat at the table across from *Sean*, and I slip into it.

"Right, I'm sure I did." He shifts his attention away from me and back to Norman. "As I was saying, you made the right decision, Mr. Whitman. Westerlyn will be well looked after. Congratulations, again."

Now I'm annoyed for a different reason.

He ditches me last night, then acts indifferent this morning as he casts me aside. What a monster! He's being so stiff and formal. Granted, the grouchiness from yesterday wasn't exactly icing on the cake, but I'd prefer *that* to whatever this version of him is.

Swallowing my rage and reminding myself to remain positive, I take a deep breath and cross one leg over the other. In no way am I showing him how much he affects me.

Does he still have my panties?

Norman sits next to me, his body somewhat tense now that he's realized Sean Blackwood and I have some kind of history.

"I don't doubt that you have Westerlyn's best interest at heart,"

Norman says to him, trying to forge ahead through the awkwardness. "I want to thank you again for your help throughout this process." Turning to me he adds, "Mr. Blackwood and his team have a remarkable history of success. I'm confident that their goals align with ours, and I'm leaving you in good hands."

Good hands.

I know *just* how good those hands really are.

Sean addresses me, saying, "Rest assured, Ms. Summers, your efforts are recognized. I know we can take Westerlyn Hotels to the next level."

Despite the predicament we find ourselves in, his words are reassuring, and I take a deep breath. I have to think of the hotel chain and my staff and let go of my anger. It's easy enough to do as I've never been one to hold a grudge. I also don't want to make this transition more difficult than it's going to be. Norman deserves to retire without worry. Not to mention, the sale is final, and there's no magical "undo" button in sight.

"That sounds nice," I say, keeping my tone light. "I appreciate the sentiment. But I do have a lot of questions about what this transition is going to entail and what our partnership is going to look like."

"I'm sure you do. As do I." Sean directs his attention to Norman. "I think we have it all covered here," he says. "Thank you for facilitating the introduction. Is there anything else we can do for you?"

Norman blinks.

Wait. Did he just dismiss Norman?

He totally did. He sure wastes no time taking charge. The ink isn't even dry on the contract yet!

"Oh, right," Norman says, flabbergasted, and stands. "Right. I think that's all. Sarah will get you the folders you requested." He glances from him to me, and his smile makes a return. "Jess, I know this is going to be a big change..."

"Norman, I'll be fine," I assure him, rising to my feet. "I'm so happy for you, and I'm going to miss you."

"I'm going to miss you too, kid." He pats my shoulder. "I'll go wrap a couple of things up, and then I'm out of here."

"Enjoy your retirement, Mr. Whitman," Sean says. There isn't a smile on his face.

I watch Norman walk out of the room, and when the door falls closed behind him, I find myself unable to keep from getting emotional.

One word: brutal.

No, scratch that—brutal doesn't even come close.

That dismissal was utterly ruthless, as if it were just another routine for him, as if he carries out such acts every day without a second thought. It sure doesn't add any sweetness to the bitter pill.

I breathe out, trying to calm myself, and sit back down. Sadness starts to well inside of me. The last thing I want to do is cry in front of him.

Quickly, I tell myself that Norman is not leaving for good right this second. Besides, it's not like now that he's retired, I'm never going to hear from him again. I hear Bali is a hoot this time of year. Sunny. Breezy. Cocktails galore. However, it still tugs on my heart. After all the long nights and hard work we've put into this place, it won't be the same without him.

My sentiments are pushed to the side when it dawns on me that I'm now alone with Sean Blackwood.

I turn to face him, only to find him already staring at me.

8

SEAN

*W*ell, fuck. Didn't see *that* one coming.

I'd say I'm surprised to see who Jessica Summers is, but the word "surprise" is a damn understatement.

My neighbor is the last person I expected to run into this morning, at least not outside of our apartment building.

The taste of her sweet pussy still lingers on my tongue.

Her pert nipples under my palms remain etched in my memory.

I still hear her plea for a goodnight kiss, and her disappointment when I opted not to grant her that wish. She slumped back, snoring peacefully.

But the moment she walked through the conference room's door, and I registered who she was, I was pissed.

There's *no* way this is a coincidence.

Okay, her being my neighbor might be. But everything that happened last night? The revealing outfit, the bedroom eyes, the flirting, the fooling around—it's safe to say she knew who I was when she spotted me at the bar. If she indeed was aware of who I was—of which

I'm certain—then I have every reason to believe that her advances were part of a rather unconventional business strategy.

It took everything I had to bite my tongue. I'm nothing if not professional, and I wanted to avoid discussions in front of Norman that may disclose information about our acquaintance. It wasn't the time, and it definitely wasn't the place. What happened between us should stay that way.

However, that doesn't mean I'm going to let her think whatever scheme she's orchestrating is working.

"I know you have questions," I say, once Norman is gone, leaving any trace of emotion out of my voice. "This is all a lot to process."

"You could say that."

I rest my clasped hands on the table. "Before we get into all of that, I want to give you the opportunity to sell to Blackwood. We're willing to pay a generous sum if you—"

She doesn't give me a chance to finish. Her answer is quick and sharp.

"No." She shakes her head. "Not going to happen."

She's got a backbone, good. Usually, I appreciate a worthy opponent —one who doesn't crumble in my presence or bend to financial temptation at the drop of a hat. However, with the board and my father watching my every move, there's no room for games. "You know, it's a professional courtesy to let someone finish talking before you shoot them down."

"I don't care," she snaps, her breathing quick, her face flushing with irritation. "I already know the answer to your question."

I raise my eyebrow. "You don't even know how much I'm offering."

"It doesn't matter. I don't want to sell."

I'm prepared for this. Over half the co-owners we plan to buy out turn down the offer when it's first presented. They all try to make it seem like it has to do with integrity or some bullshit like that. It never does. It's all about the money.

I fix her with a firm stare. "Don't turn your nose down at a payout so quickly," I advise. "There's a lot you can do with money. You've done a good job turning this place around. I'm sure there are other hotels that could benefit from your skills."

"I'm aware of that," she says. "And this has nothing to do with money. It isn't the issue. I love this job. I love the work I do and what I've done to get Westerlyn to this point." Her full tits rise and fall beneath her blouse as she glares at me. "Why would I want to buy another hotel and start from the ground up again? I've already done that, and now I'm ready to spend my time and energy making this place even greater than it already is. I don't want to sell."

She seems more determined than some of the others I've done business with, I'll give her that. But the board has a strict policy when dealing with co-owners. There's simply no way they'll let this slide. I know them and my father too well. Blackwood working with a private owner like this? Never in a million years. It's not how it's done, especially not for the long term.

"Everyone says it's not about money," I start, "until they actually see the zeros on the check."

Her expression says, "Go fuck yourself."

Keeping a straight face, I reach across the table and pluck the pen and pad of paper sitting in the center. I tear off a piece and swiftly jot down my offer, where each zero packs a bigger punch when lined up on the page. Ultimately, it matches the same generous sum we extended to Norman. "This is what we're willing to give. Take your time, think about it before you—"

She doesn't even look at the paper, instead clutches her arms in front of her breasts. "No deal."

"Don't allow emotion and sentiment to cloud your judgment. Let's approach this logically, if only briefly." Challenging a woman's logic can be a risky move, but hey, we're dealing with reality here.

She arches an angry-looking brow. "What the hell is that supposed to mean?"

"I mean you're throwing away a golden opportunity you're going to regret someday."

"I can assure you—today's interaction is *not* the one I'm regretting right now."

And there it is.

She's the first to allude to what happened last night.

"This has nothing to do with our personal lives," I say, not taking the bait. "We're both adults. I don't see why we can't act like it."

She huffs, and I can tell she wants to respond. Instead, she stares for a few seconds, takes a deep breath, then says, "I appreciate the offer, but I'm not interested in selling, and that's final. Now, if you're done trying to buy my hotel out from under me, can we talk about this transitional phase and what it'll mean for my staff?"

The switch nearly gives me whiplash.

I narrow my eyes and study her carefully, trying to figure out what angle she's playing. For once, I'm having a hard time getting a read on her. She's tough as nails.

I'm man enough to know when to back off.

This negotiation isn't over, not by a longshot. There's a time to play hardball and a time to wait. I get the sense that pushing any further is only going to make her shut down completely.

What I wrote down may be the first offer, but it doesn't have to be the last. I have a feeling we're going to do this dance for a while.

It doesn't matter. She'll wind up selling to me just like they all do.

"We won't be rushing into any changes," I clarify. "Initially, we'll maintain business as usual. Given the current tension and the adjustment to a new co-owner, it's crucial to ease into things. I plan to observe each department closely to understand their operations better. Once I have a clear picture, I'll create a detailed schedule for implementing the Blackwood standards step by step."

Typically, one of my managers oversees the adaptation phase.

This one, I'll handle myself.

I rise from my chair, adjusting my suit jacket. Her eyes wander for a moment, and though it's brief, I'm still able to clock her checking me out. At least her attraction to me doesn't seem to have been faked.

"Shall we start the tour now?" I ask, motioning for her to stand and join me. "The sooner I see how things are run, the quicker I'll be out of your hair. At least for today."

"And how often will you be gracing us with your presence?" She rises from her seat, giving me a view of those long legs, and we exit the room together.

"Almost every day for the foreseeable future. Blackwood isn't a large corporate shell. I'm not here to assume managerial responsibilities, but our aim is to make decisions that facilitate a seamless transition under Blackwood's wing. We prefer a hands-on approach when it comes to our investments."

"As long as you keep those same hands to yourself, we won't have a problem."

Inwardly, I chuckle. That's rich, considering she was the one to come onto me last night. "Likewise," I say. "But this isn't the time nor the place to talk about that."

"Agreed."

J essica proceeds to give me an extensive tour of the hotel. I've seen most of it already. Norman gave me a tour when we were first discussing the sale, and I've stayed here three or four times prior to that. It really is a nice space. They've struck a good balance between comfort and elegance, something that can be difficult. It's clear that the money they've made has been pumped back into the property.

"I'm sure you know all the specifics already," Jessica says as we walk. "But in case you need a refresher given your *extensive* portfolio," she quips, and I let her comment slide, "we are a smaller hotel by comparison to our counterparts in the city. We have eighty rooms, with forty standard rooms, twenty deluxe rooms, ten suites—including the Presidential Suite—and ten executive rooms. All the furniture was updated and replaced just over a year ago. We also just finished a major renovation of our main lobby and suites, which I'm sure Norman told you all about."

"He did. One of the things that made this sale so appealing was how many updates and upgrades the hotel has had over the last few years."

"And despite it all, we're making profit," she says with a confident smile.

"Or, because of it. What about marketing?" I ask. "Norman said that was more his department, although you did handle some aspects of it. Who are you using to handle your marketing now?"

"You're looking at her."

My eyebrows shoot up. "You're running the hotel *and* handling the marketing? You know there are professionals who handle that sort of thing, right, Jessica?"

"Please, call me Jess. I'm well aware. And I'm open to passing on the responsibility to someone with hotel marketing experience, provided it fits within our budget."

"That can easily be arranged. All the marketing for our hotels is done through the same company. I'll reach out to one of my managers to get the ball rolling," I say. "I admire you handling it yourself, but it's best to leave it to the professionals."

She arches an eyebrow. "Is this *shade* about me not taking your offer? Clearly, neither Norman nor I were completely inexperienced in what we were doing."

"I'm a grown man, Jess. I don't do 'shade,'" I tell her with air quotes. "And while we're back on the subject, you should know that I'm not going to stop trying to buy you out. Blackwood doesn't do partnerships, and once I have a strategic blueprint for the integrational overhaul, there will be no stopping the progress."

Jess halts her steps and turns to face me. The outline of her nipples hint under the fabric of her blouse. I'd like to feel them against my tongue. "You're shameless, do you know that?" she asks, poking me in the chest. "You must know that!" My cock wakes with her touch. Her sharp breaths mimic the rhythm of her poking, and a flush of redness paints its way down her neck, determined to reach the curves of her freckled breasts. "I already told you that I'm not going to sell. Regardless of the money." She pokes me again. "Not now." Another poke. "Not ever." Yet another poke.

With each poke, my dick jerks slightly, but I keep up my poker face.

"How many more times do I have to say it?" she asks, double-poking me, and my dick emulates.

"As many times as it takes, until we finally land on a number that'll change your mind."

She shakes her head, and with a final, firmer poke she says, "Not going to happen," before lowering her hand.

"It always does," I say.

"You're relentless."

"You have no idea," I tell her. "Company battles make me hard."

She gasps, and her nipples press firmly against her blouse. We stand facing each other in the hall, the air around us thick with tension. The fun tension from last night, the combative kind, the kind that gets your blood pumping.

"You know what, since you're so keen on working alone, finish the tour yourself." Jess backs away with her hands in the air in mock surrender. "I've got work to do. I'm sure you can find your way around. Just don't bother my staff."

"Our staff, you mean."

She rolls her eyes and waves me off as she marches away. I stand there, enjoying the swaying of her hips as she goes.

9

JESS

I spend the rest of the day hiding out in my office, quietly fuming. He enrages me so much, I've lost all my charm capabilities.

He can go screw himself.

Jerk.

I can't believe I was ever attracted to him.

Hot mouth and body aside, he's a pompous dick, and not in the fun way. In the annoying, I want to kick him in the knee (or better, balls) kind of way. And maybe I'm being the slightest bit childish, but can anyone blame me?

No one likes their job being threatened and no one likes someone who comes in acting like they know what's best. Westerlyn Hotels are *mine*. They carry my blood, sweat, and tears. They're my dream, my legacy. And I'm not going to let an intimidating snobby rich douche take them from me. No matter how many times he tries to throw money in my face.

Been there, done that.

I sure as hell won't set myself up for a rerun of past mistakes.

My ex-boyfriend worked in finance. He ran the show at an up-and-coming capital enterprise as CEO. His intelligent mind, quick wit, and undeniable charm captivated me from the moment I met him. He was very tall, handsome, confident, ten years older than me, and I hate to admit it, but I was head over heels in an instant. Being an investment banker, he was always looking for the next sure thing. Me? I was too young and in love to realize that when it comes to money—or love, or weddings, or happy endings—a sure thing doesn't exist.

One day, I told him about this small, beautiful Central Park Plaza Hotel I wanted to buy. He knew it was my biggest dream to run a hotel of my own and suggested we go in together.

It sounded like the perfect idea, and of course I said yes.

I still remember the way my heart dropped when I got home, and he was gone. He didn't even have the decency to leave a note. And the hotel I'd wanted to buy? Was now his and only his.

Needless to say, my trust is hard earned.

Darn CEOs.

"Whoa, you look pissed."

I glance up from my desk to see Pauline standing in the doorway. "Is it that obvious?" I have been trying to keep it all inside, not wanting to let my staff notice how upset I am.

"Considering you're always disgustingly cheerful, yes. Yes, yes, it is." She steps in and closes the door behind her. "I take it the meeting with the new co-owner didn't go well?"

"It was a disaster," I tell her, rubbing my forehead, "but not for the reasons you're thinking."

She frowns and takes the seat across from my desk. "Why? What happened?"

With a heavy sigh, I let my head fall forward onto my keyboard with a *thunk*. "Let's just say—me and the CEO of Blackwood Hotels & Resorts, Mr. Sean Blackwood, have already met."

"Really? When?"

"Oh, you know, last night at Swayze's, and before that when he answered the door naked."

Pauline gasps, recalling my telling her all about it during my round. When I look up, she has one hand over her mouth, her eyes are as wide as saucers, and there's disbelief on her face. Finally, she speaks. "The new co-owner is your hot next-door neighbor?"

"The new co-owner is a jerk. A bona fide, overconfident, infuriating, jerk."

"But also, your hot next-door neighbor."

"Unfortunately, yes."

"Shit."

"You can say that out loud. More like a *shit*rilogy."

"Is he really that bad?"

I huff and lean back in my chair, staring up at the ceiling. "*Yes*."

"This is crazy. What are the odds?"

"Slim, very slim. And yet, here we are. Dammit, why did it have to be him? It could have been literally *anyone* else."

Pauline remains silent, and when I glance over, she's studying me carefully. "Then let me ask you another question." She leans forward. "Are you really mad at him or are you mad at yourself for...," She searches for the right word, "...fooling around with him?"

"It's both." Obviously.

Okay, maybe I'm slightly angrier with myself for doing what I did with him. After all, I have an iron-clad "no business entanglements—no exceptions" rule for a reason. *Duh*, it's practically written in the stars. Especially with CEOs.

I will never date another CEO again. Ever. Even if the underworld turns into an ice rink, count me out.

Of course, there's no way I could have known who he was. We never exchanged names, and I had no idea he was the jerk Norman sold his shares to. Still, the frustration is unwavering.

"I'm sure this makes everything ten times more awkward," Pauline says. "But there's no reason you both can't be adults about this."

She's right. I know she's right. I have to think on the bright side. For one, I got to "fool around" with him before he became an insufferable prick. But I won't allow him to outdo me, that's for certain. And two, the deal with Blackwood is something that can help the hotels expand their potential. I have so many plans and ideas, ones that have seemed like a dream, things I told myself I'd try once the hotels made profit for a year. With a company like Blackwood, some of those things can become a reality now. When he talked earlier about his strategic blueprint for the overhaul—while sounding way too cocky and know-it-all about it—I didn't get mad at his immediate assessment of room for growth.

Truth is, the business and success-oriented side of me was getting excited. I understand there's potential for enhancement.

"You're right, Pauline," I admit. "And I know the pros more than outweigh the cons. It just sucks."

"I know it does," she says in her dry way. "You were really into him."

"Okay, I wouldn't go *that* far. I was drawn to him by some electric pull, yes. Call it a momentary lapse in judgment. Call it a surge of balcony-adrenaline. Call it cocktail blindness. Of course, now when I think about his face all I want to do is poke him in the eye."

"Whoa, easy there, killer, don't go too far," Pauline teases and leans back. "In all seriousness, there's a simple solution that'll help you deal with all these complex emotions."

"Please, I'm all ears."

"Sleep with him."

I burst out laughing. "God dammit, Pauline. Be serious."

"Oh, I am," she says, without an ounce of humor. "Despite how pissed at him you are, that doesn't change the fact that he made you come. That's more than your ex ever did. Seriously, Jess, what more is there to think about? I say, sleep with him and get it out of your system.

Otherwise, you'll just drive yourself crazy wondering what it would be like."

"Yeah, that's not going to happen. Any desire has been successfully stamped out after that meeting."

"If you say so," Pauline says, getting to her feet. "Can't wait to meet him. Where's he now?"

"No idea. I left him on the second floor when he tried to buy my half of the hotels."

"Oh, geez."

"Yeah. I love this place too much to simply hand it over."

"I admire you for that, Jess. I really do."

Pauline heads for the door, and just before she opens it, I ask, "What would you do?"

"Me? If I were you, I'd take the deal and count my money on a beach somewhere with my family."

Her swift response catches me off guard. She didn't even think twice. "Just like that?"

"Hell yeah. Life is too short to sit in a hotel office all day, no matter how comfy it is."

She has a point, I admit. Savoring a Sex on the Beach cocktail on an actual beach, rather than being embroiled in a brutal office war with a presumptuous billionaire co-owner, undeniably has its advantages.

"And...you wouldn't sleep with him?" I ask.

Pauline makes a mock noise of surprise. "I'm a happily married woman, Jess. Me, I would never, *ever*, dream of such a scenario," she teases. "That being said, you're not me. You don't have to like the guy to have some fun. Just saying."

Without another word, she spins on her heel, and exits my office to get back to work.

I know she's joking to cheer me up. And I get how any lingering attraction will make this whole scenario difficult.

But I meant what I said. I can't think about him without my heart spiking with indignation.

However, I know if I'm going to win his favor and demonstrate my indispensability as a team player—exceptional enough for him to knock off any thoughts of buying my shares—I must set aside last night's events. For the good of my staff and my own sanity.

Squaring my shoulders, I take a few deep breaths and bring my focus back to work, pushing away the hot memories from the night before.

I don't see him the rest of the day. Following his tour, he requested supplementary files from Sarah (with a dash of grumbling about why we still rely on antiquated paper files instead of embracing the digital era, *good grief*), and then gracefully departed the premises, en route to his office at Blackwood Inc. At least, that's where I assume he went.

It doesn't matter to me as long as he's off the property.

I've never been one to avoid my problems, but in this particular instance, I welcome the distance. It gives me a chance to decompress and figure out how I want to handle this "delicate" situation we find ourselves in.

I conclude the best way is to hash things out with him as soon as possible.

Tonight.

The remainder of my day is consumed with calming my concerned colleagues who pop by my office door. They find comfort in understanding that Mr. Blackwood is merely a new co-owner, while I firmly maintain the role of manager. In between these visits, I juggle my usual day-to-day duties and address Norman's organizational tasks. It's exhausting but keeps my mind busy, and when 7:00 p.m. rolls around,

I'm more than ready to go home—even though that means dealing with Sean Blackwood.

But I've had enough time to think about what I want to say to him.

As soon as I step off the elevator, with purpose, I march to his door and knock. After a few seconds, when no one answers, I knock again. Nothing. He must not be home yet. Deflated, I let myself into my own apartment, greeted by Pippin's delighted chirping.

"Pippin, Mommy's home!" I cross the room, open the cage door, and reach inside. Immediately, he hops onto my finger, still chirping when I take him out. "And did you have a great day?"

I stroke his little head, and he gives me an affectionate nibble before hop-flying onto my shoulder. He never fails to make me smile. I know for a fact he'll be perfectly content hanging out on my shoulder for the rest of the evening.

"Pippin, you would not believe the day I had," I tell him, tossing my purse onto the couch. "As soon as that grumpy neighbor of ours gets home, I'm going to confront him about yesterday. But first, dinner."

I bring the food app up on my phone, trying to decide what I'm in the mood for. Given how all over the place the day was, ordering in is preferred. After tapping the "Confirm order" button, I clean Pippin's cage, replenish his water, and refill his food trays. Squawking, he watches me and then hops to his food tray, eager to munch on a fresh piece of apple as I collapse on the couch. With a full belly, the little cutie pie ventures back out. He wanders for a bit and returns to my shoulder where he remains, preening himself.

As I wait for my quintessential New-York-style vegetable and chickpea curry, I get lost socializing on my favorite platform, scrolling through video after video, laughing and amusing myself.

That's when I hear footsteps out in the hallway.

Part of me thinks I should give Sean a chance to decompress before cornering him and demanding we talk. Then again, I had zero time to prepare before walking into that meeting this morning. Besides, the sooner we talk things out, the better.

Taking a deep breath, I heave myself off the couch and step out of my apartment. By now, Sean's already inside.

I waste no time knocking. "Hello?"

The moment he opens the door and sees me, I launch into the speech I prepared. "Don't say anything, just listen," I demand, my voice positive, even playful, but firm. "Abandoning you on our tour was childish of me, yes, but you have to see that I have every right to be angry. First and foremost, this entire deal was done behind my back without my knowledge. And while that's an issue I addressed with Norman, you coming in and trying to buy me out was frustrating."

"Jess—"

"Not done yet," I say, holding up my hand. "I'm already feeling like my opinion wasn't considered, and now you're trying to take away my dream. I've worked my ass off bringing those hotels to where they are now, and I don't appreciate a stranger trying to swoop in and take it all from me."

"Norman had every right—"

"Nope, not done yet." I cut him off a second time. "Secondly, if all that wasn't bad enough, now I have to deal with the fact that I..." I pause, searching for the right word, "... 'playfully engaged' with the new co-owner of my hotels." It's the best expression I can come up with to make it sound less awkward than it already is. "I can assure you, if I'd had any idea who you were last night, I wouldn't have flirted with you. And I definitely wouldn't have cornered you. Nor let you do...*that* with me."

He's giving me a funny look—has been since the moment he opened the door. It gets to the point where I have to address it.

"And *why* are you looking at me like that?" I ask.

"It's not every day that your neighbor and new colleague shows up at your door to monologue at you with a bird sitting on their shoulder."

Oh, shoot. I never put Pippin back in his cage. I immediately reach up to stroke the bird's feathers, which are slightly ruffled. He must sense my feelings toward Sean, or maybe he's confused as to why he's outside of our apartment. Realizing that my passionate speech is probably being undercut by the bird perched on me, I feel the heat rise in my cheeks.

"One second."

I storm back into my place and put Pippin (who thinks this is a riot) in his cage. When I return to Sean's, he's no longer where I left him, however, the door to his apartment is still open.

I let myself in, finding him standing at a small bar next to the balcony doors. He's making himself a coffee and begins to speak without even bothering to look at me.

"You expect me to believe it was a coincidence?" he asks. "That you really didn't know who I was?"

"How the hell would I have known?" I demand. "You and I never exchanged names, and Norman dropped a fait accompli on me after my two-week trip."

He snorts in disbelief and makes a gesture to offer me a drink, but I shake my head. Picking up his steaming cup, he turns to look me in the eye, his expression dark and serious. "Very convincing. He didn't give you the name of the company who bought his shares?"

"He sure did. Point is, I didn't know *your* name." *Or that you were the CEO of Blackwood*, but I don't say it. Everyone in the hotel business knows Blackwood Hotels & Resorts. Is my life falling apart just because I didn't make *Forbes Magazine* my bedtime reading? Undoubtedly, high and mighty Sean Blackwood's photograph graces their cover like a frequent flyer.

"I'm almost considering believing you," he growls. "I'm curious, what exactly was your plan? Seduce the new boss and use it as leverage?"

"I'm not that kind of person, and I'd appreciate you not to think of me as such," I say. "But if you're really fixated on that made-up scenario, then tell me how I tried to use last night to my advantage."

He's silent, stirring his coffee rather than answering my question. It's clear from his reticence that he doesn't have an answer, and it makes me smirk in triumph.

"*Exactly*," I exclaim. "You can't because I definitely didn't."

He puts the spoon down. "You could have been trying to gather insider information or just gain a psychological upper hand."

I can't help but laugh, genuinely amused. "Oh, come on now, Mr. CEO. You're giving me way too much credit," I say. "I had no idea who you were at the time, and trust me, if I were really out to gain an advantage, I would have used far more sophisticated methods than a tipsy 'chance encounter' in Swayze's bathroom."

There's an awkward pause where we both just look at each other.

He really has beautiful eyes, a rich, dark forest green, deep, and captivating.

Long, striking lashes.

Well-defined, masculine brows.

"What's done is done," he breaks the silence, "but I'm sure it goes without saying that it's not going to happen again."

"Well, there's something we can finally both agree on."

"Good."

"Yeah, good." I nod, slightly irritated. "And just so you know. First, I'm not interested in a repeat performance with someone after they gave me a 'hit and run.' Our encounter was rather...brief. Second, even if I were interested in a snack rather than a meal, your attitude today successfully killed any attraction I may have had."

"Same," he says.

Annoyance bolts through me. "What the hell did *I* do? *You* were the one acting like a jerk and trying to steal my business out from under me."

"I'm not trying to steal it. I'm trying to buy it. I was and still am willing to negotiate the payout, but you're being too stubborn to even listen to what I'm offering."

"Oh, I heard you, loud and clear. Yet you don't seem to hear me when I say I'm not interested in money."

"Blackwood has acquired nearly fifteen hotels in the last six months alone. I've worked with clients who were just as stubborn as you, in some cases even more. And let me tell you this: every single one of them ended up taking the deal in the end. Every. Single. One. So you can lie to yourself all you want, but *everyone* has a price."

The absolute nerve of this guy.

Keep cool. Be warm. Charm your way to victory.

It's something my mom instilled in me from an early age.

I inhale a deep breath to retain my composure and stop myself from stomping away like I did earlier. "Here's something to consider, *Sean*," I say with a (diplomatic) smile, and the use of his first name catches even me by surprise, though I keep my voice charmingly steady to conceal just how worked up I truly am. "I'll bet you a million dollars they ended up taking the payout because they didn't want to deal with *you* anymore, Mr. 'I Work Alone.' I'm not going to speak for them, and I don't doubt some of them have dollar signs in their eyes. However, I'm sure that a few of them felt forced out, felt like their life's work was being pulled away from them, and they took the money because they suspected that you weren't willing to play nice."

Okay, so all that wasn't polite or diplomatic, but the truth never hurt anyone.

"And that's why Norman sold his shares?"

I blink. "Well...that's not what I said. All I'm saying is that that's not going to happen to me," I insist, my composed smile gone. "I sank my life savings into the Westerlyn chain. I worked my fingers to the bone at each property, sacrificed birthdays, holidays, weekends, and...even a wedding." I swallow, warding off the flood of personal memories. "Any-way...I saw the potential. And now that I'm finally where I was always meant to be, where my staff has become my family, I'm not going to trade that for a few extra zeros on a check." I narrow my eyes at him. "So either find a way to set your ego aside and work with me or prepare for the fight of your life. The choice is yours."

I don't wait for a response. I don't need one.

I've said what I wanted to say and that's all that matters. Feeling significantly lighter, I turn my back on Sean and exit his apartment. Who knows if my words got through to him?

All I can do is wait to see what tomorrow brings.

10

SEAN

I don't remember the last time I was told off like that.

I'm no stranger to confrontation, especially work-related ones. Over the years, I've ruffled a lot of feathers and have had my fair share of angry arguments. But there's something different about Jess. Maybe it's because the first time we met she was so bubbly and cheerful (annoyingly so), or maybe it has to do with the steadfast claim that she doesn't care about money. How the hell—as hotel owner—do you not care about money? It could even be because during her passionate speech she had a bird hanging out on her shoulder like it was nothing.

One thing is for sure: it's enough to give me pause.

I watch her walk away, eyes on her hips, noting that she doesn't even slam the door behind her. She closes it respectfully, leaving me in silence.

What wedding did she sacrifice? She made a subtle reference to a rebound in the bar, but obviously, there's someone in her past who left a bad impression.

Sitting in my favorite armchair, I stir my hot coffee, deep in thought.

Okay, fair is fair. She *didn't* know who I was when we met at the bar last night. Thinking about the expression on her face when she walked into the meeting this morning further proves her point. Slowly, I'm starting to realize that my neighbor wears her heart on her sleeve. If she had been planning something, she'd have been smug and obnoxious about it.

I take a sip of the black liquid, and the bitter flavor surges on my tongue.

This does put me in an awkward situation.

The board is expecting me to buy her out. While there's not exactly a time limit on this, sooner is typically better. Of course, there's nothing in writing that says I can't work with her. In times of transition, we often work with current and previous owners to ensure the process is as smooth as possible. Jess is clearly willing to work with me. I don't see why I can't extend that partnership further than I normally would.

My mind jumps back to that dimly lit bathroom at Swayze's. I think about her smooth thighs and delicious clit, about how good she felt pressed against me and how eager she was. Having a woman be sexually avid like that did it for me. Don't get me wrong, I'm all about being in charge of my personal life and bedroom. Yet, that doesn't mean I don't appreciate initiative. My lips tingle at the memory, and I can almost taste her on my tongue.

I halt my thoughts.

There's no guarantee she's going to be easy to work with. There's also no guarantee that she's not going to defy me at every turn. I don't need that kind of headache. Dealing with my father is enough to last a life-time, especially considering the intensity of the process ahead.

Whatever happened, happened. It's not going to have any influence on my decisions moving forward.

My cell rings.

"Yeah?" I bark.

"Mr. Blackwood?" Jasmine's voice carries urgency. "I've identified the competitor rumored to be interested in acquiring Westerlyn Hotels."

"Who is it?"

"Richard Rutherford."

God dammit.

I knew it.

The situation couldn't be more unfavorable for us. Richard Rutherford, the CEO and owner of the globally renowned Rutherford Plaza Hotels, stands as our most formidable rival. Possessing substantial wealth, abundant resources, and the influential power to make significant moves, he effortlessly dominates the chess board. His interest in Westerlyn is far from ideal, particularly in light of his previous triumph in an overseas hotel chain acquisition, where he outmaneuvered me by presenting a last-minute offer I couldn't match.

I tell Jasmine to keep the info under wraps for now and end the call. After I polish off my coffee, I stand up to get myself something to eat.

The next morning, I head into my office before going to the hotel. I'm not exactly in the best of moods, and when I find my father already there, looking out the window with his back to me, I bite back an exasperated sigh. If I let myself into his office as much as he lets himself into mine, he'd fly off the handle.

"You just let yourself in?" I ask, sitting at my desk.

"That's no way to greet your father."

"It is when I find him randomly standing in my office."

Dad turns around to look at me, not a trace of amusement at my jab. "Where are we on the Westerlyn account?"

"Norman's signed the agreement, and I met with the other owner for our face-to-face introduction."

"You're not supposed to be meeting with her, you're supposed to be convincing her to *sell*."

"She's not interested at this time."

My dad arches an eyebrow. "You weren't able to convince her?"

"Hardly," I say, ignoring his jab, my voice deadpan. "She has invested significant time and resources into these hotels, and retirement isn't a persuasive angle, given her age. Convincing her to align with our perspective will require substantial effort. If we're not careful, we run the risk of her doubling down. She also has the respect of her staff, and I don't doubt they'd be on her side if that happens."

"Staff is replaceable. They don't have to see things our way. There are plenty of other people in the city who'd be more than willing to have the job and do it the way we want."

"I'm not going to fire her whole staff just to prove a point."

"And that's why you're not on the board yet. You're not willing to do what needs to be done."

Something inside of me snaps.

Maybe it's the cavalier way he's willing to take away people's livelihoods, maybe it's him rubbing salt in the wound when it comes to me running the board. Whatever the case, anger and defiance rush through my veins at an alarming rate.

"I'm not on the board yet because you refuse to relinquish control," I reply sharply. "Stop micromanaging me. I know what I'm doing. I've convinced hundreds of people to sell to us and my closing rate is higher than anyone else's." This includes him, and he knows it. "I'll get her to sell, and I'll do it my way."

Dad doesn't even flinch. "Do I really have to remind you that not too long ago, you encountered a significant loss to Rutherford Plaza Hotels?"

"Anything else?" I bark, refusing to revisit that topic again.

"You've always been so hotheaded, son. There's no need to get worked up over a simple conversation."

"Are we done here?"

"I'll come back later when you've had time to cool off."

Yeah, right. Of course he'd play things as if he ended the conversation. Douglas Blackwood can't stand losing, even if it's only verbally.

He turns to leave, but stops in his tracks. "Ah, hang on. But before I go," he says, handing over some mundane document, "send this fax for me, will you? My fax machine is acting up, and Jasmine isn't in yet."

"There's no fax machine in this company, except in your office. You're the only one clinging to old technology."

He exits my office, and I sit there for a moment, fuming.

Then I have an idea.

After a moment of reflection, I pick up my phone and dial the hotel's number. Soon after, I'm transferred to Jess.

"Hey, it's Sean. I need to meet with you this morning."

After a few moments of silent contemplation, she says, "Eleven o'clock, my office."

I spend the next hour preparing and make it to the hotel with about five minutes to spare. Sarah's desk is a jumble of files and thick folders, a clear attempt to fill the void left by Norman Whitman's absence. She informs me that Jess is in Norman's office—*my* new office for the time of the overhaul—and I find her standing by one of the shelves, eyes narrowed at the fax machine, meticulously entering a number. I open my mouth to speak, and before I can utter a syllable, she raises a finger and shushes me.

My eyebrows take a hike to my hairline. I'm not used to being shushed. "Did you just—?"

She doesn't even look at me. "Just give me a second."

Eventually, she draws back and finally looks at me. "Sorry about that," she says, giving me a surprisingly charming smile. "I have to send this fax to the magazine today."

"Magazine?"

"Yeah, for the hotel's ad reservations."

"You don't have to do that anymore," I remind her. "Remember, I said we'll start taking care of all that."

Jess swirls the ice cubes in her coffee, still focused on the fax machine. "You also said that for now it's business as usual. I figured I'd keep doing it until we have a solid plan moving forward."

"Fair enough. But there's a paperless way to do it, you know that, right?" I remark, as the fax machine's dialing sounds permeate the room.

Jess chuckles softly, as if acknowledging their attachment to the traditional method. "Well, Norman loved his fax machine. The magazine's department seems to prefer it too."

I walk to the empty desk so I can sit. She looks up from the paper that is slowly feeding through the machine, giving me a strange look.

"What's wrong?" I ask in confusion.

"Nothing, it's just...that was Norman's chair."

It was fairly obvious from the start that there's a father-daughter relationship between her and the former owner. I'm sure that's part of the reason she's fighting this deal as much as she is. And while I can empathize, my less emotional and more rational side doesn't have time for such nostalgia.

"It's my chair *and* office now. You're going to have to get used to seeing me sitting in it."

Finished with her task, she removes the paper from the machine and turns to me. Her expression hardens, and she grips her cup tighter. In a playful tone, she then says, "I don't have to get used to anything, *Mr. Blackwood*." She quirks her head at me. "Now, did you come here just to annoy me?"

"I had an idea this morning. One that I think you'll want to hear."

"I already told you I'm not selling."

"I'm aware. You've made that abundantly clear," I say. "So, I've decided to offer a compromise. Sit."

She perks up and proceeds to take a seat in front of my desk. "What kind of compromise?"

"The kind that's going to work for both of us."

"I should hope so, given that that is the definition of compromise." She crosses her long legs, observing me closely as she does.

I can't detect even a trace of the heat and desire that was present at the bar. Now, there's only apprehension, but also a hint of curiosity.

For a moment, I can't fathom that the Jess sitting in front of me and the Jess who cornered me in the bathroom are one and the same. That Jess was sexy, seductive, and spontaneous, eager to have something quick and messy with a near stranger. The memory of her hot body along mine, her gorgeous tits pressing softly against my chest, hits me full force, and I have the urge to press her against the wall, push up her skirt, and pick up right where we left off. I want to feel those thighs around my wrist and her arousal coating my hand as I make her moan.

For a moment, I have to remind myself of where we are and draw my focus back to work, willing my dick to stay put.

I clear my throat, and say, "The compromise is this: You sell your shares, and in return, I'm prepared to provide you with invaluable insights. You and I join forces to enhance the hotel and align it with the standards of our fellow Blackwood properties."

"That's it?" She interrupts me. "That's all you're offering?"

"Hold on a second, I'm not done, I'm willing to increase my offer by—"

"*You* hold on," she says calmly. "I chose the wallpaper, every house-plant is hand-picked, I bought photographs at the flea market, I sampled hundreds of culinary specialties, I have so many more visions, and you're offering me *money*? No, Mr. Blackwood, you have to do better than that. *Much* better."

"That's why I'd like you to remain in a managerial position."

Her eyebrows rise in genuine surprise, clearly not expecting that as an option.

She blinks. Twice.

"Once you've sold your shares to me, you *continue* in your current position," I explain, "as my employee on a payroll. Job security is a given

—in fact, I guarantee that your position as 'Director of Hotel Operations at Westerlyn Hotels' is backed. You can maintain your current role and continue to guide the staff and shape the hotel's future. Empowered by Blackwood capital, your visions can reach unparalleled heights."

Jess is quiet, slowly oscillating left and right in her chair as she stares at me.

When she doesn't speak, I add, "You'll receive a more than fair buyout amount and salary. You'll be a multimillionaire overnight. Set for life. Immune if the economy goes downhill."

Even if money isn't her priority, my offer is opening up a realm of business opportunities while preserving her decision-making power within the hotel. Her commitment to her staff, as she confided in me, will remain the priority.

Declining this opportunity would be outright foolish.

It's a win-win deal for her.

I take it as a good sign that she hasn't said no right away or thrown me out of the office—attempted to throw me out. I'd not leave willingly since this is now my office.

We sit in tense silence, although that tension is radiating more from her than it is from me.

My dick twitches in anticipation of her response.

"Quite the interesting proposal," she finally says, her tone careful and measured. "Even if I entertained your idea and become your employee—what if we don't get along?" She pauses, then shakes her head decisively, a firm no. "Too risky."

God dammit.

I was close.

So damn close.

There *has* to be something she wants. What does a woman like her desire most? What can I offer her that can't be bought? How do I get Jess Summers to sell, before my competition does?

11

SEAN

*W*hen I leave the apartment in the morning, she's already left for work early. Work has been quite demanding for both of us.

The first thing I do once I leave the apartment is stop by her favorite coffee place for an iced French vanilla with a shot of espresso. I'm aware of how occupied she is, not just with the transition, but also managing a large group looking to stay at Westerlyn for their yearly retreat. She probably won't have the time to go, considering that she occasionally uses getting coffee as a way to take a breather in the midst of her busy mornings. Maybe the refreshing chill of the cup in her hands will help alleviate some of the frostiness between us.

However, when I arrive at Westerlyn, her office door is closed. Briefly, I halt at Sarah's desk. Having learned that she prefers green smoothies over hot drinks, I'd ordered one for her too, and she plucks it out of the holder. Everyone deserves a little treat once in a while. With a delighted smile, Sarah informs me that Jess received an unexpected visitor.

"Who?" I ask, marching toward my own office.

"Mr. Rutherford."

I nearly fumble the coffee holder with the remaining two cups. Turning to face her, I confirm, "Richard Rutherford?"

"Yes." Sarah nods, taking a sip of her smoothie.

Well, shit.

I walk into my office, setting the coffees down.

The rumors and the information my PA uncovered were spot on. The shark is here to make his offer. To outbid me. To get his grabby hands on *my* hotel. To steal her shares from under me.

Dammit.

Not gonna happen. Over my dead body.

How much is the bastard willing to pay? He can easily outbid me, but fortunately, it's not money she's after. Yet who knows what else he has up his sleeve? My father's mocking face is already in my mind, taunting me about his warnings to get her to sell as quickly as possible before some savvy investor swoops in.

Richard Rutherford of all people.

I wish I could be a fly on the wall. Perhaps I should confidently walk in, hand her the coffee, and loiter around, maybe even pretend to need her printer for something? It would be completely unbelievable, considering my commitment to not wasting paper, but who would even notice? Answer: she would notice. If *anybody* would notice, it'd be her. I've given her a hard enough time about going paperless as it is.

I need a better idea.

My office phone rings. It's an internal call coming from her office.

I pick up. "Yeah?"

"Babe," I hear Jess say brightly, even cheerfully, "will you please come into my office for a second?"

My heart hammers. "Babe"? Is that what she said?

"Sure. Gladly," I say without hesitation. I don't even attempt to conceal the upswing in my mood.

Deciding to not bring the coffees along—it wouldn't be appropriate to offer her a coffee while not being able to accommodate her guest—I walk to her door and enter after my first knock. Jess is already strolling toward me, meeting me halfway.

"Hi, babe," she says joyfully, giving me a gorgeous smile, "there you are!"

Her pleading eyes are locked on mine, her expression begging me to *play along.*

Before I can answer, she leans in to give me a kiss on my lips. At least, that's what I think she intends to do. I realize too late that she was actually aiming for my cheek. She almost squeaks in surprise when I—accidentally (for the most part)—turn my head and our lips touch. Of course, I let my mouth linger for a moment. You know, playing along.

It feels good to press my lips to hers. It feels natural, as it should.

When she pulls back, I detect a micro-embarrassment-slash-amusement at the kiss mix-up, but she confidently brushes it off, saying, "Honey, let me introduce you to Mr. Rutherford." She faces the tall man seated in front of her desk, who's looking straight at us. "Richard, this is Sean Blackwood, my fiancé."

I blink.

I'm her fiancé?

I'm not just "Babe" but "officially engaged"?

Okay, why not.

She's fighting fire with fire. I can work with that.

Turning toward him, I'm trying to make sense of it all. Most likely, there's some unfinished business between the two of them, and I'll gladly portray her fake husband-to-be, shielding her from my main competitor.

This is clearly to my advantage.

Richard Rutherford, the biggest hotel mogul in the nation with wealth that engulfs his "I get what I want" approach, appears surprised at the announcement. His jaw clenches, but only for a moment, before he sets up his poker face. She called him "Richard," addressed him informally, and I get a sense they've known each other for years. For whatever reason he's here, private or business, I'm not entirely sure. What I do know is he didn't expect to see me here—engaged to this stunning woman.

He gets up and faces me. He's definitely aged since the last time I saw him, at the Grand Hotelier Convention in London a year back, and throughout the years at one of the city's high-profile fundraising galas, including, of course, the Grand Hospitality Affair. His salt-and-pepper hair adds an air of sophistication, and he stands two inches taller than me, dressed in a dark blue Brioni suit with a top-tier timepiece gracing his wrist.

"We've met," I inform her as we shake hands.

"Small world," Richard says in his deep baritone. "How do you do, Mr. Blackwood?" He smirks, just as he did when we competed in a bidding war, both of us eager to acquire a prominent hotel chain in Europe. I wasn't a sore loser, even though my father never fails to rub it in.

"Good," I reply, keeping it friendly. "How are you?"

"Honey, are you ready?" Jess interrupts, effectively putting a stop to any potential conversation. "I don't want to be late. The jeweler is wait-ing." She beams at me.

"Ready, baby," I say, and a chuckle escapes. I don't even have to pretend. It feels nice and natural to call her "Baby." Also, the whole situ-ation is hilarious. *The jeweler is waiting?*

Richard grabs his jacket, understanding the message, and heads toward the door. When he reaches for the knob, he pivots to face her. "Think about my offer, Jessie."

Jessie? They definitely have a private history.

Do I really want to know what else they shared?

"No need," she replies, her tone icy. "The answer is the same." For a moment, I'm baffled. Yes, I've seen her assertive side, but this coldness is on a whole other level. While Jess argues, and damn, argue she does, she usually maintains a touch of playfulness. Here, there's exactly zero of that.

"I'll see you at the charity auction in two weeks." He looks from me to her then back at me.

"Of course." I nod. "As is the tradition every year."

"Bye, Jessie." He faces me. "Mr. Blackwood."

"Have a good day, Mr. Rutherford," I say.

He gives me a curt nod and heads out.

My happy mood isn't an act. I'm *ecstatic* that my competitor bit the dust. The match is 1:1. Clearly, I won this one—the easiest win I've ever achieved. Somehow, the most amusing too.

As soon as he's gone, Jess quickly shuts the door and turns to me. "I'm so sorry, Sean. He surprised me, and this was the only way to make him understand that I'm *not* interested. And never will be. Thanks for playing along."

Not interested in...what? Selling the hotel? Dating him?

"You're welcome. Any time. How do you know him?" I ask.

"We were engaged at one point, and it didn't end well," she says curtly. "It's not my favorite conversational topic."

Talk about a plot twist. That, I didn't see coming.

At least the whole fake fiancé thing makes sense now. There seems to be a pattern in her picking her fiancés. Slowly, the puzzle pieces begin to fall into place. He is the "missed wedding" she referred to, the rebound, the reason she found herself drowning her sorrows at Swayze's.

"Did he make you an offer for the hotel?" I ask, getting down to the interesting part.

She shifts away uncomfortably. "He did."

"How much did he offer you?"

She turns. "A lot."

I remain standing where I am, watching her walk to her desk. "How much?" I press.

She shrugs, indicating this conversation is done, that she's ready to get back to her duties. When I don't make a move, she looks back up. "Not enough. It's not important. Also, none of your business. I'm not selling to him."

"Well, good. You shouldn't."

I'm relieved, even if not calmed. "Not enough" won't deter a man like Richard Rutherford. Somehow, he's caught wind of the chain's immense potential and expressed interest, most likely upon learning of Norman Whitman's retirement. I doubt that was his final play. My presence won't dissuade him—if anything, it will embolden him. Like the shark he is, he has detected blood, and individuals like him thrive on challenging deals.

I must stay vigilant. Unlike me, he doesn't have a board to answer to.

"You should have called security on him," I joke (not really).

"Right?" She smiles, unbuttoning her jacket. "I should have. Next time, I will."

"Be right back." Snapping my gaze away from her curves, I walk to my office, grab her coffee and head back.

When I return, she's already sitting at her computer, quietly getting into her morning duties. It's the first time I've had a moment to take in her office. It's cozy, not the typical hotel manager setup like Norman's, with two plush armchairs decked with green pillows. The walls are painted in soft greenish tones. The heavy pine desk bears traces of its previous life, and is covered with a jumble of documents and folders. My eyes land on a photo of her standing between her folks, in front of what seems to be the family hotel in a woodland area, with two Great Danes playing around. It's impossible to overlook the striking resemblance between Jess and her mother, although her mom sports glasses, and short brown hair with numerous grays. Standing firm, her father wields a quiet authority and a noticeable robust physique.

I place the French vanilla on her desk, and she looks at me with surprise. "What's this?"

"I thought it was obvious."

She looks amused by my response and lets out a chuckle. "I know *what* it is. I meant why did you get me coffee?"

"A fiancé can't get his fiancée a drink?"

She smirks. "Other people can. You usually don't. I thought..."

When she doesn't finish her sentence, I ask, "What did you think?"

Jess studies me carefully, and I can see that she's not sure how to respond. She frowns and regards me suspiciously but picks up the cup regardless.

"Thanks," she says, giving me a warm smile. She takes a big sip. "So, about that charity event Richard mentioned. You're going?"

"Yes, I attend the Grand Hospitality Affair every year, representing Blackwood. Interested in going? I can smuggle you in."

"Well, the thing is, I already have a ticket from Norman. There's an art piece that's going to be auctioned, and I was thinking of acquiring it for the lobby. It would be perfect, well, if I can get it for a reasonable price. I was looking forward to going, but now..."

"...but now it looks like we're attending, as an engaged couple?" I finish for her.

She blinks, then takes another gulp of her coffee. "Well...only so *he* thinks we're an engaged couple. Do you mind? He knows I'm going. He saw my ticket." She gestures to the burgundy auction ticket next to her laptop. "And it would be weird if I went alone. I mean...all we need to do is show up together. That's it. We keep it under wraps for everybody else."

I shrug. "Doable. For everybody else, we're just two people attending an event."

"But wait...what if people ask who I am?"

"I'll introduce you by your name and as co-owner of Westerlyn. We come late, leave early. People attending are mostly interested in their own affairs. Don't worry. Should any question arise: we're private, we haven't decided to go public yet. Done."

"Oh, that'll work." She looks at me with a thankful expression. "You really don't mind playing along?"

"Let's say, I can arrange it—if you cooperate."

Her shoulders stiffen. "Cooperate?"

"You know what I want in return," I say, satisfied with the bargaining tool she has presented to me. "How about this? If I play along as your fake fiancé for the next few weeks, you reconsider my proposal. You said it's risky, but I'll say let's embrace the challenge. What do you say? At least don't shoot my offer down right off the bat."

After a pause, she finally nods. "I won't say no right away." Her tone is careful and measured. "I'm going to think on it."

"Fine." I nod. "My offer is good, and you know it."

Jess regards me carefully, as if she's trying to gain insight into what I'm thinking. She doesn't have to look too deep. I'm not hiding anything. I have no intention of deceiving her in any way. This isn't some kind of power play to placate her.

If there's one thing I learned early in life, it's that deception and deceit won't achieve satisfactory results, at least not in my book. Besides, the way Jess acted in Norman's presence and the hurt I've seen in her eyes leads me to believe she appreciates openness and loyalty.

At least something we both see eye to eye on.

It's nice to see her softening toward my idea, if only a little.

"Are we going to the jeweler now or later?" I ask. "As far as I know, he's got a one-of-a-kind engagement ring on standby waiting for us."

She smiles, her features are half a shade brighter. It's not the smile she gave me when we first met, but it's a smile nonetheless, which is a step in a positive direction. I hope.

"Not so fast," she says. "How long do I have to think it over?"

"I can hold the board off for another day. Any longer than that will be pushing it, and then someone else from the company will likely get involved."

AKA, my father will butt in, and I'm not going to let that happen.

She sits up in her chair, placing her empty coffee cup on the desk. "You'll have my answer by then."

I walk to my office, sit down at my desk and power up my computer, occasionally taking a sip of my own drink. I can tell I've thrown her off—much like she did with me. Which means I've achieved my goal: to keep her on her toes—just as she keeps me on mine.

The rest of the day is fairly quiet as we both handle our tasks, barely speaking unless to exchange pertinent work information. Even still, my mind is on high alert, and I feel more aware of her presence than I have ever been before.

12

JESS

When I heard that Sean had arrived, I reacted without thinking. Ultimately, it was the right thing to do.

Thank goodness he's so quick-witted and played his role as my fiancé to perfection. That kiss—okay, more like a peck—was purely accidental (thanks, cosmic energies!), and, believe it or not, it ended up playing out perfectly.

In no way could I let Richard think I was sitting around, all depressed, still pining after him while he looked better than ever, all smug and mighty. He didn't even try to conceal the fact he's the most successful hotelier on the planet—*conceited prick*—and most likely privately incredibly happy too.

Sure, my initial instinct was to kick him out, but that's something young Jess would have done. Behaving emotionally like that would only boost his stupid ego, letting him believe I still had feelings for him. I don't. Not anymore.

The other reason I gave Richard a few minutes was my curiosity about the offer he wanted to present, and honestly, the deep satisfaction of telling him to screw off, no matter what he offered. It felt *fantastic* to say no.

My fake engagement was the cherry on top. Richard and his "unrefusable offer" were out of there like a bullet.

Ha!

Fuck you very much!

But now, there's this charity event I must attend with my new fake fiancé. Skipping it would raise suspicions.

I sit, thinking about Sean's offer.

I think of sitting on a beach, slurping some colorful ice-cold concoction.

One never knows how the economy will turn. Right now, we're making a little profit and keeping up with expenses—but that could easily change. I'm aware I'm very much in a David and Goliath situation. That doesn't mean I'm not gonna put up a fight, if necessary, but I know I have to think about what would be better for the business in the long run. And mostly, what would be best for my staff.

I n the late afternoon, once Sean has left for Blackwood, I call Norman and tell him that Sean wants to buy me out.

"I was afraid of that," he admits. It sounds like there is wind and waves in the background.

"You were? Geez, thanks, Norman."

"Which is why I made it a point to tell him that you won't sell."

I lay out the pros and cons, tell him that I'm not a fan of the idea of being beholden to *anyone,* let alone Mr. Blackwood and a faceless board I haven't met.

"I don't envy you having to make that decision," Norman says after listening carefully. "If he offers you what he offered me, you'd recoup twice your life savings you invested. But keep in mind that Sean Blackwood is a very smart and incredibly powerful man. He didn't get to where he is by making emotional decisions. So, if you decide to sell *and stay*, don't let your heart sway you when dealing with him. I don't wanna see you get hurt again."

Norman knows how shattered I was when my ex dumped me and robbed me of my dream. It's his way of subtly cautioning me to not fall for Sean Blackwood, not lose my heart to him, not to repeat my past.

"I appreciate that," I say confidently, "but you don't have to worry about me. He's a CEO. He has a VIP seat in the 'Above All, No Way!' section. Besides, any feelings, emotional or physical, are long gone."

W hen I get home in the late evening, before even stepping foot in my apartment, I stop at Sean's door. Having made my decision, I want to start the morning off with a clean slate and a clear direction on where we're going.

I knock on his door.

It takes him a second to open. When he does, I have a brief déjà vu of him being stark naked—and I have to squeeze my legs together at the memory—but alas, he's not (dang it).

Instead, I get the sense he's just gotten home.

His suit jacket is gone, as is his tie. The sleeves of his crisp white shirt are rolled up past his strong, manly elbows and the top three buttons have been undone, revealing just the barest hint of chest hair and a tattoo. I try not to stare. Try not to think about him rolling those sleeves up over his muscular, tattooed arms (a geometric design spreading across his shoulders and chest) as he walks toward me, a hungry, smoldering look in his eyes. My body reacts instantly, and I involuntarily clench around nothing, thinking of his thick fingers.

No. Nope.

Wrong time and wrong place.

Also, wrong person. He's not that same stranger from the bar.

He's the man who's more than off limits, and in more ways than one.

An elegant African American woman emerges from his apartment, walking toward the front door. She wears an expensive outfit, and her makeup is flawless. A wave of "oh, no" hits me.

Who is she?

An intense feeling of jealousy almost overwhelms me as I stare at her. *Oh, my green monster is fierce!*

Is that his girlfriend? Did I just interrupt something?

It's only her clothing style that hints at her age. With that smooth skin of hers, she could well be in her late thirties. Sean, he's likely somewhere in his early forties.

By the looks of her, she takes good care of herself. Unlike me, she has not one extra pound on her. Is that his type?

When she walks past him, she touches his arm, saying, "The copies are on your desk, Mr. Blackwood."

"Thanks, Jasmine." Sean goes to introduce me to his PA, Jasmine Williams, and from the conversation with the beautiful, lively woman, I gather that she only dropped by to obtain his signature for an urgent business deal that came through shortly after he'd left the office.

Thank goodness.

Relief washes over me as she walks toward the elevator. Not that I care whether he has a girlfriend or not.

We're strictly business.

"You're really making this a habit," he says once the elevator door closes, crossing his arms and leaning against the doorframe. "I don't know whether to be concerned or flattered."

"Neither. I just wanted to let you know that I accept your offer. The one about working together, not the one about selling," I quickly add. "Not right now at least."

He raises his eyebrow but remains silent.

"Well, see," I continue, "I appreciate your proposal, and I'm open to exploring this option. But here's what I suggest: instead of an immediate sale, let's have a trial period where I join your team as an employee. This will allow both of us to assess how well this arrangement fits."

Sean studies me carefully for a moment. "Go on."

"Ninety days. That's the trial period I suggest. If, at the end of these ninety days, things go smoothly, I'm willing to commit to becoming a long-term, dedicated employee within your organization, and I'll proceed with selling my shares to you—after re-negotiating your offer, that is."

The firm lines of his lips turn up at the corners. "Fourteen days. Let's do fourteen days. Some wars have been shorter than ninety days."

"Well, this isn't war." *Or is it?* "Sixty days," I counter.

He remains firm. "Fourteen days. It's the perfect adaptation time frame to introduce the transitional changes."

"Let's not jump the gun. We might need more days to adjust. Let's do forty."

"Fourteen."

"Jesus, Sean! Don't be such a stubborn mule. Give me at least a month."

I bet nobody has ever dared to sass him like that during business negotiations. His mouth curves *almost* into a smile, and his expression mirrors a silent "look who's talking."

"One month," I repeat, poking his chest. Surprisingly, he lets out a growly chuckle. Since when does the man chuckle?

"Done," he agrees, and we shake on it.

His grip is firm, and a tingling sensation runs through my body as his hand envelops mine, akin to a subtle electric current. He holds on for a moment, and then he lets go, sealing the agreement.

Despite my satisfaction, I get a sense that I made it way too easy for him.

The idea of Sean being my boss still doesn't sit well with me, at least not yet, and even less so with a significantly shorter trial period, but hey, I can deal.

"Perfect," I tell him, disregarding the fact he not only halved my suggestion but reduced it by a third. Nevertheless, it could have been an outright refusal. A month is preferable to a flat-out rejection.

"I believe this approach will provide a fair opportunity," I continue, "for both of us to make an informed decision about our future partnership. You may have your company's best interests at heart, but I have my staff's. And that's always going to come first over corporate necessity."

"You make it sound like we're some random faceless organization trying to bend everything to our will."

"Aren't you?" I mean it as a joke, something to break the tension. (By that, I mean the tension in *me*. *He* looks calm as a cucumber.)

"Allow me to clarify: I am also genuinely concerned about the well-being and best interests of the staff," he assures me.

"I mean it, Sean. You can't meddle in my role as a director."

He nods. "I won't interfere in your responsibilities. We'll work together to put Blackwood's strategies into action, and it will be your duty to implement them."

"Naturally, our relationship will remain strictly professional," I continue to recap, keeping it professional. "We work on a smooth transition, and in two weeks, we attend the charity event together."

"I act as your fake fiancé in front of Richard."

"Yes," I say. "After the month is over, we're free to date again."

Sean nods. "If he asks, I'll tell him you broke it off because you met someone else."

"Good idea," I admit. "If we're compatible as business partners, I'll sell my shares."

"I'm sure we're compatible."

I blink, ignoring the way he said it.

"Your reassurance is noted," I tell him. "However, let me be honest. The likelihood of me selling my shares by the end of the month is miniscule at best. Don't assume it's in the bag, because it is not."

"All I want is a fair shot."

"A fair shot it is, no more, no less. Let's see where it takes us. We'll need everything in writing to make it official of course," I insist with a winner's smile.

"Sure thing," he says. "Tomorrow morning, I'll have our legal team draft the necessary agreements to formalize this process. Besides, I've worked in hospitality my whole life. I've been where you are, and I think you'll find I'm very reasonable."

"You've proven that by offering a compromise and agreeing to mine. Don't make me regret trusting you."

"I'm not one for regrets."

Something in the way he says that gives me pause. I see him standing there relaxed and at ease, so very different from how he is while we're working. That damn night at the bar tugs at the back of my memories, and for the briefest moment, I feel that heat simmer below the surface. My eyes stray to his lips. His beautiful, full, masculine lips. The ones I felt on mine for one too-short second. It would be so easy to lean in, to feel the press of that mouth to mine and really indulge. My thighs clench harder.

Is he a good kisser, I wonder?

Clearly, he's not.

That's probably why he refrained from kissing me at the bar. It's likely he's out of practice, and, if I had to guess, not particularly skilled either.

"Other than that," I say, "we will be strictly professional, no funny business."

"We already agreed on that. Wouldn't even cross my mind."

What a jerk.

"I was just making sure. I'll see you in the morning then," I say before my eyes have a chance to land on his lips again, backing away in the direction of my apartment. "Good night."

"Good night."

He closes the door, and I step into my place, leaning against the wall as I will my thumping heart to slow down. In his cage, Pippin cocks his head and squawks at me, almost as if to suggest, "Dun-dun-dun-dun! Kiss him!"

"Not now, not tomorrow, not ever, you little matchmaker!"

Then I remember. Darn it. I forgot to retrieve my panties. *Again.*

13

SEAN

*W*ell played.

I commend Jess for having the business savvy to make such a request, and I'm happy to sign a contract. My cock twitches in anticipation of the thirty days I'm going to officially be her boss.

The next day, we sit down together, and I present her with a digital legal agreement, describing the deal Blackwood Inc. is willing to offer. She dedicates a full day to meticulous reading, with the document undergoing a thorough review by her legal counsel. Following this, she provides me with several minor revisions and proceeds to sign it once she's entirely satisfied.

Over the course of the next week, I dedicate most of my time to working directly with Jess on the property, getting familiar with WH policies, staff, and procedures, being on site full time. To her credit, once we review the transition process, Jess is positive and upbeat, sharing her thoughts, lighting up every room she walks into, and at times, providing suggestions. It seems now that she's on board, she's ready to hit the ground running.

In the late evenings, I swing by the Blackwood office to attend to my company responsibilities. Often, it's deserted by the time I arrive. However, today I get there earlier, and several lights are still on. I immerse myself in work for two solid hours, including finally finishing my report for the board and sending it out.

Just as I'm ready to head out, I notice an email from Jess pop up in my inbox. It's a contract she drafted for Schuster and Flint—the large group interested in hosting their retreat at the Westerlyn hotel. This falls in line with our prior understanding, as I expressed to be involved in substantial business dealings (including overseeing reservations, book-ings, or negotiations), to gain insights into their procedures.

I pull it up on my tablet and study it.

My father chooses that moment to walk into my office, holding a paper. Noticing my pensive expression, he takes the tablet out of my hand, scrolling through the contract. "This cannot be how she's run this business up until this point," he says, wrinkling his nose. He looks at me, shaking his head. "Ha-ha. No wonder it took them so long to actually turn a profit."

"I'm sure she did what she had to," I say, taking the tablet back.

He points to the document. It's a printout of my report.

"This whole timeline is ridiculous," he says. "Thirty days! What good does it do us to drag this out until she's ready?"

I grab my suit jacket and slip it on. "This is a win as far as I'm concerned. Jesus Christ, Father, did you really have to *print* out the report?"

"A win? How is that—"

"The sale will happen eventually," I interject. "I don't see the harm in letting this play out."

Dad waves a dismissive hand, leaving my office. "But don't come crawling back to me, expecting me to step in when it goes wrong."

. . .

Connor and I meet up at our bar. We have some buffalo wings and lose ourselves in the football game.

It feels good to kick back and turn my brain off for a bit. And yet, Jess creeps back in. I chalk it up to not being in the right headspace. Connor erupts in laughter when I fill him in on the whole Jess-being-the-beautiful-bar-girl revelation followed by the whole Jess-being-my-fake-fiancée-to-fool-Rutherford unfolding.

"Can't fecking wait to properly meet this new woman at the auction," he playfully remarks.

"You better behave." I signal the waiter for another round of fries, making sure they're extra crispy.

"Oh, I'll be on me best behavior. I promise!" he declares. "Like a good little altar boy at mass—halo included."

By the time I get home, I'm relaxed. Perhaps too relaxed, because before I go inside, I pause to look at Jess's door. Almost instinctively, I reach into my jacket pocket, the very same one I wore during our bathroom encounter. I retrieve her panties and press them to my nose. My dick jolts awake. For fuck's sake, I'm turning into a first-grade creeper. Thankfully, the rational part of my brain kicks in, and I let myself into my apartment before further complicating an already-complicated matter.

Before I call it a night, I fetch an envelope. I tuck her panties inside and place it next to her door—a subtle memento of our night.

That's all it is, just a memento. It can't happen again.

My body doesn't get the message.

I strip down and fall into bed.

Even if hooking up again was on the table, she's probably asleep. With that thought, I wonder what she sleeps in. Short-shorts and a tank top? A thin nightie? Nothing? I doubt it's nothing.

My dick, being the persistent bastard that he is, twitches and swells.

If I had it my way it would be nothing.

Reaching down, I cup myself and close my eyes, picturing Jess standing in the sunlight without her towel. Automatically, my imagination connects those visuals to our hookup in the bathroom. I work myself up, jerking off as I think about lifting her and tossing her onto my bed. I'd kick the towel down the balcony, run my hands up her smooth skin, and squeeze her curves. In the fantasy, she's wet. She's as eager and ready as I am, tugging at me and bringing me down against her.

It's like she's taking her frustration out on my mouth, kissing harshly and biting at my bottom lip as her nails dig into my shoulder blades. She distrusts me—for the most part. But she can't deny the tension that's there, can't deny that I make her weak in the knees. And I can do it again.

I want to do it again.

My heart starts to race as my movements grow faster. The way we move together, the way she doesn't melt, doesn't let me take control but tries to wrestle it from me, makes it that much sweeter when she eventually does cave in. It's a punch to the gut when I come, harder than the first time I thought about her. Lying there panting, a calmness washes over me.

I clean up and fall back into bed, exhausted.

14

SEAN

*T*he next morning, as per usual, Jess is already at her desk when I arrive, wearing a lavender outfit. I wonder how early she gets up and if this is a regular occurrence, or if she's just doing it to avoid seeing me at our apartment building. Either way, somehow, she always manages to arrive before I do.

"Hey," she says, glancing up at me. "Thank you for my...for the envelope."

Every time I see her, she's more beautiful. "You're welcome."

"Did you get a chance to check over that contract I sent you yesterday?"

It's hilarious how she changed topics.

"I did. We need to change it."

Her face falls. "Why? What's your problem with it?"

"My concern is that we aren't charging enough for a group that will be reserving seventy-five percent of the hotel's capacity. In New York City, I know for certain, there's no other hotel in our quality range charging less."

"This isn't about the numbers. Or at least it shouldn't be. Schuster and Flint have been having their corporate retreat here for *years*. They were one of the first groups I booked when I bought the hotels and they've been supporting us ever since."

"Your loyalty is commendable, but not sustainable. Furthermore, the cancellation policy is not up to our standards."

"Our policy is lenient, given our high occupancy in this area," she argues.

"We need to be stricter. We should firmly enforce a seven-day cancellation policy and charge for one night if they try to cancel within that time frame. It's common practice in NYC and will help us manage reservations, ensuring rooms aren't left unoccupied due to last-minute cancellations."

"Well...for new reservations," she says, "it's not a big deal. But for returning guests, I know there's going to be pushback. How about we grandfather them into the new price and policy?"

"This is revenue that you're missing out on by being too nice," I argue. "We make the rules here, not them. It's going to ruffle a few feathers, but they'll get used to it."

Jess leans back in her chair as she spins from side to side. "We have older clients who have been coming here for years, and I don't want to lose their business just because we're changing things."

"Jess, you can't please everyone, and you're going to drive yourself crazy if you keep trying. We're running a business here, they know that, and know that. We can't make exceptions for everyone just because they piss and moan about it."

"It doesn't sound right to me. The reason why we're doing so well is because I've cultivated relationships with our guests. I hate the thought of throwing that aside just for corporate sake. How about this? Let's bend the rules a bit for Schuster and Flint, just this once." She pauses her spinning, meeting my gaze with a playful twinkle in her eyes. "I'm confident that Mr. Sean Blackwood, our undisputed CEO, can effortlessly accommodate, don't you think?"

I suppress a smile.

Quite frankly, I anticipated more resistance, and I'm pleased we can navigate constructively. Enduring daily battles with my father is sufficient—I have no desire for them in other aspects of my life.

I don't have to contemplate.

"All right, we make an exception for them," I concede with a nod. "However, all reservations in the future will need to follow the new policy. Let's hope they don't cancel on us."

Her face lights up. "They won't, I'm sure! They're a group that indulges in the restaurant, and you'll see they make their stay worth our while."

"All right."

She studies me for a moment, eyebrows suddenly knitting together with concern. "Are *you* all right?"

"I'm fine—why do you ask?"

"I don't know. You gave in *way* too easy."

"I didn't give in to anything. I see your point. You know your customers and you know what their expectations are, that's good enough for me."

She gives me another bright smile, and it makes my stomach clench. "Thanks, Sean. I appreciate that. And no worries, I can talk to my contact at Schuster and Flint and prepare them for the changes. We've been working with them for years, and you're right, I should update the contract to be aligned with industry standards."

"See what you can do."

I head to my office, and work on my usual morning tasks in comfortable silence.

In the late afternoon after her break, Jess stops by my office, lavender sunglasses perched on her head, matching her outfit. "I meant to tell you: the interior designer put a couple of small finishing touches on the

Presidential Suite. That means all renovations are officially complete. Do you want to go check it out?"

"Yeah, sure." I get up, ready to stretch my legs for a bit.

We exit the office.

I bring the conversation to the marketing agency's plan, suggesting exclusive partnerships with local cultural institutions, curated in-house experiences, and a strategic social media campaign—to elevate WH's status in NYC.

"I read the email this morning. I'm glad I don't have to take care of it in any way," Jess says, her voice filled with relief.

"I told you Blackwood was here to make your life easier."

"I will admit that you did say that. And I love the practices that they're going to implement to streamline things."

"See? It won't be so bad for Blackwood to run things."

She smirks at me, saying, "Don't push your luck, CEO."

"I would never," I say, strolling with her through the sunny lobby.

"I was wondering about the charity event next week." She gestures to the wall behind the lobby. "How much budget do we have for the art piece?"

"One hundred thousand dollars," I suggest.

"*One hundred thousand*?" she whispers in shock, looking at me in disbelief. "Are you serious, Sean?"

"Yeah, why? Not enough?"

"No, I didn't expect that much. With that amount, we'll snag the piece for sure!" She enthusiastically explains how the timing lines up perfectly with Schuster and Flint's arrival, how she appreciates that the hotel will greet them in all its glory. She's convinced the artist is a hidden gem in New York and predicts a significant spike in the price. According to her, the artist's drawing will not only enhance the lobby's atmosphere but also turn it into a go-to spot for magazines looking for a captivating backdrop.

"Why do you go to the yearly event?" she asks as I press the elevator button.

"My late mother founded the charity," I inform her. "'Grand Hospitality Affair' was her idea."

Her eyes widen in surprise. "Oh, I had no idea!"

"Yeah, it was her vision, despite my father's protests. She and one of our board members brought it to life."

"I'm sorry to hear your mother died."

"It was a long-term illness. She was battling it for several years before she eventually passed."

"I truly am sorry."

"It happened a long time ago," I assure her, sparing her from how watching my mother's strength gradually diminish during my childhood years affected me. How angry I was at my father's denial of the severity of the situation. The sleepless nights I spent wondering if there was more I could have done to influence my father's decisions. "She was an influential and compassionate figure. You could say she was a marvel of productivity who handled various responsibilities. Despite her impact, she remained humble, generous, and genuinely connected with people."

We step into the elevator. "What's her name?"

"Mary. Mary Irene Blackwood." I pull out my phone and scroll through my photos as we ride up. Most of them are hotel location photos. Some are goofy pics of Connor insisting I capture "the Irish hunk" and me—there are tons of him or us posing in front of our bikes in the middle of nowhere. Jess leans in when I find my favorite pic. In it, my mom is in the middle of planting flowers, holding a well-worn yet cherished hand trowel she inherited from Granny. She's wearing a big summer hat with a huge yellow bow. Even though the hat casts a shadow over half her face, there are crinkles around her eyes formed by her infectious laughter. My father is crouching beside her, casual in khaki shorts and a white T-Shirt, with a tender smile on his face. It's a smile I haven't seen in years.

"It's a beautiful photo. I bet she was a wonderful woman."

"She was." I pocket my phone.

The Presidential Suite looks satisfying. I've seen pictures of how it looked prior to the renovation, and Jess had certainly done a good job in picking the interior design firm. The room features serene, earthy tones, a king-size bed with luxurious linens that match the harmonious color scheme, next to an opulent marble bathroom with a deep soaking tub. Tasteful decor accents and fresh white tulips in white vases add to the welcoming touch. I pull out my phone and add the firm to Blackwood's list of vendors.

"I'm never gonna get tired of this view," Jess says, wandering over to the large windows. It's a bright day outside, the sky a clear blue without a cloud. From where the suite is positioned in the building, it offers a nice view of the NYC skyline.

"I've lived here a long time, and I still never get tired of it myself." I move to stand next to her, my hands shoved into my pockets, facing the skyline. I maintain a gap from the window though. "But I'll admire it from a distance. Heights aren't my thing."

I don't know why I choose to stand so close nonetheless—the drop below is quite daunting. There's ample space, and I could shift a fraction to the left to create a more reasonable gap from the edge. Yet, doing so would also increase the distance between us, and I choose not to. I enjoy her citrus perfume subtly wafting my way.

When she glances over at me, those lips of hers are curved into a smirk. "So...you are human after all," she says softly.

Unsure what she's talking about, I grumble, "Why do you say that?"

"Because the only thing you ever talk about is work. Even in the morning, when you greet me, you immediately launch into professional matters. To hear you admire something, let alone share a personal family photo, is surprising. Not to mention to hear you have a fear of something is rather human."

"Did I strike you as inhuman?" I ask.

Redness blooms across her cheeks, and I notice her chest move as her breathing picks up. "Do you really want to know what I thought about you when we first met?" There's a playfulness in her tone, and I'm intrigued and curious.

"Humor me."

She studies me for a moment, as if she's unsure how best to answer. Then she turns around to face me and rests her back against the window.

I resist a sudden urge to reach out and prevent her from falling.

Instead, I focus on what she's wearing. Today she's in a form-fitting pantsuit. Normally, that doesn't do anything for me, but for some reason, on her it looks good. The lavender jacket is unbuttoned, revealing a tight white shirt, with a neckline that dips tantalizingly low. Seeing it so close reminds me of when her body was pressed against mine and the tops of her breasts spilled out of that dress.

"Think you can handle it?" she challenges, smiling, tilting her head playfully.

That's when her sunglasses slip off her head, hitting the floor with several *taps*. We both kneel to grab them, and our hands touch in the process. Energy shoots through me at the skin contact, and my dick twitches.

When we get back up, she's closer than before, showing no inclination to retreat.

I'm even more curious where this is going than I was a second ago. I'm startled to realize the expression on her face is pretty damn close to what I pictured it being last night in my fantasy, and blood travels straight south.

I place a hand on the pane of glass, resting against it casually next to her head, bringing us face to face. My other hand stays in my jacket pocket, preventing me from touching her.

"I can handle anything," I rumble.

"Are you sure?" Her voice sounds breathy.

"Tell me."

She drops her hands and arches her back just enough without actually touching. Her voice is hoarse when she says, "Mr. Grumpy King... the undisputed grumpiness monarch."

A bit lengthy, but I've been called worse. Actually, "undisputed" and "monarch," has a ring to it. "Clearly that wasn't much of a deal-breaker, considering what happened later at the bar."

She laughs, a low giggle that I feel as much as hear. The warmth of her body calls to me, mixes with my own, and my breathing matches hers.

"At the time, no, it wasn't. Especially since I had already gotten a glimpse of what you had to offer."

"And you liked what you saw?" I ask in an undertone.

"The jury's still out." Our gazes lock. "Yes," she says, softly, breathless. "Because I always wondered..."

She blinks, as if contemplating whether to share it with me. Just when I think she might have reconsidered, and I'm about to urge her with an "Out with it, now," she says, "Why didn't you kiss me that night?"

Not what I expected.

Her breath hitches, and the air between us crackles with anticipation. She isn't just referring to the clumsy opportunity when she slipped and her chest collided with me, but to her award-winning late-night plea for a goodnight kiss. My veins ignite with heat. My cock stiffens in response to her. Her blue eyes remain fixed on mine, drawing us into a magnetic, charged moment.

"Kissing is something to be done with a clear mind," I rumble. "I didn't want you to live with regrets."

She lifts her head, bringing her lips closer to mine. "I wouldn't have." Only a few inches separate our mouths. "Maybe...you know..." she whispers hoarsely, "we should practice kissing for the charity event?"

I can feel her breath on my lips.

All I need to do is dip my head.

Nobody will expect us to kiss at the charity event next week. That's what my expression tells her.

Her expression nonchalantly tells me she couldn't care less.

I want to close the distance between us. Not that there's much of one right now. She lessens it even more by lifting her head a little higher. Now that there's hardly any space left between us, everything we said about sticking to professionalism doesn't matter. I think about last night, about picturing her in my bed, my dick inside her, and how hot and heavy we would be. It'd be so easy to follow through, to lock the door to this suite and take advantage of that king-sized bed. Or that bathtub. Or just my strength.

Her eyes grow hooded as they flicker to my lips and then back up to meet my gaze, telling me that she's thinking the same exact thing.

Her citrus perfume invades my nostrils.

With each breath, her breasts graze my chest.

With each graze, my cock jerks.

Almost instinctively, my hand withdraws from my pocket, and finds its way to cradle her face. She lets out a small gasp. Softly, my fingertips begin grazing her cheek. At that simple contact, I feel her heartbeat echo against my chest, her nipples pressing into me with each exhale.

I cradle her neck and dip my head, slowly.

Deeper and deeper.

Until our lips touch.

When our mouths finally meet, it's a soft collision.

I'm struck by the feel of her, the softness of her lips, by the taste of her. It's a subtle mix of coffee and something uniquely her own. It's intoxicating, a flavor that lingers in my senses. But there's more. I can taste the tension, the thrill of breaking the rules, and the sheer intoxication of crossing that line. We both know this is forbidden territory.

Neither of us cares.

The moment my tongue finds hers for the first time, she releases a soft moan.

With a delicate urgency, her fingers reach to cling to the lapel of my dark-blue jacket.

We're not just kissing.

I *devour* her mouth, and she devours mine.

The more minutes tick by, the more I lose myself, the more intoxicated I feel. My hand holds her neck, then brushes to her throat and from there, slides farther down. We kiss like we're in a trance, like we're possessed.

My hand glides over her breast, and her nipple puckers under my touch.

After what seems like an eternity of shameless making out, I start pulling away. There's an immediate protest. Her hands cling to me, and she utters a whispered "Not yet..."

She doesn't want my kiss to stop.

So, I don't.

Both my hands fully cup her breasts as I deepen the kiss again, finding her tongue, tracing her firm nipple through the white cotton. She lets out several soft moans and bucks her hips against my thigh.

I'm hard as a rock. How long does it take for the tub to fill? Already, I picture myself hoisting her over my shoulder and marching toward our wet destination.

Just when I reach for her hips, from outside the suite door, there's the unmistakable rattling of the housekeeping cart.

There's a glimmer of disappointment on Jess's face, but she immediately straightens herself and steps away.

"This didn't happen," she says. "I mean, it was fake. Just a training exercise," she adds and increases the distance between us, straightening her clothes and adjusting her sunglasses.

It was fake?

Just a training exercise?

What the fuck?

Is she having regrets?

When Pauline walks in, conducting a quality inspection and providing instructions to the housekeeper next to her, Jess is adjusting one of the paintings on the wall while I remain standing by the window. If I wasn't thrown off by what she said, the entire situation would be hilarious.

"Oh, I'm sorry, I didn't know you were in here," Pauline apologizes, swiveling her gaze from Jess to me and back to her. "So? What do you guys think?" she asks, seemingly oblivious to the tension she just interrupted.

"I think it looks great," Jess chirps with the usual pep in her voice, as if I only imagined having her tongue in my mouth. "And I'm glad all the renovations are finally complete." She looks at me. "Right, Mr. Blackwood?"

"Right. The interior designer did a good job," I agree with a nod. "I'll leave you to it then. Don't forget we have a conference meeting tomorrow morning."

"Don't worry, I have an excellent memory."

The double meaning isn't lost on me.

15

JESS

*W*hy did I kiss him?

I shouldn't have done it.

Sweet Jesus, is he a good kisser.

It took everything in me to stop and not to beg for more. My brain has never been mushier. My nipples have never been harder. My panties have never been wetter.

It was a mistake.

But a good one.

I mean, it was good practice, just in case we have to kiss in front of Richard.

No problem. I can maintain a distinction between our fake relationship and work.

Before the "brief" moment in the Presidential Suite, I was hopeful about this new partnership with Sean. He's been surprisingly reasonable, enough so that it almost made me forget who I'm dealing with.

Why, oh why, did I forget *myself*? The way my knees turned to jelly should have been my first warning—a big red stop sign. The way my heart skipped several beats when our lips touched should have been my second—a neon sign blinking "danger ahead." The way my muscles clenched should have been the third—and final—siren blaring in my head.

But clearly, I missed every cue to run for the hills.

What did I do instead? I went for seconds.

It's proximity. If I didn't have to see him almost every day, either at work or home, I'd be able to put him out of my mind. But it's just that occasionally, rarely, I can't help but notice that his dark gaze lingers on me, intense and prolonged, and it does something to me.

Work has never been a worse distraction.

But rest assured, it won't happen again.

Next time I'll have my running shoes on.

He's Sean Blackwood, for crying out loud: the epitome of a ruthless, emotionless rich tycoon who steals your senses in a heartbeat—oh, and your panties, too (though he's generous enough to kindly return them when you least expect it).

W hen I arrive home, even though I'm sure he's not home yet, I tiptoe past his apartment so quietly that you'd think I was facing a life sentence for a crime as daring as a forbidden kiss from my neighbor, rival, secret fake fiancé, and boss, all rolled into one.

T he meeting we have the next day—luckily—puts a damper on my attraction to him. While some of the policies he wants to implement make sense, there are a few that I can't get behind.

Yesterday, he tried to change guest policies and pet policies. Fine. Today, he's trying to change policies when it comes to the staff, and that's where I have to firmly put my foot down. Things like planning vacation time now require our staff to log into an online portal and do everything that way.

While I'd been the spearhead of the paperless movement when it came to Norman and our guests, for staff it's different. I've left those decisions up to the department heads, giving them a chance to decide how they want to run things. A lot of our employees, such as the hotel's housekeeping staff supervised by Pauline, don't work at a computer or have one readily available, so the department heads take that into consideration in terms of scheduling. It has been functioning effectively thus far, granting the managers a degree of flexibility.

Although I have managed to negotiate in certain situations, unfortunately I don't have a chance to cut this one off at the pass. It's like he's immune to my top-tier charm and negotiation finesse—courtesy of Mom, who honed these skills navigating Dad.

Sean announces these changes, including the ones we discussed, in his typical Mr. Grumpy King rules fashion, all stern and untouchable during an 11 a.m. conference meeting with the managers and higher-ups. He informs them that all departments are going to handle things the *exact same* way, and that they will be responsible for training their staff on how to handle the new app. Needless to say, this causes quite a stir, especially for some of our older employees who aren't tech savvy. Pauline looks unhappy during the whole meeting.

"You're not going to fight me on this one, Jess," Sean says after the meeting when I corner him in his office. "There are certain things that are nonnegotiable, and this is one of them. Every Blackwood property does this the same way, and it works the best. There's less chance for misunderstandings."

"But we're not like every property you own, we're smaller, more intimate. By changing that, you're going to make us just like everybody else." I give him my sassiest stance, poking his chest. "Do you *really* want to be like everybody else, Mr. Blackwood?"

He leans in. "No, I don't, Ms. Summers," he rumbles in *that* voice, and I swear, I get a little wet. Then he stands back to his full height, towering over me. "We're not changing the core of what Westerlyn is, we're tweaking, which will make your life easier. Trust me, you'll thank me in the long run."

Tweaking, *pfft.*

Pretty much every conversation we have about staff changes goes like that.

I get that he has experience, and he's been doing this for a while, but so have I.

His way isn't the only way, despite what he thinks.

But I have to admit, apart from that and as far as the rest of the integration goes, we find compromises, good ones even. We butt heads less often than I first anticipated. Perhaps the most remarkable and unexpected aspect is that Sean consistently listens attentively to me, intervening only when he sincerely believes I should reconsider. I admit: he breathes competence. He *does* know a lot. He's certainly not the "smash-through-walls and leave-no-trace" monster they paint him to be, well, not so far, at least.

At one point, though, a suspicion starts to creep in.

Something's up, I keep thinking.

Something's fishy.

And over the next couple of days that follow, I still can't shake my suspicions: Is he being cooperative and playing my "kissing-friendly fake fiancé" for diplomatic reasons, to encourage me to sell? Or is he acting as he does because he genuinely thinks I'm the embodiment of perfection?

My ex was the epitome of male sweetness and awesomeness—before he ripped my heart out and trampled all over it, before he swiped my hotel, and with that, fundamentally changed my beliefs about love.

I keep all this in mind and prepare to tread carefully.

16

JESS

A couple of days before the charity event, I have a meeting scheduled with Emma Simpson from the front desk. She appears worried, which is out of character for the peppy young woman. It immediately causes me concern, and I offer her the seat across from me.

"Everything okay?" I ask, noticing her eyes dart in the direction of Sean's office, which is empty. "Don't worry about Mr. Blackwood. He won't be in for a while. You can talk freely."

"I don't want to ruffle any feathers or cause any trouble, you know," Emma explains.

Her comment puts me on red alert and my back straightens as I lean forward. "I would never think that's what you're doing. I've known you long enough, Emma, to know you're not that kind of person. Now, what's going on, what's wrong?"

"Ms. Summers, I do apologize. It's just that there have been some rumors circulating..."

My heart plummets to my stomach, and my skin suddenly feels warm. There's no way, absolutely no way anyone at the hotel knows what's happened between me and Sean, except for Pauline. And she's not one to gossip, when it comes to stuff we share in confidence.

Have they noticed our glances, or heaven forbid, did some eagle-eyed observer witness our kiss?

"What...sort of rumors?" I ask, hoping my tone sounds as neutral and innocent as I mean it to. I'm sure the redness has already spread across my face.

"People are saying that Mr. Blackwood has a habit of buying up these properties and then replacing the staff with his own people. A lot of us are concerned that with all these changes, our jobs might be for the chop."

I relax, grateful the rumors have nothing to do with our fake kiss. But I'm deeply troubled that my employees are scared and none of them have come to talk to me about it until now. It's been almost two weeks, and I highly doubt these are new concerns. "Emma, please believe me when I tell you this: no one's jobs are on the line." I give her a reassuring smile. "Nobody is going to get fired without me knowing or without my approval."

She smiles and seems to relax as well. "I hoped that would be the case, but it's reassuring to hear you say it."

"You guys know my door is always open. That hasn't changed just because Norman isn't here anymore."

"Oh, I know that, thank you. It's just that Mr. Blackwood is usually next door, and it feels a bit awkward coming to talk to you and asking for privacy."

"Let me worry about that."

"Thank you, Ms. Summers. Honestly, I feel much better just for having had this chat. How are you managing in all this, by the way? If it's overwhelming for us, I can't imagine what it must be like for you."

I appreciate her concern.

She's right.

This is a significant undertaking for me, and everyone involved. But

I'm not going to let her see how it's getting to me. "I'm doing what needs to be done. Don't worry about me, Emma," I assure her, giving her a warm smile, and a cheeky wink. "I can handle Mr. Blackwood."

Rising from her chair, Emma shoots me a grin. "Oh, I don't doubt that at all. You're one of the nicest bosses I've ever had. But I've also seen what happens to that pleasant exterior when people cross you... and I'd rather not be in that position. Have a lovely day, Ms. Summers."

I grin back. "You too, Emma."

She exits my office and I sit there for a moment, processing what she told me. For once, my usual calm demeanor is difficult to maintain. My staff is worried, not just because of the overhaul and the time to get used to the new adjustments, likely more so because they sense my inner turmoil. People don't like change, especially if it's a change that basically turns everything upside down. It's a lot to take in and, despite what Sean thinks, I'm not going to change the way I work and interact with them.

That's the one thing I will never compromise on.

I get back to work, wishing Sean was the only man giving me grief. We're all hands on deck, preparing for the upcoming corporate retreat with Schuster and Flint. The repeated calls from Mr. Grant, the group's new event coordinator—a rather difficult and hard-to-please character —are also putting me on edge. Oh, how I miss handling everything with the now-retired Mr. Schuster. I try to be friendly, but Mr. Grant certainly has a knack for testing my patience.

H alf an hour later, as soon as Sean walks by my office, I spin my chair to look at him.

"Please come in and close the door, Sean," I tell him, with absolutely no charm in my voice. I'm dead serious. "We need to talk."

Sean raises his eyebrow, since I prefer to leave the door open (a point we have argued back and forth repeatedly). He does as I say, glancing at me over his shoulder.

"Is this about tomorrow's charity event?" He closes the door, then turns to face me. "Or about what I can offer for your half of the hotels?"

"You wish. It's more serious than that." I take a deep breath, trying to steady myself and not let him see how worked up I am. "There seem to be some misconceptions about the hotel's future."

"You think so?"

"I know so."

He stands there, in the middle of my office, hands casually in his pockets. "Didn't we discuss all this at the conference meeting?"

"I was just speaking with one of my employees, and they told me everybody is worried about losing their jobs." I'm careful not to mention Emma's name to avoid any retaliation on Sean's part.

He has the nerve to roll his eyes. "That's it? I thought it was something serious."

My temper flares. "It is serious to me! Don't brush it off like it's nothing."

"If I'm brushing it off it's because it *is* nothing. I'm too busy to deal with staff drama. Staff is replaceable. If this person is going to come running to you every time she hears stupid rumors, then maybe we should think about that person's future here."

"Staff is replaceable? Isn't that what Blackwood is renowned for? Taking over and letting go of staff?"

His facial expression darkens considerably. The shadows carve deep lines of menace across his features, a brooding intensity that sends a shiver down my spine. He shakes his head, growling, "Not under my leadership."

I try to steady my heartbeat. "Are you sure?"

"I'm sure. Not unless absolutely necessary. You have the wrong impression of me. Not everything you hear or read in the press is true," he assures me, his gaze still dark. "I value our team."

There's something in his sincere tone that immediately puts me at ease. For some reason, I find myself believing him, trusting his words.

He's not that good an actor.

"Can I get that in writing?" I tease (but not really).

"Are you ready for tomorrow?" he asks, ignoring my question, and instead, jerking his chin toward the charity auction ticket still proudly displayed on my desk.

Happiness surges within me when I pick it up.

"I am. I've picked a stunning cocktail dress and shoes. I have an appointment at the hair salon tomorrow afternoon. Do we still plan to arrive fashionably late and make a quick exit?"

"That's the plan. We'll show face, scope out the drawing, and make our exit with it." He nods. "In and out."

I smirk, liking the notion. "A heist at a charity event. I'm in." I relax in my seat, confident in our plan to navigate the event and sidestep unnecessary encounters with Richard. "What time are we leaving? It's starting at 6:00 p.m."

"Events like this never start punctually. I'll pick you up. Be ready at six sharp."

"Perfect! We'll arrive just in time for the auction."

"Timing is everything in this game."

"Anything else we should discuss?" I ask, putting the ticket in my purse. There will be enough time to cover any last-minute details on the ride over, to align our answers just in case we get busted, but when it comes to fooling Richard, there's nothing like overpreparing.

"What about what's happening between us?"

My head shoots up and I almost drop my purse. He's talking about the kiss. The real fake kiss. It catches me off guard that he's mentioning it. "What do you mean?" I ask.

"You know what I mean."

"Nothing is happening," I insist.

"Are you really going to look me in the eye and tell me you didn't feel anything, that it was just for show?"

"When?" I ask.

"You know when," he huffs. "In the Presidential Suite."

"Maybe you're the one feeling something."

"Smooth deflection."

I know I shouldn't have kissed him—be it a pretend kiss or a genuine one. I've never encountered a man who stirs such a whirlwind of mixed emotions within me.

I don't know whether I want to tell him this meeting is done or get up and yank on his suit jacket and pull him against me. At least it would shut him up for a moment.

Luckily, I don't have to make the decision.

Before I can make up my mind on what to say next, he's gone.

17

JESS

$\mathcal{G}$rand Hospitality Affair

"It's so good to meet you, Mrs. Sanborne," I say to the sophisticated white-haired woman in her late sixties. Sean introduces her as one of the board members of Blackwood Holdings and co-founder of the event. I learn that she's been with Blackwood for decades and is an active participant in various community events, aimed at making a positive impact in the city.

"Please, call me Daniela. How wonderful that you could make it." She reaches out both hands to take mine. "I assume it's your first event?"

"It is, and I'm excited to be here." It's a huge event! There are *so* many people, and all dressed to the nines. I survey the crowd, but I can't seem to locate Richard. Finding him is like searching for a needle in a haystack.

"My dear, our events are a great way to connect, and you'll find some of the most influential figures here tonight," she says, and I'm almost surprised when she brings me into a hug. From what I've picked up from Sean, I didn't expect any warmth from a Blackwood board member, but I'm only too happy to return it. I assume everybody is friends on special occasions such as this one.

She continues talking about the charity and what it stands for. The Grand Hospitality Affair is a yearly event dedicated to supporting local communities in the hospitality sector. Scholarships, training programs, and local business partnerships are the heart of this wonderful initiative. I get a sense that, despite Sean being a regular attendee, his involvement in the charity isn't widely known.

"Ye're runnin' a bit late. The show's about to start," a man with a thick Irish accent says as he joins our group. He pats Sean on his shoulder, then faces me and reaches out his hand. "Connor O'Malley. Who do we have here?"

"Jess Summers. My pleasure."

"Jess Summers, is it? Well, the pleasure's all mine." He smirks, eyes twinkling with mischief. "So you're the one who has the big man here blushing like a schoolboy."

"Oh, I wouldn't say I have him blushing," I quip. "I'd like to think I just caught him off guard with my irresistible charm."

He laughs. "Nicely done, and damn right."

"Connor here is the resident trouble-maker," Sean interjects, shooting him a stern look. "Officially, he holds the prestigious title of VP of sales at Blackwood. Unofficially, he's the reason we have a 'Fun at Work' policy."

"You mean 'No Fun at Work' policy, Chief?" Connor retorts, a smirk playing on his lips.

"*Precisely.*"

"Guilty as charged."

"Oh, I've had my fair share of experiences with his strict policy rules," I chime in.

"I bet ya have. But don't be fooled by his Metropolitan slickness and sulky face, Jess," Connor says, pausing for effect before adding, "There's more to him than meets the eye. It's not all business meetings and bedtime prayers. He's just hidin' it well. Once it's out, mind yourself!"

"Well, isn't that a revelation," I say in a playful tone. "I better watch out then."

"Don't say ya weren't warned." Connor smirks, shooting a glance at Sean. "That's the cat out of the bag now, Big Man."

Sean raises an eyebrow at Connor's remark. "The cat might be out, but remember, I'm the one holding the leash."

"Ya don't have to remind me. I'm well aware, Chief. Now, pints?"

Right on cue, Jasmine Williams, Sean's friendly PA I've met before, welcomes us warmly, offering drinks. She informs Daniela and Sean that there's a slight delay due to an unexpected issue—one of the art pieces, surprisingly large, is proving challenging to maneuver through one of the narrow entrances, causing a temporary hold-up. When I look at Sean, he gives me a "We've got this, no problem" nod. True to Sean's prediction, nobody pokes into our relationship—or why I'm here in the first place. My mere presence by his side automatically grants me acceptance into the inner circle.

No, it's more than that. I feel like I truly belong.

With my hair and makeup all set, I'm wearing a breathtaking red cocktail dress with a sleek silhouette, a neckline that's making a cheeky statement, and I've paired it with golden-beige heels that lace from my ankles all the way up to just below my knees. I mean, this outfit and my matching red nail polish, who can have doubts?

Sean stays at my side as we engage in small talk with other guests, each one eager to greet him. He introduces me to a diverse array of influential individuals. Through these encounters, I'm carrying a profound understanding of not only Sean and the people that make Blackwood, but also just how tight-knit the NYC hotel circle is—everybody knows everybody.

With the second ring, Sean offers his arm, and heat floods my veins at his closeness while my hand grips his muscle as he ushers us to our seats. My chest swells when Connor insists on sitting on my other side.

A few moments later, the grand hall transforms into an auction arena, and the Grand Hospitality Affair unfolds.

It isn't just huge. It's grand. Nowhere I can spot Richard.

When I take my seat, I take one more look around, absently twirling a ring on my ring finger, the pretty piece of jewelry we made a surprise pit stop for at the jewelers. I did protest, but Sean had insisted the jeweler was waiting, and who was I to argue? Of course, I'll return the ring after our time as a fake couple is up. Its placement among my other rings is intended for an audience of one. While it might give off the impression of an engagement ring to a particular observer, the intention is to keep everyone else blissfully unaware is working perfectly.

Such a bummer he isn't here. Oh, well, he'll likely see one of the photos in tomorrow's paper. There are photographers everywhere. Now, I'm not a spiteful person, but for some reason, there's something oddly satisfying about the idea of Richard discovering me in the midst of success—it's like a balm for my wounded heart.

Moments later, bidding paddles are discreetly distributed.

The auctioneer, an elegant figure, takes the stage, introducing the first item—a rare piece of art starting at five thousand dollars.

I'm not bidding, but watch when other bidders enter the fray. With a calculated glance, Sean makes his move now and then, subtly escalating the bids.

"Jaysus, Sean's makin' sure those art pieces go for a pretty feckin' penny. Owners will be thanking him from their new yachts," Connor whispers, sitting next to me. He can't help but offer a low whistle. "He'd usually be quiet enough about any contribution, but he's making his presence known today, whatever's goin' on." He smirks, but I don't have time to react.

A masterpiece of modern art takes center stage, and a hush falls over the room.

The auctioneer introduces the *Metropolitan Reverie*.

It's the drawing I've been waiting for, the reason why I'm here.

It looks even better than I imagined.

The canvas is an impressive twenty-one by ten feet, and it's an abstract piece that captures the skyline of New York City. After several recent exhibitions, Josephine Ashford's artwork is gaining recognition in the art world, sparking rising demand both nationally and internationally. By the looks of this piece, the artist utilized her entire arm length to blend bold, swirling charcoal strokes to represent the city's vibrant energy. The skyline is powerful, with subtle references to iconic NYC landmarks. But wait...no...is that what I think it is? Amid the abstract forms, I discover something that quickens my pulse. There's a hidden figure that resembles Spider-man swinging through the city! I know it's just in my imagination—but I'm sure it's a sign.

Now I know it for certain: I have to have it. Oh, it'll look more than wonderful in our lobby. It's perfect!

"We're starting the bidding at fifty thousand dollars for this exquisite piece," the auctioneer begins.

My heart races, and the air is thick with anticipation.

Of course, Sean notices my excitement, and he turns to me, his brow going up just a millimeter. *That's the one?*

I offer him a subtle nod.

Go for it, his eyes say. *Show's all yours.*

All right, I eye back.

The bidding war for *Metropolitan Reverie* begins, and I join the action, bringing the bid up to fifty-five thousand dollars.

As expected, several paddles rise at the next amounts, but my eyes remain fixed on the artwork. Soon, the increments become smaller, and one by one, bidders start bowing out. With each increase, my determination intensifies, and soon we reach the pivotal moment.

The auctioneer asks, "Do I hear one hundred thousand dollars?"

At that, I raise my paddle once again, my hand shaking a little. That's so much money. But I'm ready to claim what I think will be an amazing investment, both financially and aesthetically.

My heart quickens when no one else matches the auctioneer's next bid suggestion.

Connor leans in. "That's the job done now, I'd say," he whispers to me, and even Daniela, sitting front row, turns to offer a warm smile.

"Going once... going twice..." the auctioneer begins, and just as the realization of triumph settles in, a sharp voice sounds from the back.

"Two hundred thousand dollars."

The room buzzes with surprise. I turn, disbelief written all over my face.

It's Richard.

There he stands, paddle raised.

Tall, confident, with a perfect poker face. He has always had a knack for making a grand last-minute entrance (especially when it comes to breaking hearts).

But right now, it feels like two hundred thousand bricks have dropped on me.

The auctioneer seamlessly adjusts, acknowledging the new bid. "We have two hundred thousand dollars. Do I hear two hundred-fifty thousand?"

I clench my paddle. I can't match him.

In our talk beforehand, Sean and I capped the auction budget at one hundred thousand dollars.

When Richard's gaze meets mine, anger roars inside of me at his smug face. It wasn't a mere coincidence that he arrived late and over-looked my bet—no, he's well aware I want it. I know what Richard is doing—because I've seen him do it before. If he thinks he can gift it to me later, arguing that he just tried to raise its value for me, he's wildly mistaken. While I don't doubt the drawing is going to be worth much, much more in a few years, I can't get into debt. I can't push the limits for this piece that has captured my soul.

Sean looks at me, aware of my turmoil, leans in and whispers, "May I?"

Yes, I nod.

His lips brush against my knuckles before he faces the auctioneer.

"One million dollars," he says, his voice cutting through the room.

The crowd gasps.

Faces fall.

My heart leaps.

He said it as if it were nothing. Like he ordered pancakes. Like he asked for a napkin.

"Two million dollars," Richard counters.

More gasps.

Double jerk.

"Three," Sean says without blinking.

Holy moly.

The atmosphere is charged with the thrill of anticipation. All eyes swivel back to Richard Rutherford. My heart is about to pound out of my chest. Its rhythmic thumping echoes in my ears.

Do not match, do not match, I think.

Richard seems to assess the situation, then shakes his head—no. Art has never held much interest for him, and he's unaware of its value. What he isn't unaware of is Sean's determination. He recognizes my fiancé would sell his soul to bring joy to my heart.

He gives Sean a nod of acknowledgment, a silent and polite concession.

"Going once... going twice..." The room holds its breath. Me? I'm sitting on the edge of my seat, wondering if I'll need CPR by the time the hammer falls.

"Sold, for three million dollars."

The auctioneer brings the hammer down. *Thunk!*

I let out a breath, my shoulders drop, and tension melts away in my body.

It's ours.

The room erupts into a wave of applause, not just for the victorious bid but for the intensity displayed by both men in the epic exchange. I fight to hold back my too-obvious delight at Sean securing the most significant piece of the evening. Undoubtedly, the art magazines will be full of the dramatic showdown at the auction. Critics will analyze the significance and catapult the artist to new heights of recognition.

Connor leans in with a grin. "Told ya, job done."

We leave swiftly during the break, with warm goodbyes from Daniela and Jasmine, and my hand firmly around Sean's arm.

"Christ alive! Life's too short for these borin' charity auctions, isn't it? You'd have more craic at a funeral," Connor teases with a knowing grin, patting Sean's shoulder as we walk past him. "Enjoy the evenin', you two." Connor leans into Sean, lowering his voice conspiratorially—but just enough for me to hear. "Word to the wise, lad. Keep this one. She's good for ya."

I'm filled with pure joy.

I've made the right decision.

As we ride the elevator down to the parking garage, Sean shoots me a triumphant smile. It's one of those smiles that steals your breath, and for a moment, I find myself almost needing to gulp, struck by the sheer beauty of it. Everything went off without a hitch.

Yes, his smile is triumphant, but oh, boy, so is mine.

"Thank you for doing that." I beam at him, unable to hide my joy. "Our lobby will look spectacular."

"It's a good investment, I'm sure. And now, for the fun part of the evening. Are you hungry? Dinner's waiting."

I stare at him. "Dinner? As in a business dinner?"

He shakes his head. "No, it's not a corporate dinner. I want you to come to dinner—with *me*."

I lean against the shiny elevator wall. "You know, it's common courtesy to ask if a woman wants to join you for dinner..." I raise my hand to playfully poke his chest. "...instead of assuming she will."

He catches my hand in the middle of the movement, wraps my fingers in his and kisses my fingertips before he lets go. "Are you saying you don't want to go?"

My heart flutters, and I try to act nonchalantly while grabbing onto my purse. "I'm not saying that at all. Dinner sounds *great*."

I believe I have gotten to know Sean pretty well over the last two weeks, and he's a straightforward kind of guy. Chances are if he really needed to talk to me about business, he would just do it. It's one of the things I have come to expect, which is why our "faking an engagement" has been hard for me to process.

But is this a casual dinner or a date? That's the three-million-dollar question. Not that it makes a difference—or concerns me.

It's a date, I decide.

A fake one, of course, but still, a date is a date. Or is it real?

I mean, he bought a three-million-dollar art piece because of me. I'm aware he didn't buy it *for* me, it's for our lobby. But it still counts.

Sean Blackwood, the most irritable, utterly commanding, supremely authoritative, yet undeniably most eligible billionaire bachelor in NYC is out on a legit frickin' date. And who's the one he managed to rope into joining him? Yours truly!

How fortunate *he* is. Ha!

"So, where are we going for dinner?" I ask, once I'm seated in his luxury Mercedes, fastening my seatbelt. Nervous excitement flutters in my belly. Taking a first date with a guy I've been fake-engaged to should be a walk in the park. Yet here I am, proving that even a seasoned faker can't dodge the fluttering nerves.

"We're going to one of my favorite little Mexican restaurants," he says. "I don't go nearly as often as I'd like, but when I was first starting out, it was where I would treat myself."

He's taking me somewhere that's important to him. Oh, if that doesn't tug at my heartstrings and make my stomach burst with butterflies. I honestly half-expected him to take me to the bar again or some super-duper fancy place that matches his expensive taste. But this? This is better.

"Mexican sounds perfect," I say, giving him a warm smile. "It's been a long time since I've had good Mexican food."

"Then prepare yourself, because Montaña serves authentic Mexican cuisine."

"Hey, I'm sure it's better than the last time I had Mexican food."

"Where was that?"

"It was at Taco Bell."

Sean laughs, a sound I hear so rarely, but when I do, it instantly makes me happy. His gaze travels across my body as he watches me laugh too.

"Have I told you how stunning you look tonight?" he asks before facing the road again.

"Thank you, you clean up well yourself." Sean is impeccably dressed in a form-fitting dark-gray suit, and his tie adds a touch of flair with its deep, rich shade of orange. There's something about a man in a finely tailored suit that will always be sexy. Especially if that man has muscles that look like they were chiseled from stone, and the suit highlights every one of them, and I swear, he can probably flex the buttons off. At least he can in my fantasies, and oh, my God, do I have plenty of those running through my head on a daily basis.

Passing another car, he turns to me, rumbling, "Are you wearing panties tonight?"

OMG. Naughty. I'm wearing a thong. The dress is smooth, and it leaves no room for traditional undergarments. A thong was the only practical choice to ensure that no lines disrupted the silhouette of the dress along my hips.

"I'm wearing a thong," I tell him.

"Take it off for me."

"Sean!"

"We're going to behave, relax," he assures me with a wink. "I just like knowing you're not."

Okay, there definitely seems to be a pattern here. I do as he says (not hesitating all that much). In one swift motion, my fingers slide into my thong. I roll it down over my hips, pushing them past my calves and heels.

"Much better," he praises while I open my little golden-beige purse to deposit it.

"Give it to me." He holds out his hand, eyes back on the road.

"Sean?"

"I'll give it back."

I pass him my thong, and he smoothly tucks it into his side pocket before placing his hand on my knee. There's definitely a pattern here. With just his left hand, he navigates the road, and the other rests casually. Just as he promised, he refrains from making any advances. It's both tantalizing and scorching, *scorching* hot.

We pull up to the restaurant, and Sean gets out first. I barely have a chance to unbuckle my seatbelt before he has the door open for me and extends his arm. Feeling giddy and not even attempting to hide my pleased blushing, I accept, and we head into the restaurant arm in arm. With my dress being knee-length, I don't have to worry of unintentionally making it into one of NYC's infamous gossip magazines, gracing the pages under a "flashing" headline—ultimately ruining the charity article I had envisioned as a beacon of respectability.

The restaurant is small, as he mentioned before, but traditionally decorated. Ornate wooden carvings and vibrant Talavera tiles provide an elegant cultural touch, while elaborate wrought-iron chandeliers cast a warm glow. It's evident a lot of love and pride has been put into the space. It's equally evident that he comes here more than he lets on, because they know him on sight.

Judging by the ambiance and the impeccable appearance of the women around, I surmise that I may not be the sole attendee who's opted for a thong-less approach, and Sean's hand on my hip reminds me of his appreciation of this choice.

It feels delightfully naughty, with no one in the know.

We're greeted like royalty and whisked away to the only empty table. The waiter arrives, and we give him our orders. Sean orders the nachos with extra guac, and I'll try the tamales—without the avocados (they never made it to my list of favorites). Unlike the margarita I order.

When the waiter leaves, I say, "Don't even think about kissing me after all that avocado."

"I'll make sure to rinse my mouth out first."

"Good." I take a thoughtful sip of water. "So aside from your love of Mexican cuisine, tell me something else I don't know about you."

Sean leans back in his seat, relaxed in a way I haven't seen in a while. "What do you want to know?"

"Something personal. Something fun."

"Ask me a fun question," he challenges.

The question pops into my head instantly. "Your middle name isn't Peter by any chance, is it?"

He looks puzzled. "Actually, it is. Named after my grandfather."

"No way!"

"Yep."

"Oh, my gosh, just like Peter Parker!" I beam at him, intrigued. My chest rises, and I'm hoping my dress doesn't reveal my perky nipples beneath the fabric. "You know, Spider-Man? Besides Mary Jane, he had a thing for a Jessica."

"Seriously?"

"You bet."

He chuckles. "Believe me, no Spidey-skills here. Heights aren't my thing. You're looking at a guy who wouldn't even climb a ladder."

That explains why he was so concerned on the balcony the first time we met and didn't politely suggest 'handling' things. I flash a grin and reply, "Well, I guess we won't be plotting any daring rooftop getaways together, then. But hey, at least we can enjoy...well..." My eyes fall to my lap and slide back to him. "...ground-level *adventures*?"

"Who needs heights when there's so much to explore down here."

"*Exactly.*"

"Got any more burning questions?" he asks.

"I sure do," I say brightly. "Do you have siblings?"

"I'm an only child. I was raised by both my parents. I told you about my mother passing away. I was thirteen when it happened. After that, my dad was pretty busy, so it was one nanny after another until I was old enough to work, and then I started working at my father's properties, learning the ins and outs of hospitality. It was one of my mother's final wishes. She told me that she knew how important it was to him—to stay."

"Oh...so did you like it?"

"Thankfully, I did. I wanted to make it a career. That was the last time my father and I ever agreed on anything."

"So, you really were born and bred in this business, huh?"

There's a smile on his face, and when he speaks, it's full of sarcasm. "I think if I had wanted to go into any other profession, my dad might have had a heart attack."

"It sounds like he cares for you."

The waiter pops by to drop off our drinks, which we thank him for. I pick up my margarita and take a healthy swig. It's really good, and I take another right away. Sean asked for a black coffee and a soda with lime which he sips thoughtfully as he watches me enjoying my cocktail from across the table. It's dangerously good. I feel so comfortable I almost forget I'm not wearing any underwear. I don't think I've ever been on such a deliciously hot first date.

"What about you?" he asks. "I know you've told me a little bit of how you got into this business, but I feel like there's more to the story."

"There's not much to tell. I had your standard childhood: raised by two parents, and luckily, they're both alive and well. I've worked in hospitality since I was a kid. My parents own a successful small hotel on the West Coast, in Cedar Cove, and I knew from a young age that I wanted to do what they did. So, I got a job at a hotel and loved it so much that I decided that's my calling."

Sean raises his eyebrow as he stirs his coffee. When I don't immediately continue, he asks, "That's it?"

"Why? What were you expecting?"

"There's gotta be something else. A few interesting tidbits that you're not mentioning."

"Of course there's more, but I really wouldn't call the tidbits interesting. More like..." I pause, trying to find the right word. "Sad. Devastating. A hard lesson I had to learn." I take another sip of my margarita.

His expression turns hard and serious, reminding me of our first encounter in our apartment's hallway. "What happened?"

Normally, thinking about what happened stings even after all this time. I regard him for a moment, my fingers tracing the rim of my glass. "To be honest, I haven't talked about it with anyone else besides Pauline, my neighbor Lottie, and Norman. It's not something I typically dive into on the first date."

Shit.

First date.

I wish I could take back those words the moment they leave my lips.

Or at least said "fake date."

Sean arches an eyebrow, just as I expected. "Given everything that we've done up until this point, I don't think we can label this a 'typical' first date."

"Fair point," I say casually, pondering what exactly he means.

Is it atypical because it's not a date, or is it atypical because, in his mind, it *is* a first date but not in the conventional romantic sense—you know, not your run-of-the-mill dinner-and-a-movie date?

"But I still find it quite enjoyable," he rumbles.

Even though it doesn't answer my question, my heart swells.

That's when the door opens and Richard walks in, accompanied by three suits.

Speak of the devil.

The four men look like they own the place, even though Richard is clearly the leader. His commanding presence suggests that this insider restaurant is the ideal setting for a business meeting. The ambiance, neither too opulent nor too casual, seems perfectly suited for business deals. Richard glances across the room, and when he sees us, he nods. Sean nods back.

"Small world," Sean says, after turning back to me. "Do you want to leave?"

"Absolutely not," I say firmly, but appreciating his question. From the corner of my eye, I notice Richard and the three impeccably dressed individuals being guided to sit a few tables down.

"Fine by me, my soon-to-be wife," Sean says, a mischievous glint in his eye.

And just like that, the question is answered. Our "no clue what it is" date morphs into a fake date, with Sean game for extending the performance.

I try not to let my inner turmoil rear its ugly head.

"You were saying?" he asks. "Please continue."

"Well...the main reason I don't like to bring up what happened before I bought Westerlyn is because even after all this time, I feel incredibly dumb for not seeing what was coming…" I pause for a moment. "How much did Norman tell you about me or my past while you two were putting the deal together?"

"Not much, really. I knew something significant happened to you before. Or at least, that's the sense I got. But if it's really not something you want to talk about—"

"No, no, it's okay. I don't mind talking about it now," I assure him, crossing my legs and leaning back in my seat. "As you know, I was in a relationship with Richard. Back then, he handled investments. He knew that I wanted to own my own hotel, and one day, I found one that was exactly what I wanted. It was my dream place, a plaza hotel. All I could think about was all the changes I'd make and how I could improve it. I was so excited. But I was young and in love, both of which make you blind. Anyway, the hotel was way too expensive for me alone, so he offered to buy it with me, together." I sigh. "The one thing I'm proud of myself for doing is keeping our bank accounts separate. Otherwise, it may have turned out far worse than it actually did. Which isn't saying much because it was still pretty bad."

"What happened?"

"Just one day before our wedding—he bought the hotel for himself."

Sean leans on the table, and his expression is darker than I've ever seen before. It's the definition of brooding intensity, a thunderstorm brewing in his gaze.

I can't take my eyes off him. It's frightening, in a good way—in a good way because he's completely on my side.

Sean shakes his head as he crosses his arms. "That's unacceptable."

"I know. The funny thing is, it catapulted his career, turning a small hotel into a billionaire plaza mogul empire."

"That's not funny. It's fucked up."

"I know. But honestly, Sean, in the end, I had to stop thinking about it or what I should have done. I had to accept that it is what it is. If I was ever going to be happy, if I was ever going to move on and make some-thing of my life and live my dream, I couldn't live in the past. That's what I told myself every day, until I believed it. My approach was to find the silver lining amid the turmoil, the glimmer of light in the storm. I couldn't keep thinking about him. I wouldn't give him that power. Not then, not now."

"How does he dare show his face in our hotel, let alone try to buy it?" This time, he has a "I'll burn the world down, and this guy first" death glare. My nipples prickle against the fabric of my cocktail dress.

"I know. The audacity, right?"

"Didn't you wish he'd regret the crap he pulled?"

"Of course. Especially in the beginning. But somehow, deep inside, I knew I dodged a bullet. He chose the hotel over me. Goes to show how much he truly loved me. Thanks—*next*! I knew I'd find a better opportu-nity. And I did."

Sean reaches across the table and takes my hand. In my mind, I hope it's as real as it feels. I also hope Richard is watching us, that he sees this. But when I glance over, he's occupied by studying the menu.

"You're definitely the most positive, steadfast person I've ever met," Sean rumbles. "I can't imagine the strength it must have taken to pick yourself back up and start over. A lot of people would have let that situa-tion turn them bitter. But you didn't. You still managed to save up and make your dream happen. You should be pretty proud of that."

"The gown, the engagement and wedding ring all ended up in the pawn shop. Without that cash, I might never have secured a stake in Norman's shares. Crazy, isn't it?"

There's a look of understanding that passes across his face. "That's why you were so upset about Norman selling to me. Old wounds and all that."

"Well, that was only part of it. The main part is because I swore I would never get involved again with someone I was working with. No sex, no dates, no feelings with coworkers or business partners, in short:

no business entanglements, especially with Chief Executive Officers. It's my number one rule. It encompasses the 'don't kiss the CEO' and 'never date the CEO' and especially the 'wear panties at all times' clauses—no exceptions." I smirk as Sean's eyes light back up. "Clearly, I fell *somewhat* off the wagon."

"I'm glad you somewhat did. It's proved beneficial for the both of us." Sean pauses for a moment, and then he says, "And now it's making a ton of sense why you refused for so long."

"I'm not sorry about anything."

Sean's thumb strokes my palm. Just that little touch is enough to stoke those flames between us that never seem to burn out. They only lie dormant until the next time we're together.

"What do you see yourself doing next?" Sean asks.

I consider his question. I love how he's always interested in me and my thoughts. "Honestly? I feel like the sky's the limit. With everything running so well, there's always room for expansion, and I've been considering exploring the adjacent building for the possibility of expanding our New York property. If our occupancy rates remain consistently high, we're going to need more rooms."

"I don't think it's for sale, the adjacent building. I already had Connor look into it."

"Oh, not yet, but soon," I say, smiling, squeezing his hand. "I've got a real estate agent with some top-notch insider info. Jane Deets. I'll reach out to her and see what I can do."

There is genuine excitement in his eyes. "Excellent," he says. "If that's the case, increasing the amenities would be good. If we expand, we can make space for an indoor pool, which is always a draw to guests. Especially in the city where swimming isn't easy to come by. And a spa. Spas are a great source of income, not just from guests but from locals as well."

"Norman and I always wanted to explore this option, but the limits of financial resources have held us back. But what about you? Where do you see Blackwood in the next five years?"

"That's easy. International. Hands down, we're going to be in many countries across the world. We've already started and we're in the process of acquiring smaller chains in some of the bigger tourist areas, like the Caribbean and Europe." The darkness in his eyes returns. "That's if my father will ever get off the board and let me do what needs to be done."

It's what it always seems to come down to for Sean, getting out of the tight hold his father has on the company. That's got to be frustrating, and annoying. I lucked out meeting Norman and connecting with him as well as we did. I have no doubt that if he hadn't been as open-minded and understanding, it would have been impossible for me to implement the necessary changes.

"Can I ask you something?" I request once the waiter brings our food and we start to dig in.

"Sure, go ahead."

"I find it strange that your father is so fixated on the idea of you buying me out. I mean, it's kind of flattering that he's so interested, but isn't there a more significant business he should be focused on?"

"He's a, let's say, *difficult* figure. It's evident that fellow board members are growing weary of his approach. But it's challenging to take action against the man who built and owns the majority of the company shares. He possesses sufficient leverage to prevent a vote for his removal."

"You've proven yourself time and time again. Magazines are filled with your praises. He shouldn't be micromanaging you."

"You're preaching to the choir, Jess."

I'm intrigued to learn more about his relationship with his father and late mother. In the photo, his dad didn't strike me as a "difficult figure," but I hesitate—it's not my place.

Instead, I say, "His mood, his burden. Don't make it yours." His brow furrows, but a flicker of something unreadable crosses his features. "So, when you're head of the board, when you finally have the reins, what's the first thing you're going to do?"

He seems to consider my question for a moment before he says, "As mentioned, we're set on expanding internationally. But the initial step I'll take upon gaining control is to assess our existing properties and concentrate on enhancing their potential. Focus on quality over quantity."

"Smart. Exploring the opportunities right in front of you is a fantastic way to foster growth."

"We have a separate team who deals with the management side of things, but I always felt we could be doing more. We bought these places because of their potential, and we've continued to work to make them profitable, but profit isn't everything."

"Right?" I smile at him. "If we wanted to, we could really go ham and focus on the latest technological advances for hospitality. For example, implementing in-room tablets for guests to control room settings and request services."

"What other changes do you want to make that you haven't been able to?"

"Oh," I wave my hand, "don't even get me started."

"Too late." He gives me the cutest smile. "I'm invested. Tell me."

The rest of the evening dissolves into a sort of impromptu business meeting. The food is excellent. And while, yes, this had started off as a thrilling-auction-turned-hot-fake-date, I don't really mind the conversation switching because there's something different about it. It feels like a true collaboration, a true meeting of the minds. I forget everything about me, and there's only him. Sean Blackwood. Dominant, powerful, with his all-encompassing presence.

The plans we talk about are plans we want to make together. We're a team.

In fact, I feel like we're really onto something, and that together, we're an unstoppable force.

It's good this isn't a real-real date.

In a way, it's for the best. A professional partnership shouldn't be jeopardized by something as delicate and fleeting as love.

"Wanna have some fun with him?" he asks after the waiter takes our orders for dessert.

"With Richard?" I glance over, and notice two more businessmen have joined his table. While we're anticipating our final course, they're still in the midst of savoring the main meal. "Sure."

"Get up and walk to the washroom. I'll meet you there in a minute."

I nod, excitement swelling in me. I get up, and from the corner of my eye, I catch Richard following my movements. He's about to get up too, but changes his mind when Sean stands.

Once I'm in the beautiful, huge washroom that serves as a front room to the guest toilets, filled with a couch, seats, mirrors and two lavish sink areas, Sean arrives only a few seconds after.

Before I can even get a word out, he rumbles, "I've been meaning to do this all evening."

Before I can react, his lips are on mine.

Before I can even process what's happening, my brain shuts off.

No power.

Not even a flicker.

Except for the surge of electricity that courses through me with his earth-shaking kiss. It's brimming with such emotion, passion, and tenderness that it almost moves me to tears. Nothing else exists. We kiss and kiss, unable and unwilling to stop.

Without breaking the kiss, he attempts to lock the door behind us. "Fuck, there's no way to lock it," he mutters against my lips before pulling away, but not losing touch of me.

He looks at his watch, and I can tell what he's thinking. His intentions are clear—he's not inclined to venture into *that* territory, and he'd rather spare me the walk of shame in front of Richard. Instead, he chooses to relish a touch of playful torture.

"We don't have much time, let's make it count," he murmurs. "Two minutes, max."

He brings me back into another kiss and pushes me toward one of the sinks. My hands are all over him, tugging at his shoulders, at his muscular arms. He wrestles control, pulling up my dress so he can slip his hand underneath. His mouth is hot and hungry, just like his gaze had been. His tongue pushes past my lips while his hands grab my naked ass.

He hoists me into a seated position on the vanity, never breaking our kiss. Nearly every inch of us is touching. His hands are back on my breasts, my waist, my hips, squeezing hard, as if he's never touched me before in his life.

"We can't keep doing this, Sean," I whisper between our kisses, breathless.

"Jesus Christ, I want to fuck you so bad, Jess," he rasps, "but this isn't the time."

When there's a noise, we whip our heads toward the door, but it's nothing. He kisses me more, his hands back on my breasts, teasing my nipples through the cloth.

"Those damn nipples have been driving me insane all night. Lower that top for me."

I do as he says, not questioning anything, pulling my dress down, exposing my naked breasts for him.

"A bit more."

Before I can blink, his lips are circling my nipple, then sucking it in, pulling it hard and releasing it with a *pop*. "Fuck, you're perfect." He repeats the same thing with the other nipple. The sensation makes me moan, and warmth blooms between my legs.

"Oh...Sean."

His palms skim along my thighs and all I can think about is him touching me between them. Gosh, I'm so relieved I opted for comfort over potential panties struggle.

His hands slide to my knees. "Open your legs. Quick. Spread them. Spread them."

I hesitate, my head light. "What if someone walks in?"

"I know who's in charge, Jess. *And it ain't you.* I need to taste you. Now." He's already lowering himself as I'm opening my legs, my golden-beige strappy heels dangling to his left and right.

"Wider. Relax."

The next thing I know, he has my clit in his mouth.

"Naughty girl," he rumbles teasingly. "No underwear? Living life on the edge, I see. Brave move."

I can't even joke at this point because his tongue swipes over the sensitive skin, oh-so-gently massaging the sensitive bud, and oh, God, I'm trying so hard to be still. He's sucking on my clit, teasing it, doing things to it that make my head fall back and my back arch.

One swipe later, I start panting.

Two swipes later, my thighs start shaking, and when he sucks it into his mouth, hard, sending pulses throughout my whole body, I can't stop a low groan from escaping my mouth.

Three sucking motions later, I'm ready to erupt. We're talking a volcanic explosion, massive, earth-shatteringly violent, and downright cataclysmically cosmical.

Making sense of things is a challenge right now.

I want to ignore the noise outside the door so badly. But suddenly, he's back in a standing position, and I follow his lead, standing (all wobbly), while I adjust my top over my chest and he's helping to smooth my dress down.

The door opens, and an elderly lady with an elegant white bob walks in, her walking stick in hand. We nod at her innocently, and she gives us a warm, cute little smile and proceeds to the ladies' room in the back.

Once we hear the click of the door behind her, he leans in, and I'm so glad his hand reaches back below my dress and softly starts rubbing my clit, around and around, rumbling, "Once we get home, there's no mercy."

My hips buck against his hand as I'm hovering on the edge while he continues to brush his finger against my swollen, aching clit. I can feel how soaked I am for him and let out a desperate whimper.

I'm so wet.

I'm so close.

I'm so very close.

"It won't be sex," he rumbles in that low voice against the shell of my ear, stroking me. "It won't be love making. It'll be hard fucking, and you're gonna take that cock like a naughty little thing."

I nod, fully agreeing. "Sounds like a perfect plan." At this point, I would have agreed to paint the entire hotel lobby pink and fill it with real flamingos strutting around.

He circles my clit one last time, pinches it, then removes his hand. "I propose that we scarf down dessert and make a swift exit."

"Yep, my plan exactly," I manage to breathe out.

My clit protests loudly, screaming, *please please please continue.*

He gives me a quick kiss, licks his finger clean, reaches up into his hair and dishevels it a bit (the part that hasn't been disheveled by my thighs), giving me a smirk.

"Good. Let's go." Oh, I get it. He's planning to straighten his hair as we're walking toward our table, in perfect line of sight of Richard.

I smile. "Okay."

Sean reaches for my hand, and when his fingers find mine, the touch sends a delicious shiver racing down my spine. He leads me toward the exit, fingers interlaced, then we're out the door. We're holding hands, like a real couple. It's not just the firm touch of his hand or the cute wink, it's the side-glance when he squeezes my hand and his thumb softly brushes over my knuckle. He's acutely aware of his actions and what they do to my heart.

Oh, no. This is bad.

Very bad.

Worse than I thought.

I might not only break my cardinal rule.

I might commit an unforgivable act.

I might be falling in love with Sean Blackwood.

18

SEAN

*a*fter scarfing down the churros with chocolate sauce, the drive home definitely intensifies the suspense when she places her feet on the console and my fingers onto her clit and begs me to let her come.

Teasing her, I slowly rub her clit up and down then circle it with my thumb.

Being the gentleman that I am, I don't edge her too much.

When I open her car door, the air is alive with the warmth of the evening and the exhilaration of a hot car drive.

Once the elevator doors close, she turns to face me, her eyes shining.

"I had a great time tonight," she says as we ride up.

"So did I."

She inches closer, and the air crackles. I can taste the desire, feel it in every nerve.

A charged silence hangs between us, thick with unspoken desire. She's close, so close, and I can feel the pull between us intensifying. I tug her to me until her tits graze my chest, and her hands settle against my arms. It takes everything in me to keep the beast in check. I stop myself from grabbing her hips, turning her around and bending her over, asking her to hoick that skirt up, and making her scream my name.

Sure, sex in the elevator sounds like a hot idea, but it's not what I have in mind for tonight.

Tonight's going to be on a whole other level of heat.

The elevator dings at our floor and we step out.

"Oh, there you are, Mr. Blackwood," my assistant greets me with a warm smile. "I just dropped by to finalize the documents. Wrapping things up with Mrs. Sanborne took longer than expected."

I sense it before it happens.

I can feel Jess's immediate retreat. She removes her hand from my arm.

The moment is broken.

Shit.

"No worries, Jasmine." I nod, understanding the intricacies involved in the aftermath of a high-profile auction. "I appreciate your dedication." She likely called, but my phone stayed on silent after the auction —I've been too distracted to turn it back on.

"I'm off next week, as you know," she continues, a hint of exhaustion in her eyes. "But I wanted to make sure everything was in order before I left. Hi again, Ms. Summers."

"Hi Jasmine, how are you?" The women hug like two long lost friends and exchange warm words.

"Oh, well, it seems time has slipped away on us," Jess says with a charming smile, but I detect a touch of awkwardness in her tone. "I suppose I'll be on my way. Good night, everybody."

She discreetly retreats into her apartment.

I immerse myself in the paperwork, signing the necessary documents to initiate the transfer of funds.

As soon as Jasmine is gone, I knock on Jess's door.

It takes a while.

When she opens, there's a flicker of hesitation—only a flicker. But it's enough to give me pause. She has changed her mind. This isn't the time to push her past her wishes, past that rule she set for herself. I sense what she's thinking: there are many more things standing between us.

"Sean, I..." she whispers, then trails off.

"I know," I stop her, stroking her chin. She doesn't need to lay her cards on the table. The night took a turn she wasn't ready for. "We won't do anything until you're sure about us," I rasp against her ear, my voice low, tinged with a raw honesty. "Not until you're sure about me."

Her eyes widen.

She studies me, her eyes searching mine for answers. The fake engagement, the shared intimacy, and the connection we've been building in the past few days hang in the air.

"I don't want this to be just a moment," I rumble, trailing my thumb down her chin. "I want it to be everything, but only if you're ready for everything."

"I appreciate you saying that," she whispers, her body visibly relaxing. "I can't deny that tonight was exhilarating, an all-time high. But you're my boss...a CEO...well, and the emotions, they're not quite there for me in the way they should be, and I suppose I'm not ready to peel back those layers again. I'm sorry, and I promise I'll be more careful next time." She leans in for a short hug, and as she pulls back, she says, "It was a glitch, a momentary lapse after the adrenaline rush of a successful evening."

I nod, and my dick weeps.

I release her gently, allowing her the space she needs.

Every logical part of my mind screams that this is impossible, that emotions don't just glitch into existence, but there's no sense in pushing her.

Time is a small price to pay for something real, something worth waiting for. I reach up, brushing a strand of hair from her face, my fingers lingering against her cheek.

"I understand," I say. "I'll wait. As long as it takes." I wink at her, "You and I both know you can't help but fall in love with me."

Shaking her head with a smile, she replies, "As tempting as that sounds, I don't make exceptions. So, everything back to normal?"

I nod. "Sure."

"Good. See you tomorrow, *boss*."

"Wait." I pull her back.

She gasps when I hand her back her thong, then enter my apartment.

I wake up bright and early as usual, with one slight change. Ever since our kiss in the Presidential Suite followed by our date after the charity, my dreams have been plagued by images of my neighbor, and my dick is already at attention. Apparently, my imagination has decided to run wild with all the things I can't do to Jess. According to her, we are a glitch. According to her, it was a solo act on the feelings front.

It takes an hour on the treadmill and a cold shower to calm myself down.

She's right, of course. The more distance between us, the better. I am her boss, and she is my employee. Nothing can happen between us.

Fuck.

No woman has ever had this power over me, and there's way too much on the line to rewrite the script.

The next few days, conversation is focused on work and work alone.

But physically? That's a whole other ball game. Jess is no longer avoiding me, no longer hurrying out of the room with one excuse or another. In fact, it's almost the opposite. When we're talking or looking at paperwork together, she's close and a bit more in my personal space, letting her perfume hang around me.

I'd be lying if I said it isn't working.

Being that close and feeling her body heat draws my focus every time.

Each time I accidentally (or not) touch her, I hear her inhale sharply before slowly exhaling like she's trying to calm herself down. I have an excellent poker face—unlike Jess, especially with the paleness of her skin. The flush easily spreads across her freckled cheeks, giving her away every time. It's cute.

After a couple of days, it starts to feel natural. I don't even notice the switch at first. Mostly, I want to keep touching her and being close to her because I know we both enjoy it.

Despite her denial before, I've caught her leaning into my touch on more than one occasion. A hand on my arm. Her body pressing into my side. Once, she even leans back against my chest when I glance over her shoulder to look at a document we're reviewing.

My resolve almost slips—*almost*.

Nothing can and will happen until she's ready.

19

JESS

*I*t's the day before Schuster and Flint, the big retreat group that books with us every year, are set to arrive. After a hectic morning, I collapse with an exhausted sigh. I just finished meeting with maintenance about a couple of minor room repairs and informed Pauline regarding several various last-minute wishes and preferences, such as bedding, room amenities, temperature, decorations, and concierge services, and stopped by the front desk to let them know I had emailed an updated reservation list. We've had several unexpected last-minute additions—the new coordinator Mr. Grant sure likes to keep me busy—and we need to have extra special welcome packets (that include personalized handwritten notes) put together. One of our guest specials includes a delightful assortment of original NYC-style cheesecake bites sourced from that charming local bakery just around the corner, a hidden gem cherished by the locals. I call Sarah to ensure we have enough pieces on hand.

Sean walks in a moment later and slides an iced coffee toward me. "Here, you need this," he says with a rare smile.

I take it graciously, saying "Thank you" before consuming a giant swig. The liquid is cool and invigorating, and the instantaneous shot of caffeine lifts my spirits. With a smile, I lean back in my seat and look at Sean. His lips curve at my reaction.

"Thanks. I owe you one."

"You don't owe me anything. You've been working like a boss," he says, smiling. "The least I can do is get you coffee and maybe dinner if you're up for it."

Dinner? He's asking me on another date? My heart leaps until I remember I can't.

"Dinner sounds great," I tell him, "but this is going to be another late night. We've had some last-minute requests from Mr. Grant that I need to supervise myself before they all arrive tomorrow."

Sean leans against my desk and shrugs. "That's fine, we can have it delivered. Personally, I could devour some sushi right now."

I'm touched that he wants to stay, although I shouldn't be surprised given how equally hard—equally boss, no doubt—he's been working. It's easy to see why he's in the position that he's in. He has an insane eye for detail, not to mention his willingness to roll up his sleeves and jump right in is admirable. Trust me, I've met plenty of CEOs over the years and can tell you that's not a common occurrence.

Also, I'd be lying if I said I wasn't excited to spend more private one-on-one time with Sean—and his lips. Ever since the charity auction, something has changed. He spends much more time at Westerlyn than he used to. Working these longer stretches of time with him has shown me a side I wasn't prepared for, a softness I'm privy to. The way he's been looking out for me and checking in to see how I'm doing shows how much he cares. It's not just me he's been sweet with. The other day, Emma had a family emergency, and he immediately called her a car and even followed up with her.

Why has everyone been warning me about him? After our "rough start," and a few glitches here and there, he's been nothing but rational, attentive, and even sweet.

The devil on my shoulder tells me it's the calm before the storm.

The angel on my shoulder tells me it's perfectly fine to allow myself to fall for Mr. CEO.

"You don't have to stay, you know," I tell him, getting up to stretch my legs and pick up the folder I (lovingly) labeled "Operation Retreat Rescue" from one of the piles on my desk. "Don't get me wrong, I appreciate the help, but I don't want to take up another one of your evenings. We've been working late all week."

"If you're working, then I'm working," he says firmly. As he speaks, my gaze involuntarily shifts to his lips, their every movement captivating me. "I'm not one to sit on the sidelines when there's stuff that needs to be done."

Those lips will be the death of me.

And not just those lips.

The words he said with those lips.

I want it to be everything, but only if you're ready for everything.

I'll wait.

As long as it takes.

Deafening echoes of déjà vu scream in my heart, but I tell myself this time it's different. Because Sean isn't Richard.

The problem is: I can't trust myself to know. Nor can I scold myself.

Here's the thing.

Everything was going fairly well. Then somewhere along the way, there was a switch. I'm not sure when it happened, how, or why—but it did. Probably somewhere between kissing me stupid and kissing me stupider.

I hated that I liked it.

Apparently, now that I've had an appetizer (multiple, in fact), my body wants the whole meal. Every time I feel he's close, like right now, it's like someone takes the dial of my body heat and cranks it up all the way. Not only do I sense the familiar spicy scent of his aftershave, but I can also feel the heat radiating off his body in waves. It's intoxicatingly inviting.

I don't even hear my desk phone start to ring.

It can ring and ring and ring, and I don't care.

His green eyes stroke over me. "You want me to get it?" Sean rumbles.

"I got it," I say, coming to my senses, and regaining enough body control to detach my eyes from his lips and reach for the phone.

It's Emma from the front desk.

After she explains her issue with the guest, I straighten. "All right, don't worry, I'll be down in a second. I'll take care of it. Offer him drink vouchers for the bar and tell him dinner is on us."

As soon as I hang up the phone, Sean reverts to Mr. Grumpy King, likely alarmed by my facial expression. "What's wrong?"

"The new group coordinator arrived a day early, Mr. Grant from Schuster and Flint. Which wouldn't be such a big deal, if we weren't still deep cleaning his suite for his arrival."

A dark shadow crosses his features, then he asks, "Can't we put him in a different suite until then?"

"Emma told him that, and he started getting belligerent."

"Oh, fantastic," he says sarcastically.

"I'll go talk to Emma, do damage control."

"Good luck."

B oth of us leave my office, heading in opposite directions, him for his room and me for the front desk. Before I even get there, I already know the situation has escalated. I hear a rough male voice drowning out Emma's soft, musical one. I brace myself for the confrontation and plaster on my best customer service smile.

When I round the corner, I find an older gentleman, in his mid-to-late sixties, with jet-black hair, which is obviously dyed, and an expensive suit that likely costs more than a week's stay in our Presidential Suite. His hands rest on the front desk, and I notice a glittering gold Rolex just under his sleeve. His expression can only be described as disgust, like he stepped in something that smelled. I don't think I've ever seen a snobbish person with their face physically turned up, but there he is.

The bold, abstract strokes of *Metropolitan Reverie* in the back of the lobby instantly catch my eye, effortlessly calming my mood. The art piece wouldn't grace these walls if not for Westerlyn's proven devotion to excellence and, let's not beat around the bush, some downright unmatched *triumphs*.

"This is unacceptable," he's saying, his hoarse voice unnecessarily loud. "What kind of *dump* is this? The hotel knew I was coming, and my room should have been made available in anticipation of my arrival. Where is your manager?"

"I'm right here, sir," I say as I approach the desk. "Are you Mr. Grant?" I ask, keeping my tone friendly.

"Obviously that's who I am. Are you the manager?"

"I'm the general manager, yes. I'm Jessica Summers, pleasure to meet you, Mr. Grant."

I extend my hand for a shake, and he looks down at it with a sneer, as if he's surprised I dare try to shake his hand. He ignores it. Ooo-kay. I lower it to my side.

"Well," he says, "then maybe you can make sense of this enormous error on your hotel's behalf. How is it that my suite is unavailable?"

"That particular suite will be available tomorrow, which is what we have on file for your scheduled check-in. The suite isn't quite ready, seeing as it's a day early. However, we have another lovely one that's available that I'd be happy to show you to."

"But isn't that going to require me moving tomorrow? I'm a very busy man, Ms. Summers. I'm running this retreat and will have my hands full when the group arrives tomorrow, especially since we may be a handful of people short and won't require all the rooms. It means I'll have to juggle and adjust plans, thanks to this headache. As you can tell, I'm juggling a million things right now. Trust me, young lady, I do *not* have time for your nonsense because you were utterly unprepared."

I'm not impressed with how he's speaking to me and how he obviously was speaking to Emma. Never mind the fact that he definitely was not intending to check in early, nor did he seem to consider his early arrival as an issue. The man hasn't even stayed here, and he's already kicking up a fuss.

"The hotel would be more than happy to facilitate the moving of your belongings once the room is available," I state calmly, forgoing to point out that if he had called in earlier, we might have easily accommodated. I doubt the fault is on our side, however, it *is* possible. "We understand that you're a busy man, and we'd be more than happy to have our bellman take care of the change. You'll be able to pick up your new keys right here at the front desk whenever you have a moment."

"What about compensation? The hotel should do more to correct this oversight."

There it is.

There are two types of people who complain at a hotel. Type one: people who genuinely have valid concerns that require attention. Type two: people who use such situations as a way to obtain benefits. I'm starting to see that Mr. Grant is the second kind.

Sean was right, dammit. I really should have insisted on the new hotel room prices for a group of his size, *and* the cancellation policy. Especially when Mr. Grant conveniently "forgot" to inform the bookings department about the guest shortage he just mentioned, as I was sure he had.

Still, having this guy causing a fuss over something that can be solved professionally and in a timely manner is really testing what little patience I have left.

I can't believe I skipped my date for this.

I keep reminding myself to stay on the sunny side just like my parents taught me—no matter if it's a person or a challenge—and channel my "I-so-want-to-kick-him-in-the-balls" energy into a beaming smile and a voice that could soothe a room full of squawking Pippins.

Ah, the liberating power of staying the course with style.

"Well, Mr. Grant," I start, "I'd be more than happy to look into that. In the meantime, why don't you enjoy a complimentary meal and drink while we take your belongings to your room?"

"That's it?" He huffs out a mocking laugh. "That's all you're gonna give me for this inconvenience?"

I open my mouth to respond, but before I can, Sean's voice sounds from behind me, loud and clear.

20

JESS

"*I* think Ms. Summers here has offered you quite a bit by way of compensation," Sean says, "given that we're almost booked out and you were not on the schedule for arrivals today, Andrew."

Mr. Grant's eyes widen as they fall on Sean, who now stands by my side.

"Sean?" he asks, surprised. "What...are you doing here?"

"Westerlyn Hotels has been acquired by Blackwood. I'm here working with Ms. Summers on the transition of the acquisition."

No surprise, he knows Mr. Grant—of course he does. He's been in this game for almost two decades, unlike me, juggling months away at my other hotels on the East Coast in Maine, Connecticut, and Massachusetts before working out of the New York City branch.

Mr. Grant puts on a cheerful smile, which I can't tell if it's fake or not. "At least there's someone running this hotel who knows what they are doing," he says to Sean, completely ignoring me now and somewhat turning his body away in the process.

The audacity. I feel the heat rise to my face and my annoyance at this man switches to indignation. "I have been running this hotel for five years, Mr. Grant," I tell him. "And before that, another hotel. I know what I'm doing."

He side-eyes me but otherwise ignores me completely. Instead, he full-on turns his back to me and gives Sean his undivided attention. I catch Emma's eye over his shoulder, and she looks as irritated and insulted as I feel.

Sean doesn't seem like he's willing to let the slight go, saying, "Ms. Summers deserves the credit when it comes to running this hotel, Andrew. She has been more than charitable, especially considering the challenging circumstances." He lowers his voice, hinting at a private conversation, yet it's loud enough for me to hear. "I don't understand why you insist on doing this every single time your company sends you on a business retreat, Andrew. It should be more than enough that you are already compensated for your time by your company and don't have to pay a penny. And even if you did, we both know you can afford it," he says, fixing Mr. Grant with a knowing look.

It takes all my willpower not to react to Sean's burn and laugh out loud.

I've already been getting the sense that the man is quite shrewd, but to hear it confirmed by Sean, and that he's not standing for any of this man's crap, has me feeling all kinds of ways.

I allow myself to smile, and it's more than a little smug.

One of the pet peeves I've had over the years is hearing about and seeing managers bend over backward to cater to these "rich people types" who show them no respect. To know that Sean is not one to tolerate such behavior, to know that he's going to call someone out for their rudeness with such elegant grace, and, even more importantly, back me one hundred percent, makes my heart skip a beat with sheer excitement and awe.

Mr. Grant becomes noticeably flustered. He opens and closes his mouth a few times before words actually come out. "You have to see things from my perspective, Sean," he says with a friendly smile, his voice much calmer and lower, like he's making an effort to appear benevolent, unlike two seconds ago when he was yelling at Emma. "Travel plans can change unexpectedly, and it's possible that there was a...well, miscommunication somewhere. You will admit that it's inconvenient to not be able to check into your room when you intend to."

In Emma's expression and her subtle shake of her head, I'm certain there had been no "miscommunication" on our part. Pauline has somehow materialized out of nowhere and communicates a "Not that I know of."

"It may be what you intended," I say, making my voice stern enough to draw his attention, yet maintaining the professionalism I take pride in. He reluctantly turns to face me, as I continue, "But we were not made aware of your early arrival. However, we're more than happy to accommodate, and as I said, we do have a suite available, and dinner is on us."

The man glances at Sean, almost as if he's expecting him to say something, maybe even chastise me. Sean doesn't say a thing, only stands there, confident, unwavering, like he owns not only this hotel, but rather every hotel that was ever built and the cosmos itself.

Mr. Grant finally gives me his full attention. "Yes, yes, good. That sounds acceptable. Thank you, Ms. Summers."

Sean clears his throat. "It would be advisable to consider extending an apology to Ms. Summers and Mrs. Simpson, wouldn't you agree, Andrew? They were both doing their jobs, and there is no justification for the manner in which you addressed them."

I swear it looks like the guy swallowed a lemon.

The way his face pinches together makes me want to die laughing.

I feel like he has never been told to apologize in his entire life, or at least in his adult life. There's a quiet pause where nobody moves or says anything, but the men stay locked in this intense staring contest.

They stare.

And stare.

Eventually, Mr. Grant nods. "Oh, why not?" He glances at me and Emma. "My apologies, ladies," he says, a sheepish grin appearing, as if he's suddenly realized he's treading on thin ice. "I will be sure to watch my tone from now on. Must be the jet lag talking, you know, ha-ha." He nods again, trying to ease the tension, and it's evident that he's chasing his tail, realizing he overstepped and needs to regain Sean's favor.

I go to accept his apology, which is more than I ever expected from this encounter, but Sean speaks up again.

"Oh, come on, Andrew. You can do better than that." The hint of a smirk graces his lips. He's loving making this guy squirm and giving him a taste of his own medicine.

Mr. Grant's cheeks redden, and his back straightens as he adjusts his already-immaculate suit jacket, then looks at me and Emma. "Of course, of course. I'm sorry," he says, releasing another awkward chuckle. "I appreciate your help, ladies. I will take you up on the offer for dinner and a drink, Ms. Summers. And, I'll make sure my tone is as smooth as a freshly buttered biscuit from here on out."

"Apology accepted, Mr. Grant," I tell him in my cheerful voice. I try so hard not to glance over at Pauline, because I know if I do, I won't be able to hold back a laugh at seeing this jerk of a man put so firmly in his place.

With a nod, he takes the vouchers Emma hands him and walks toward the restaurant. While his steps are slow and leisurely, I notice the tension in his shoulders and the tips of his ears turn red the farther he walks away.

As soon as he's out of earshot, I turn to Sean, but Emma speaks first.

"Mr. Blackwood," she says, beaming at him, "I don't want to sound unprofessional here, but *that* was *the* best thing I've seen in a long time."

"I agree," Pauline says.

Sean chuckles—actually chuckles!—completely unaccustomed to

all these Westerlyn hearts swooping his way. "I don't have use for guests who try to nickel and dime, and he has no business being rude to either of you when you were just doing your jobs. Make a note on his account. Let the others know if he tries anything during the rest of his stay to inform me, and I'll take care of it."

"Perfect!" Pauline inclines her head eagerly.

"Of course, sir!" Emma continues to beam at him, and then I hear her fingers dancing across the keys as she pulls up the guy's information. Sean and I share a brief glance before he heads back to his office while I hang around for another minute or two, just to make sure no one else shows up, or Mr. Grant doesn't come back.

When we're alone, Emma gives me the biggest grin.

"Oh...goodness gracious," Pauline says dryly, giving me a "WTH was that?" expression.

"That was bloody *amazing*!" Emma swoons, practically bouncing up and down on her heels. "I mean, it was lovely of him to back you up and call out Mr. Grant's behavior, but I was *not* expecting him to make him apologize, let alone literally demand the words 'I'm sorry.'"

"Neither was I," I say, equally flabbergasted, still contemplating his unexpected reaction to the difficult guest who clearly had ulterior motives.

"Oh, my God, the way Mr. Grant turned his back on you?" Emma lowers her voice. "What an absolute tosser—pardon my French."

"A douchebag par excellence," Pauline agrees.

"It's all right," I say. "I think Sean embarrassed him enough to make up for it."

"I never would have guessed he would have that reaction," Pauline says.

"No, me neither!" Emma exclaims, her hand on her heart, looking back in the direction Sean left. "I was convinced he was going to fire me."

"Well, it seems he's got a knack for keeping us on our toes!" I say and we all lock eyes, smirking at each other.

I don't quite realize the depth of his defense and what it means to me. All I know is that my mind is reeling. All I wanna do is chase after Sean and do...I don't even know what. Something. I want to do something with him, to him.

Pauline is the first to glance at her watch and call it a night.

Just as I'm about to storm off, she turns back and tells me that she almost forgot why she's been looking for me. She reports that her staff is slowly adapting to using the new computer we provided for those who aren't tech savvy. In fact, some of them even find it "cool" and "hip," earning a thumbs-up from their grandchildren. A deep satisfaction settles in my soul, and I bring both women into the happiest hug the world has ever seen.

"Are you all set, Emma?" I ask after we finally wish Pauline a happy evening. "I'm gonna head back to finish my work if you're good here."

She waves, a smile still on her face and returns to her screen. "Oh, yes, I've got it."

With each step toward Sean's office, I move faster and faster, until I'm power walking down the hall.

I need to get to Sean—and quickly. The moment I see the door of his office, I know exactly what I'm gonna do when I get there. Sarah is gone by now, but he's waiting for me, leaning on the edge of the desk, with his arms crossed. When I approach the doorway, his dark eyes meet mine.

"You all right there, Jess?" he rumbles.

Without second-guessing or really thinking about the consequences of what I'm about to do, I cross the threshold and quickly close the door behind me.

Sean meets me in the middle of the room.

We throw our arms around each other, pressing the other into a stormy kiss.

Words cannot express the heat between us. All the stolen looks, all the innuendo and soft touches, culminates in a frenzy of hands and mouths. I now know what that shift has been and why I'm throwing caution into the wind. He respects my staff and me. He holds us in high regard. Despite his meddling and initial dismissals, he has my back when it counts.

We really are in a partnership.

He pushes until I hit the wall with a soft *thud*. I peel his suit jacket off his shoulders and his hands tug my skirt up over my hips. It's finally happening. All the fantasies and desires flow out of me, and there's no reining them in. Instinctually, when his hands reach the back of my thighs, I lift myself up to wrap my legs around his waist. His solid strength reassures me that he's not going to let me fall. He holds me there, hands still stroking my thighs as his mouth ravages mine.

This is happening.

I don't only cross the threshold of the room, I'm crossing the line I drew in the sand due to my "never date the CEO" rule.

It's no longer an option, a limit that for the last month has seemed so important and so necessary. Now it's ridiculous. This isn't about physical attraction or desire. It's about two people giving into their true emotions that have been scratching to be set free.

I can feel him through his pants. The heat and thickness calls to me, makes me want to rip off all of our clothes and ride him until morning. And if we were home, that's exactly what I would do. But right now, the only thing I keep thinking is more. I want more. I *need* more.

"Sean," I whisper hoarsely. I don't even know if I'm begging, pleading, or asking. His name is all I can convey in that moment.

"I know, baby, I know."

He called me "baby."

This time, it's not to fool my ex. This time, it's real.

His hand slips into my panties, and my head falls against the wall when I let out a low moan. My hands clutch his shoulders, fingers digging into the fabric and wishing I was touching skin instead. The way he touches me makes my body come alive again. There isn't much he needs to do before I'm ready for more. It's like my body is begging for him as much as my mind is. One of my hands finds its way into his hair, and I pull him into another soul-crushing kiss.

The sound of his belt buckle echoes through the room and sends a shudder of excitement through me. He draws back to look me in the eye, his lips parted as he breathes heavily. There's a flicker of something unspoken passing between us, a silent agreement that needs no words. No condom. I'm on birth control, and we don't want anything between us. The way he's staring as he lowers his pants takes what remaining breath I have left.

And then he's slowly pushing the full nine inches into me and capturing my lips with his when my mouth falls open. His cock is rock hard, thick, and soft, and oh so impossibly long. It's all too much. Yet it's not enough.

I close my eyes, losing myself in the sensation of him stretching me, taking his time.

Shockwaves of pleasure shoot through my veins, and my heart feels like it's about to burst from my chest. No one has ever made my body feel like this. No one has ever taken my breath away in a single moment. And he's only halfway in. I have seen him naked but now to feel him entering me bare, it's more exquisite than I ever imagined. He's not just invading me—he's claiming me. I whimper as his cock is filling me, unable to breathe.

When his hip meets mine, his body pressed against mine, it's like being engulfed in a hurricane of heat and need.

"Look at me," he whispers a soft command when he's fully inside of me, his voice barely more than a breath against my ear, stilling, allowing me to adjust to his size. I struggle to follow his order, completely over-whelmed by his presence.

"Behave, or else there will be repercussions," he rumbles.

Oh shit.

So hot.

Filled to the tippy top, I open my eyes, meeting his gaze. Long lashes frame his eyes, casting delicate shadows against his skin. His deep forest-green eyes collide with mine. His gaze hits me with such force, I feel the sting behind my eyes. Locking eyes with Sean tugs at something deep within me, and feeling his heartbeat against mine, I'm drowning. But, if I have to drown, I don't want it to be in anyone else's arms.

He starts to move, rocking maddeningly slowly, ruining me slowly, and any lingering thoughts are promptly shunted from my mind.

It's like a switch has flipped. I'm his.

"Sean..." I breathe hard when he changes pace, fucking me in long, smooth strokes and I grip onto him. This is meant to be, far, far beyond a silly crush.

"Yeah, baby...so good," he pants in rhythm, branding me as his own with every possessive thrust. "You feel fucking perfect."

Shudder after shudder passes through me, making me clench and cling to him.

We're in our own little world, where nothing else matters except the connection between us. We fall into a rhythm, rocking together. With the hard wall at my back and his solid frame against my front, I feel weightless. It's like I'm floating on a cloud, like I'm about to float up through the ceiling and into the stars. And Sean? He's a towering beast of masculinity, making me feel tiny and safe all at once.

"Am I fucking you good, baby?"

"So...perfectly good," I moan, unable to put a sentence together. My brain has gone offline, not that I mind. Honestly, I could die and be happy.

Sean's hands are clutching my thighs with each thrust of his hips, his fingers digging into my skin and keeping me grounded. I hope they leave marks, that I'll have some tangible proof that this rush of passionate energy is actually happening. Because right now, with my desire-addled brain, it feels more like a fantasy than reality. I can't believe how impossibly perfect it all feels.

His pace is quick and relentless as he, too, is caught up in what's happening. Our lips are never far apart, oftentimes simply touching without kissing as our heavy breathing mingles. After a time, my body starts to cramp. My legs are screaming to be stretched out, but I ignore them because the pleasure is building, and there's no way I'm gonna stop just to readjust.

Sean shifts my weight in his hands as he starts to reach his physical limitations too. But like me, he seems unwilling to slow down.

We've stopped too many times and have been interrupted more than enough. This time neither one of us is stopping until we reach our peaks, until we come together and find some much-needed release.

Suddenly, my body shifts, and I grip Sean's shoulders as he pulls me from the wall.

He slips out of me, and for one dreadful second, I think this is it, he's going to pull out and leave me panting and begging. To my relief, he doesn't. My ass comes down hard on the top of my desk, and he immediately thrusts back in, using the desk for leverage.

It bumps and scrapes across the floor, sending various items onto the ground. I don't even know or care what falls. A burst of pleasure flares when he circles my clit.

I come first.

Hard.

Loud.

By "hard and loud" I mean I arch my back and let out a scream of pleasure that could wake the dead (luckily, there's nobody but Sean around to witness—or complain about—it).

The way Sean's grinding between my legs and the way he's filling me becomes too much, and when my orgasm peaks, I clutch him to my chest, my hand still gripping his hair as I chant his name into his ear: "Sean...Sean...*Sean*..."

His grunting and moaning coaxes me through the waves of pleasure, and in a soft voice, one I've never heard from him, he says my name, "Yeah, Jess," and that's the last thing I remember as my vision goes blurry.

When I return to myself, he's gently lowering my legs onto the floor. His touch, it's different—so tender, so soft, like he's holding something fragile for the first time.

Slowly, I sit up and try to stand.

The room spins as I lose my balance, and he catches me before I fall. It sends me into a fit of giggles while I attempt to balance on my unsteady legs.

Sean's lips tip up in amusement. The way it lights up his face makes my stomach drop and my heart skip a beat. I've never witnessed him smile like that. Also, I've never seen him look at me with such admiration. His thumb trails down my chin, and it's like a tidal wave crashing over me, sweeping me away and leaving me breathless, exhilarated, and utterly captivated. And now that it's here, I'm whisked away to paradise by its intensity. It's not just his piercing eyes that overwhelm me, it's what they signify: hope, longing, surrender—the beauty of dreaming about what's to come. It's like living a dream I never dared to dream.

"You all right there, Jess?" he asks. "I don't want to have to call an ambulance because you fell over. It'd be really hard to explain."

His unexpected question catches me off guard, and I can't help but laugh. "I don't care. Seriously, the hotel could explode right now, I'd just grab some marshmallows and call it a cozy night in."

Sean kisses my nose, and he adjusts my panties and skirt back into place. "Why don't we call it a day?"

Somewhere in my fuzzy brain, I remember the meal he suggested for us. "We didn't order dinner yet."

"We'll grab something on the way home. We're going to need it as fuel for the rest of the night."

The side-eye he gives me has my knees quaking again.

"You realize that you're in for a very long night?" he grumbles.

"My place or yours?"

He hooks his arm around my waist and pulls me against his chest. "I don't care as long as I can finally get these clothes off you. Let's go."

"K."

21

SEAN

$\mathcal{W}$e wind up at her place.

Jess and I abandon the hotel in a hurry. She leaves her car behind in favor of riding in mine. With my hand on her knee, I speed the entire way as we keep exchanging knowing glances. The redness hasn't left her face and there's a sparkle in her eyes. Both are driving me crazy. I want to make her even more disheveled, panting, and needy. I *have* to feel her tightness around me again as soon as possible.

After a lively visit to a sushi drive-through, where she declares to the drive-through guy, "Hold the avocados, please!" I swiftly order the avocado-free version for both of us. Soon after, I pull into the garage.

By the time we get inside, I'm ready to explode. The sushi gets tossed into the refrigerator as an afterthought as clothes are shed, bodies are grabbed, and we stumble our way into her bedroom.

I need her again. Right this second. I've never wanted anyone as much as I want her. I want her to writhe beneath me, moaning my name as I fuck her all over the apartment. When I finally get her into bed, sprawled out underneath me like I've been imagining, I don't waste any time.

Kissing my way down her body, one hand holds me up while I slip her hardening nipple between my lips. Her back arches beautifully into my touch. Those smooth legs of hers slide around me, and I know in that second that I want them over my shoulders as soon as possible. I leave a trail of wet kisses between her tits, down the swell of her stomach and then finally her wet folds.

Her moans fill the room the second I descend between her legs. She's soft and warm, sweet on my tongue just like before but so much more addictive. After the days of torment, I know this isn't going to be a one-night thing. I don't want it to be.

I'm addicted to the way she touches me.

I'm addicted to the sensation of her kisses on my lips.

I'm addicted to the sound of her calling my name.

Despite her urging voice (and despite my urging cock), I dial down the speed and frenzy.

There's no rush and no chance of being interrupted so I'm able to go slow.

I have to take it slow, I tell myself with determination.

I know her, but now is when I'm able to learn her, figure out what she likes and how she likes it.

So I take my time, drag out her pleasure until she's begging for more.

I kiss her, I lick her, I tease her into oblivion. "See how perfect you are for me?" I rumble.

"Yeah..." she whispers.

"You were made just for me."

Her back arches and her hands twist the bed sheets when she comes.

I drink it all in. The image is burned into my mind, and I know I'm never going to forget it. In the dim lamplight, she's cast in an ethereal glow, appearing more angelic than human. I commit the image to memory as I kiss my way up her thighs, along her stomach, between the valley of her tits, which I stop to pay extra attention to. She runs her hands through my hair, and I hitch her legs around my waist while my tongue lavishes her pert, pink nipples. Only when she tugs my hair do I continue my journey upward to her neck.

"I want to be on top," she breathes.

"Go for it," I encourage her.

There's movement, and I find myself on my back with her straddling my waist. She grins proudly and I tuck my hands behind my head, smirking at her.

"I'm surprised you still have the energy to move so fast," I say. "I must not have done my job right."

"Oh, you did plenty right...my knees are still quaking."

"That's what I like to hear."

"Don't look so smug."

"I'm allowed to be smug."

Jess rolls her eyes, yet she's still smiling. She runs her hands up and down my chest. "Yeah, well, I got you off too, and you don't see me being all smug about it."

I open my mouth to say she's more than welcome to be smug, but then all thoughts drain from my brain as she shifts and grinds herself against my dick. My hands fall to her hips to give myself something to grab onto and ground myself. She does it again, watching my face with rapt attention.

"If I had only known sooner," she says, sounding amused.

It takes me a second to respond, and when I do, my breathing is heavy. "Known...what?"

"That grinding on you is one way to instantly get you to stop talking."

I tighten my grip on her waist and thrust upward so she can feel the full friction of my dick between her legs. "I would deny it, but you're not wrong."

She grins wider and is now rocking against me steadily, rolling her hips as she does. I can't take my eyes off her and how goddamn gorgeous she looks like this: sex-mussed hair, lips swollen from our kisses, her skin flush, gorgeous tits swaying. She lifts up, placing her hand next to my head to steady herself and bringing our faces closer together. While kissing me, she reaches between us, wrapping her hand around my shaft. She begins to work me with quick, firm strokes, forcing a grunt out of me, which is promptly swallowed by her eager mouth.

Everything besides Jess fades into the background.

She's all I know, all I can and want to focus on. Her warmth and citrus scent hang around me, invading every one of my senses. I don't know how long we move this way. She also wants to take her time, to draw this out for as long as we possibly can. When she finally does lift enough to put me between her legs, all I have to do is flex upward before I'm enveloped by her tight heat.

The way her head falls back as she moans, knocks any remaining breath out of my lungs. She takes the lead, rising and falling on my lap with the same steady pace she established earlier.

Her eyes are closed but mine stay open.

I want to keep this image of her in my mind.

I don't know what's going to happen after tonight. I don't know what this is going do to our working relationship or how it's going change our day-to-day. However, I'm also not in the mood to think. All I want to do is be in this moment and stay here for as long as possible. I slide my hands up her torso to give her tits appreciative affection. A lazy smile forms across her face, and she drags her eyes open to look down at me. It's like we can't keep our eyes off each other.

I wrap my arm around her waist, and just as quickly as she had me on my back, I now have her on hers. The motion makes me slip out, and there's a loss in her eyes and a protest on her lips. I'm faster. I thrust my hips forward to get back where I need to be. She pulls me into a kiss and it's soft, gentle, and sweet—a vast contrast to the heated grappling we did earlier.

When I start to move faster, her heavy breathing and the delicious noises spilling from her spur me on. She chants my name again and again, and I don't think I'll ever get tired of that sound.

It unlocks a feral, possessive side of me.

I know it's the only name she will ever utter.

Her body locks around me as she hooks her ankles together behind my back, drawing me in each time I pull out.

I'm starting to reach my own end, and I take her harder, faster, pounding her into the mattress while she keeps moaning my name over and over. I can tell she's getting close, already familiar with the signs, and I slide my hand between us. My thumb swipes around her swollen, sensitive clit, and she clutches me to her chest, pulling me into a kiss when she comes.

I briefly pause, enjoying her squeezing me, rumbling, "I love how you feel when you come on my cock," then resume my movements, working her through it, continuing the same pace to ensure she has the longest orgasm she's ever had, my hips jerking to meet hers again and again and again.

Minutes later, we lie tangled together, her bed sheets wrapped around us in a warm cocoon. I trail my fingers absentmindedly up and down her arm, marveling in the softness of her skin, occasionally tracing her freckles. She shudders and slots her fingers through mine, taking my hand. Lips meet mine, and we quietly kiss for who knows how long.

When we draw apart, she smiles and leans in for another kiss, which I happily grant. When she pulls away, the smile slowly fades, and she gives me a pensive look.

"What you did earlier in the office," she says, "I really appreciate it."

"Everyone needs to be fucked against the wall at least once in their life."

"No! Not that," she protests, laughing. "With that jerk at the front desk."

"It's no big deal."

"But it is. To me, it is."

"We're working together with this, remember? We need to have each other's backs. I wasn't about to let that asshole speak to you like that and just walk away unscathed."

"But you didn't have to say anything, and you definitely didn't have to make him apologize."

"You're right. I shouldn't have had to do that. He should have been man enough to do it himself. At least now he shouldn't give you any more trouble."

"It bugs me dealing with guests like him, particularly older rich men. Not only because of the rudeness and all that, which is annoying on its own. But with the misogyny on top of it. It just makes the whole situation ten times worse."

"He'll go the extra mile now, tipping the staff generously, as a way to make amends for the embarrassment he caused. You'll see."

"Tipping his way out of trouble, classic move."

"I know, right?"

I can still picture the way he turned his back on her, and it seriously infuriated me. It took all my willpower not to grab the man by the collar and literally shake some sense into him. I've worked with plenty of women over the years, some in very high positions within their companies. I never got the whole male supremacy bullshit that other guys in my position spew. I've met plenty of tough women who are more than capable of holding their own. I've known Jess long enough now to know that she's one of these women and seeing her disrespected like that was unacceptable. There was no way I could let it go.

"I can't even imagine having to deal with that bullshit on top of everything else you're doing," I say. "You have a hell of a lot more patience than I do, baby. That dude had some serious nerve, talking to you like that, and you still smiled at him and treated him with a hell of a lot more respect than he was giving you."

"You wanna know a secret?" she asks.

"Sure."

"I learned a long time ago from my mom that people like that, you know, folks who are rude and pissy about getting their way, cannot handle being met with someone who keeps smiling and gives zero concerns about their attitude. They're fishing for a reaction, hoping to escalate things so they can exploit the situation, and when you don't give them one, they have no idea how to handle it, and it gets under their skin."

The idea that her cheerfulness is being used as a weapon breaks me, and I start laughing. Amazing. Simply amazing. I know exactly the type of people she's talking about, and I can see how having this bright, bubbly, smiling person in front of you can be disarming. Hell, didn't it work on me right from the get-go?

I always knew Jess was bright, but I never fully, fully grasped just how clever she can be.

"That's actually a little diabolical," I tell her.

"Coming from you," she beams, "I'll take that as a compliment."

"Good because it was meant as one."

Her eyes dance, and I pull her in close. Her lips find mine, and we settle into a chill make-out session, my arms tight around her.

It doesn't even occur to me that I should go home or not spend the night. She seems to be settling in for sleep, and I don't feel like she's expecting me to leave, so why not stay? What harm could it do? I'm too warm and comfortable. Besides, if I leave, I can't nip at her skin and make her moan.

Eventually, our kisses slow to gentle pecks, then fade away altogether as we nestle into each other for sleep. It's not too long before her breathing evens out and she's out cold. I lie there for a time, feeling her body cuddled up against mine, watching her with affection blooming in my chest. The feelings are a little daunting, and yet, unsurprising. I'm too tired and relaxed to decipher them at this moment.

Instead, I adjust the blankets around us, slip my arm back around her waist, and let her rest against my chest. She nestles closer into me, and I drift off to sleep.

22

SEAN

*T*he next morning I'm woken by a strange sound. First, I think it's Jess's phone, and I gently shake her awake. "Jess, your alarm."

She giggles, and I feel her warmth roll away from me. "It's not my alarm, it's Pippin."

Frowning, I crack my eye open to look at her in confusion. "Pippin?"

"My bird."

Right. The little yellow fella she had on her shoulder when she told me off.

Jess leaves the bed, and I glance over at the clock on her nightstand to see what time it really is. A quarter to six a.m. It's early, even earlier than I normally get up to do my exercises. I was hoping to sleep in a little, considering the workout I got last night was more than enough to make up for it. Now that I'm a little bit more coherent, I can tell what I thought was an alarm definitely is a bird singing or screeching. I don't know. I'm not familiar enough with birds to tell the difference.

Whatever Jess does stops the noise, and I relax against the pillows while I wait for her to return. She does, carrying one of the food containers from last night.

"Sushi for breakfast?" I ask, raising my brow.

Her mouth is filled with one of the rolls, and she shrugs as she climbs back into bed. "Hey, why not? I'm *starving*. We didn't actually eat last night."

"I did."

She playfully nudges me with her elbow. "Quit it, you goofball."

I reach over and snag one of the avocado rolls (a clear fuck-up from the drive-through). "Goofball? Well, that's a first."

She chuckles. "Ha! Breaking new ground, aren't we?"

We keep eating while we watch the sun rise through her bedroom windows. The sky goes from dark blue to light, broken by the occasional fluffy cloud. Once all the rolls have found their way into our stomachs, Jess cozies up on my chest. Her gaze lingers on my right arm, where a geometric tattoo wraps around my bicep, its lines subtly resembling tulip leaves.

"What's the tattoo for?" she asks, her voice curious.

"It's for my mother," I reply softly, leaving it at that.

Her eyes flicker with understanding.

"I see," Jess says quietly, letting the matter drop. "Too bad we have to go to work today," she remarks and runs her fingers across my skin. "I'm too comfortable. I don't wanna go *anywhere*."

"Indeed, it would be rather pleasant to indulge in a whole day of lovemaking and sushi consumption."

"It would definitely be an amazing day off. Too bad we have a group in, otherwise I definitely would suggest we do that."

"I mean, we're the bosses. We could do it."

The idea of staying here, further exploring Jess's body while the rest of the world gets shut out is tempting. Which is saying something, considering I'm not the type of man to miss work at the drop of a hat. I can count on one hand the number of times I wasn't in the office last year.

Jess looks up at me with those wide blue eyes. "You continue to surprise me."

"What do you mean? I've unleashed my wild side more times than I can count. You've witnessed it, if memory serves."

She laughs out loud. "True, but that's not what I'm talking about." She pauses for a moment, almost as if she's not sure if she should say what's on her mind, which is funny, considering she's never been shy about sharing her feelings before. "I'll be honest, when I woke up this morning, I half-expected you not to be here."

Huh.

Now I know why she hesitated. I don't know how I feel about that.

Then again, I really can't fault her, considering the first time we were together I ended the show early. I assumed she'd moved past it, but clearly it still bothers her to some degree.

"You have my assurance that I'm not going to leave you high and dry like I did the first time," I assure her. With a smirk, I add, "Plus, you know where I live *and* work, and disappearing on you would be hard to pull off."

My tone is light and teasing, meant to put her at ease but also reassure her that I'm not considering this a one-time deal. After all that we've tackled together, it's clear that's not going to happen. I don't want it to happen. Even now, I want to run my hands up and down that soft, freckled skin and kiss her neck until she's squirming underneath me, pleading for my cock.

She laughs, her arm sliding around my waist and her leg tangling with mine. "You're right, I know how to find you. If you had tried that stunt this morning, I definitely would have given you a piece of my mind." She pokes me in the chest, hard, and yep, my body reacts to her touch.

I playfully bite her poke-finger, eliciting a surprised squeak from her.

"I'd rather have a piece of something else." I reach down and give her ass a small slap.

She twitches in response and lets out a surprise squeak. "Play your cards right...and I may just let you."

My dick's twitches intensify. I pull her onto me, burying my hand in her hair and pulling her into a kiss. Jess responds, stretching along me like a feline. I lay us down, losing myself in her touch and eager mouth.

That slow steady pace we started last night hasn't left. This time, it's Jess who starts to kiss her way down, starts to explore with her hands and mouth.

I'm more than happy to let her.

My breathing picks up as her tongue traces the hard lines of my chest. I move the tangle of brown hair away from her face so I can watch her expression as she descends. She looks up at me through her lashes, her warm eyes filled with that mischief and fire I'm quickly learning to appreciate.

She pushes the blankets aside as she settles below my waist. That mouth and that tongue I've been kissing are now wrapped around my dick. I groan, my head falling back as my hips jerk.

Staying the night is definitely proving beneficial.

Jess knows what she's doing. She has me fully hard within seconds, and I watch her with rapt attention, committing every line of her face and every minute expression to memory. The visuals are fucking spectacular. The attention and care I've seen her display on a daily basis is now focused on me, and *fuck* if she's not doing a good job of it.

Why haven't we done this sooner?

We're definitely going to do this on a regular basis.

My fingers caress her cheeks as she gets me to the edge, right on the brink, but before I can finish, she pulls off with a gasp and squeezes me just around the base. I grunt in frustration and shoot her a glare.

"You're a monster," I grumble.

Jess laughs and slides up my body again. "Only on Tuesdays…"

Oh, shit.

It's not even Tuesday. What day is it?

I don't give a fuck.

"…and you love it," she adds with a smirk.

Just like last night, she straddles my lap and sinks onto me.

Oh, *fuck*. Even better.

"I do love it."

I reach up and grab her ass, squeezing roughly as I yank her back down so that she takes me all at once. We rock together, falling into a steady rhythm of give and take. Her hands are splayed on my chest as she uses them for momentum. I take in all of her, still focusing on her expression. Watching her lose herself in pleasure isn't getting old, and I don't think it ever will.

There's a freedom there that I don't see in our day-to-day. It's intimate. It's different. It's profound. This is something deep and personal that I consider myself fortunate to witness.

I don't roll her over this time.

I can't bring myself to.

Letting her take the lead and set the pace, I watch from beneath, running my hands up and down her thighs while my hips meet her grinding. We move in sync, rocking together almost as if we're one person. Our bodies become slick with sweat, which helps our movements, and as she starts to grind harder, I know her orgasm is coming. I'm familiar with the signs by now and am more than happy to give her a hand. Her voice breaks as my thumb rubs firm circles between her legs over her drenched and swollen clit, and her body clenches deliciously.

When she comes, her nails dig into my chest and leave half-moon indents.

Now it's my turn.

I pound into her, eyes taking in her lazy smile and the afterglow that washes over her. Sliding my hand up her back, I cup her neck and pull her all the way down so I can feel her close while I finish. She moans, and it gives me that final push I need.

Spent, she lies flat across my chest, her face buried in my neck.

"Today is going to be a good day." I rub soothing circles on her back.

Humming in satisfaction, Jess giggles. "It's definitely off to a great start."

We fall silent for a time, neither wanting to say anything or move. At least, I don't. I'm aware that the real world is calling and we're going to have to answer at some point. Once that happens, work responsibilities will take precedence.

Jess is the first to speak after craning her neck to check the time. "Ugh, we need to get up."

I grab my phone and glance at the time. "We can afford to stay for a few more minutes."

Jess rests her chin on my chest to look at me. "True. But if we get up now, we can take a shower together."

I raise my eyebrow. "You make a compelling argument. And I'm tempted to accept. But if we do, I know for a fact we're going to be late."

"It'll be a quick shower."

"Jess, if I get you naked, wet, and soapy, I can guarantee the shower won't be quick. Rain check?"

"Rain check."

As she makes a move to get up, I stop her, cupping her cheek. Her eyebrows draw together as she meets my gaze, looking at me questioningly.

"You know what," I tell her, "fuck it."

She squeals in delight. I toss the phone somewhere and chase her to the bathroom.

23

JESS

*T*hree weeks later (One week left)

I t certainly is an interesting next couple of days.

Once Sean and I hook up, that intense tension between us doesn't go anywhere. I was *all* wrong in thinking it would. In fact, things only amp up. Every time we're in the same room it's like there's an invisible tether between us. We're drawn together no matter how hard we try to put distance between us. And by distance, I mean physical distance. Not because we don't want to be in each other's company, but because we wouldn't get anything done otherwise.

When we're alone, all it takes is one look before we're going at it. It's been a long time since I've had sex on a regular basis and my body definitely is thanking me for it.

Our sex is hot.

Our sex is quick.

Our sex is mesmerizingly and luxuriously long.

No room or surface is safe from us.

That's not to say that during business hours, Sean and I don't disagree once in a while. But we're able to figure things out. No matter how slow or quick we come to a solution, it typically leads to sex, which is honestly a win-win for everyone.

Sex aside, our working relationship makes me feel better about Blackwood buying Westerlyn.

I trust Sean, and even though I know he wants to buy me out, the idea doesn't fill me with indignation anymore. I even entertain it from time to time.

S ean and I see each other after work most nights after he returns from Blackwood Inc., unless either of us gets stuck late, like today. Today, he got caught up at Blackwood. Usually, we're not texting each other unless it's work related. Not only that, but we also have this unspoken understanding that nothing's ever strained between us. That's one of the things I cherish about us.

My phone buzzes just when I turn off the bedside lamp, eyes heavy with sleep.

SEAN:

Stuck at work. You still awake?

ME:

Just climbed into bed.

How was your day?

thumbs-up emoji

Glad to hear it. Night, Jess. Sleep well.

Did he just reach out just to see how I'm doing? Could it be that he's been missing me? The smile on my face doesn't fade even when I fall asleep.

In the morning, it takes me a little longer to get out of the warm cocoon of my blankets and into the shower. I'm just finishing getting ready when I hear Sean's front door open and close.

Knock. Knock.

I'm surprised to find Sean standing there with his signature well-fitted suit. Despite the fact he worked an extra-long day yesterday—I only heard him arrive home after eleven p.m. before I dozed off again—he appears well rested. He hadn't texted me or anything saying he was going to pop over in the morning before work.

I want to ask, *Hey, you missed me that much?* but instead, I ask, "Hey, everything okay?" and point at the clock. It reads 7:32 a.m.

He doesn't usually stop by in the mornings, and it's hard to tell by his expression how he's feeling. "Yeah, everything's fine," he assures me. "I figured since I'm up early, and on property today, I'd save you some gas and drive you in."

His response takes me by surprise. Aside from the one time I left my car at the hotel, we drive separately because we typically don't leave at the same time. It's also more discreet that way.

"Oh, okay," I say. "Are you sure?"

Sean slips his hands into his pockets and shrugs. "Sure, why not?"

"I just assumed it wasn't appropriate or so people would get the wrong idea."

"I don't care about that. It just makes more sense to take one car since I'm going to be at the hotel all day."

"Driving together sounds great. Goodbye, Pippin!" I call into my apartment. "Be a good birdie while I'm gone." Pippin twitters in response, fluffing his feathers and giving a little hop.

I lock the door behind me, and we walk toward the elevator.

I understand there are practical reasons for carpooling, like convenience and being eco-friendly, but perhaps he genuinely missed me. "You just want us to drive together for the hell of it?" I ask.

"Is that such a strange concept?"

"For you? Yes."

"All right, well, that's vaguely insulting," he grumbles. "There are no ulterior motives."

As we step onto the elevator, and he presses the button next to me, he leans in and growls into my ear, "Well, maybe one."

"What?"

He slips his arm around my waist and pulls me close. "I enjoy the distraction you provide."

"I distract you?"

The next thing I know, his mouth is on mine, and I'm pressed against his chest. I melt into his kiss, sliding my arms around his strong shoulders. When he draws away, he fixes me with a mind-numbing look. "You have no idea," he grumbles darkly, "how much you distract me."

Instant desire.

God, I can't handle it when his voice is *this* low and he's leaning in *this* close.

I swear this man is going to kill me before we even get to work. "Oh, yeah? Good distraction or...bad distraction?" I manage to ask, sounding way too breathy.

"Bad," he rumbles and winks at me. "So very bad."

Sean Blackwood has the cutest wink.

It's a rare sight, but when it happens, his long lashes do this flutter that somehow highlights the depth of his dark, forest-green eye color. There's an undeniable charm in the way his eye crinkles slightly. It's one of those things that always catches me by surprise and never fails to make my heart skip a beat.

When I keep staring, he winks again (can he read my thoughts?), even cuter this time.

Without a second thought, I press the "Emergency Stop" button.

I mean, any rational person would.

The elevator jerks to a halt, making Sean raise an eyebrow, and a tiny grin tugs at his lips. I take full advantage and throw my arms around his neck. His mouth crashes onto mine as he shoves me against the wall. I hook a leg around the back of his so that every part of us is touching.

"You want us to be late, huh?" he mumbles against my lips, hands already shoving my skirt up. His cock presses into my pelvis, hard, long, thick.

"Not if we're quick about it."

"Excellent thinking."

Giggling, I reach down and unbuckle his belt as his hand slides into the back of my panties. He squeezes my ass in appreciation, and it makes me fumble with his dumb zipper, feeling his steel-hard cock bulge against it. I don't know what's come over me. I'm all for spontaneity, yet this is more than that. Something about Sean makes me want to act absolutely feral (he wasn't off with the monster thing, and it's not limited to Tuesdays) when we're alone together.

He doesn't even pull my panties down, only shoves them to the side before thrusting into me with a quick jerk of his hips. I gasp, and my head falls against the wall, my body already shaking in anticipation. Heavens. No one ever made me as full as Sean makes me. I barely get a chance to adjust before he's grinding into me.

All I can do is cling to him and enjoy the ride.

"Fuck, Jess," Sean groans into my mouth. "Do you know how much you drive me crazy?"

I want to say, "Oh, believe me, it's my special talent." All I manage to utter is "Huh?" My brain is off-line. Sleeping. Undergoing some major update.

"You look perfect like this," he rumbles, thrusting, "with my cock inside of you. Your cunt is mine and only mine."

God, I could hear him talk this way for hours.

At least this quickie will hold us over a minute.

Or two. Ha!

When I come, it's because of how he's grinding into me. I moan his name and crush my face against his neck as I ride out my orgasm. He keeps thrusting, his fingers digging into the tender flesh of my thighs from holding me so tight. He comes a few seconds later with a deep groan that is the hottest sound I've ever heard in my life. "Arghh."

Unfortunately, there's no basking in the afterglow.

We're acutely aware that we're holding up the elevator, and it's only a matter of time before someone calls for it, and creepy superintendent Mr. Fletcher shows up. He's the last person I want to see on a fiery morning like this.

With matching grins, we pull ourselves together and Sean presses the button to resume our trip to the parking garage.

The elevator grinds to a halt with a cheerful ding.

As the gap between the elevator doors widens, there he stands. He's furiously whacking the elevator button: the superintendent, Mr. Creeper himself, with a protruding belly and a few wisps of hair attempting to cover his bald head. It's as if he has an uncanny sixth sense for inconvenient moments.

At first, he looks annoyed, as if the elevator had taken a detour to Mount Vesuvius, the infamous volcano in Italy, known for its historic eruption that buried the ancient city of Pompeii under layers of ash and lava. And well, it basically had. Judging by the scorching heat in here, we might as well be roasting marshmallows. However, as soon as the doors open wide enough for him to spot Sean, his demeanor changes in an instant.

"Good morning, sir," he oozes, laying on the charm. (That kiss-up!)

"How are you doing, Mr. Blackwood? It's a pleasure to see you. Is every-thing in order? Did you notice the elevator took longer this morning?"

"Yes, *of course* I noticed." Sean gives him his signature curt dark nod, a clear signal that he's not in the mood for pleasantries.

"Oh, I see. How unfortunate, Mr. Blackwood. I'm very sorry about that. Just a minor delay, I suppose."

"Make sure it doesn't happen again."

A smile settles on my lips, and I quickly wipe it away.

"Of course, sir." Mr. Fletcher steps aside for him, and when his eyes fall on me, he gives me one of his intrusive stares with his unblinking eyes. Ugh.

Before he can utter a word, Sean steps forward and leads me out, blocking Mr. Fletcher's view of me. He's not allowed to even look in my direction. That legendary grumpy glare on Sean's face says it all: *Hands off, buddy. Watch your eyes—if you wanna keep 'em.*

He might as well have said it out loud, because Mr. Fletcher's expression shifts abruptly, his smile vanishing into a nervous one.

With a fawning tone, he quickly says, "Thank you, Mr. Blackwood. If there's anything you ever need, don't hesitate to ask. We aim to ensure your stay is nothing short of perfection. Have an excellent day ahead."

"Have a good day, Mr. Fletcher," Sean says as we head out the door.

It's official. I've got the best bodyguard in town.

24

JESS

*W*e drive into work together, stopping briefly at a coffee shop before continuing on our way. Over fresh coffee and bagels, and the satisfaction of a quick, hot elevator encounter (turned into sheer awesomeness), morning traffic is a breeze. The time passes with idle chit-chat and discussions about work, including the final transition points we need to hit.

I'm aware that our partnership as co-owners does have an expiration date: In one week exactly, they're going to expect me to sell and join their organization, like Sean and I discussed early on.

By now, I have definitely warmed up to the idea, and I'm starting to feel excited at this new chapter in my life. In my continued position as a director, and with the backing of Blackwood Inc., I'm going to be able to take Westerlyn farther than I thought possible, and in a much shorter period of time.

Of course, I don't know what that means in terms of me and Sean.

Already things are murky, given the circumstances and our habit of hanging around volcanoes each morning and every night, but I'm confident we can figure things out.

. . .

In the afternoon, Pauline pokes her head in.

"So what's the deal with you two?"

I lean back in my seat, silently gesturing for her to close the door and sit. "We may not have a label, but well... I care about him."

"Just care about him?" She takes a seat and crosses her legs. "Your face lights up when you two talk, and I've never seen you more comfortable with someone as you are with him. Are you sure there isn't a little love peeking through?"

Love? That's a big word and one I don't throw around lightly.

After all, I thought I loved Richard and look where that got me. I haven't known Sean for long, and I can't say what I feel for him is *love*. At least I won't say it, not now, not when we're in this odd in-between—not quite only colleagues and almost like a real couple.

"Like I said," I tell her, "I definitely care about him. I wouldn't go as far as to say love."

"Uh-huh."

"Okay, maybe a bit of affection."

"Uh-huh."

"Okay, definitely deep infatuation...with the potential for...love."

"Ah, the 'L' word! *Finally*."

I mean, what isn't there to love about Sean? He's smart, successful, ambitious, and honest. Not to mention generous. All the traits any woman in my position would kill to have in a partner. He's tough, sure, but there's this underlying sweetness, a gentleness that I believe I'm one of the few who have been lucky enough to experience. That's the part of him I'm most attracted to. The part that draws me in and keeps me coming back, because the longer we spend time together, the more he reveals that side of himself to me.

I may not be able to say that I fully, deeply, madly love him, but...

sigh...okay, who am I kidding? It's obvious that I've tripped and fallen headfirst into the deepest love pit there is.

Thing is, ever since the charity event, I've tried to convince myself that I haven't, but I have.

"I know," I say, "it's *way, way* too early to be in love, I know! I can tell he likes me, sure, and he has said really sweet things to me, but whether he loves *me*—no, that's *not* a thought I'm entertaining right now."

"Do you want my opinion?"

"Of course I want your opinion. You found your soul mate years ago. If anyone knows anything about complicated relationships, it's you."

"Well, as the wise, old, married broad, he *has* to be in love with you."

I seriously didn't expect her to say that. "Why?"

"I don't think he'd put his job and reputation on the line just for sex."

"How do you know we have sex?"

"*Girl.* Don't you?"

I shrug. "We do."

She shrugs. "Duh-uh."

"And you think he put his job on the line for me?"

Pauline gives me a pointed look. "From what you told me, he was told to buy your properties and decided to compromise and work *with* instead of against you. Now that you two are sleeping together, if he were using it as leverage to manipulate your decisions, you'd have caught on by now. You really don't see how that clearly means he genuinely cares about you?"

Now that she puts the thought out there, it's all I can think about.

It didn't occur to me that by sleeping with me Sean was putting himself at risk.

After all, I was putting myself at risk doing the same.

I'm sure his dad and the board wouldn't be too pleased to learn he's been sleeping with a client-slash-coworker-slash-employee. Yet, he did it and continues to do so on a regular basis.

"Well," I admit, "this is way more serious than I originally thought."

"Ah, the joys of love. Just wait—sooner or later, the truth pops out." She rises from her seat, a knowing expression on her face. "Trust me, he's head over heels for you. It's glaringly obvious."

Deep down, part of me hopes he is.

If we hadn't been sleeping together in the dazzling manner we are, I would be able to convince myself all our dinner dates were casual meals between neighbors or friends.

But we're *way* past casual.

It's in all the things he *does*.

It's in the sense of security and warmth I feel that I haven't known in a long time.

It's in the subtle (but real powerful) connection that has grown between us.

I mean, from the fake engagement rescue to entrusting him with decisions for the team, and ultimately leaning on him to support me in business matters, Sean has proven himself to be a reliable partner, and for that, I'm beyond grateful.

When Pauline leaves, I have to bring my focus back to work. We're busier than ever. There are several conventions throughout the city, and nearly every hotel in the surrounding area is booked solid. Including ours. But everything is running smoothly, and it requires very little extra work on the managerial side of things.

In fact, when it nears 6:30 p.m. and all of our major tasks are accomplished for the day, Sean and I don't have to stay any later. It's a rare opportunity that we're both seizing, especially with dinner plans already in place. We have been going to dinner on the regular. This time, we find ourselves at a beautiful new Japanese restaurant I picked, having a laid-back evening.

Sometimes, I feel that his mother's memory burdens him. The relationship with his father seems like another weight on his shoulders. Even though he doesn't make it obvious, I get a sense that he relaxes when he's at WH (and not just because of me). Tonight, I gather my strength to ask him about his late mom. He opens up, sharing details about the sad circumstances—why she passed so soon, how much she worked until the end, how much he wished she had spent time planting yellow tulips (her favorite) instead of answering damn phones as his dad's executive assistant, and how much he regrets his inability to persuade his father to take drastic steps to stop her from overworking.

"As if a thirteen-year-old has the power!" I blurt out, feeling agitated.

"I know," he says darkly, but I can tell that this time, even though Sean is one of the best listeners, my words barely register with him. I meet his black gaze. It feels like his soul is gone.

When I reassure him, pointing out that he simply couldn't have borne such responsibility at that age, and that every single person on this planet would agree, he says nothing and hugs me close. In that moment, everything in me melts.

Over the rest of the delicious meal, we talk about God and the world. Culinary adventures, pets, futuristic technology, space exploration. Our discussions fade to places we've never traveled to but dream of seeing. For me, it's Tokyo; for him, it's Prague.

When the waitress serves us my favorite dessert—Dorayaki, fluffy pancakes filled with sweet red bean paste—Sean mentions he'll be on a few (boringly local) business trips tomorrow and over the next week, and I can already feel a tinge of longing. Teasingly, I remind him not to let my bed get too cold, and he responds with his signature "cutest lashes in the whole wide world" wink.

We're a couple. That's what we are.

Not officially, no, but that's what it feels like. I can feel it in my heart. It can't get any more real than this.

"I propose that we scarf down dessert and make a swift exit," I suggest playfully (but dead serious). Truth is, I'm insatiable for Sean

Blackwood, it seems, seriously yearning for all the one-on-one time with him I can get.

I don't want this to end.

Without even blinking, Sean faces the waitress. "Can we have that to go?"

25

SEAN

We talked for hours. But the moment we're in the elevator, I hoist her up, pull her thong down and put it in its usual spot, and sink into her.

The moment I cross the threshold to her place with her around my hips, I find myself tearing off her dress and losing myself in that soft body of hers.

"Yeah, there we go," I growl.

The moment I'm ready to come, she has other plans, steering "our conversation" to a different topic.

She pushes me to sit on the edge of her bed before sliding onto her knees.

Being with a woman who knows what she wants and isn't afraid to go for it? That's always a win. But throw in smartness, loyalty, and the occasional surprise—instant marriage material.

I lift my hips, and she tugs my pants down, not even bothering to take them all the way off before she runs her tongue up my shaft.

I'm hard as a rock. Achingly stiff. The goddamn visual of her lips stretched around me doesn't ease the situation. I lose myself in the wet heat, my fingers buried in her hair as she has me panting and praising within seconds. "That's it, baby, yeah, that feels fucking amazing." Every time I try to take control or pull her off to get my mouth on her, she resists, unwilling to relinquish control.

And after a time, I don't care enough to keep trying.

She takes me right to the edge, and only stops right then, ignoring my warning.

Enough is enough.

I yank her onto my lap, position her where I need her the most, and waste no time sliding her down onto me. Her pussy is tight. Dripping. Perfect for me.

With a heavy moan and a hand on my chest, she pushes me onto my back and rides me with reckless abandon, her tits a sight that leaves me breathless. She throws her head back and purrs like a newborn kitten when my hands slide up and over her stomach to those gorgeous nipples. My eyes never leave her tits as she continues to move on top of me. She squirms in delight when I roll her nipples between my fingers and lightly pinch them.

I spin her around, grab her wrists and place her arms above her head, locking her in. With my thigh, I spread her legs wide apart and angle my cock at her entrance.

I thrust into her, my whole length.

We lose ourselves in each other for the next several hours, nothing on our minds but each other and releasing the need within us. By the time Jess has her fourth orgasm, we're ready to call it a night.

Still inside of her, I pull her on top of me, her tits plastered against my chest. "My cock stays inside of you. If you wake up early, you can ride me awake. That clear?"

"I was just about to suggest that," she says.

She's destroying me.

Fuck. Me.

Jess *is* perfect for me.

My attraction to her grows stronger by the day.

I'm certain we both pass out the second our heads hit the pillows.

Two hours later, I stir awake, my dick hardening. Jess is still in my arms, cuddled on top of me. Her eyes are closed, and she's slowly circling her hips and squeezing my waking cock. My hands help, grabbing her ass, moving it in circles.

"Yeah, baby. Take that dick like a naughty girl," I rumble.

We lazy-fuck until we come, then pass out again.

Unfortunately, we can't continue our conversation the next morning. Nor enjoy our Dorayaki. My cell pings with a text while Jess is curled across my chest. It's from my father, which never bodes well. I have to be at Blackwood HQ for another meeting. I'm not particularly jazzed about it, mostly because I'm not sure what it's about.

Reluctantly, I extract myself from Jess's warm embrace. She wakes, but I urge her to go back to sleep, which she immediately does. Before I leave, I place her thong on her nightstand, lean down to brush a soft kiss on her forehead. This naked girl will be the death of me. Not wanting to wake her (or my twitching cock), I cover her with a blanket.

Back in my apartment, I do my quick morning routine and prep my compact travel bag before getting ready to head out.

I'm just hopping onto my motorcycle when I get a text.

JESS:

Hey, where'd you go? Your flight isn't until later.

ME:

Impromptu meeting at the HQ.

Good luck out there. Call me if you need anything.

Likewise.

Here's a snack for the journey. ;-)

She sends me a pic of her in the bathroom, smiling. My dick jerks. She's in front of the mirror, holding her thong. I can see the top of her tits. The photo cuts right off where her nipples begin.

I find myself smirking when I pull out of my parking space. Little tease. It's amazing what frequent sex can do to your morale. On top of that, our date last night was fun. It brought a depth of connection that I haven't had in a long time. Being able to talk shop with someone who knows what they're talking about and discussing fresh perspectives brings a unique satisfaction, but there's more to life than work. The way our conversation flowed between professional and personal was effortless.

A lot of things with Jess are effortless.

This time when I get to Blackwood Inc., I don't even bother going to my office first. I immediately head for the conference room, which Jasmine is in the process of prepping. When she sees me, she gives me a bright smile.

"Good morning, Mr. Blackwood. Can I get you a coffee or anything else?"

"Yes, please, thanks." She prepares me a cup of coffee, finishes up her work, and pats me on the arm as she leaves. When my father arrives, he takes the seat at the opposite end of the table.

"You're early," he says by way of greeting.

"I'm only here for the meeting. I have a plane to catch."

"You've been spending a lot of time at Westerlyn. I haven't seen much of you lately."

"So? You know how much time goes into transitions."

"Is that the only reason?"

His tone and hard expression are difficult to read. Luckily, I have years of experience recognizing when my father is trying to verbally goad me.

"Look, we don't have much time before the rest of the board arrives," I tell him, "so, just tell me what you're trying to say, and we can move on."

"Always so quick to be defensive, son. Fine, we'll skip right to it. Are you sleeping with the co-owner of Westerlyn Hotels?"

What the hell?

That's not what I thought he was going to ask or say, but I don't let it show that he's caught me off guard. Where would he have heard this? I know Connor definitely wouldn't have told him. The question is out of the blue because he's never asked me about my partners in the past. Why is he asking now?

"Care to explain this?" he says, dropping a shiny art magazine on my desk.

I glance at the opened page, and there it is—several photos from the charity event. Jess and I, looking like more than just colleagues, especially in that photo where she embraces me after the winning bid for the art piece. The press certainly knows how to twist a moment. Dammit.

"Just a friendly gathering," I say, trying to keep it casual.

His eyes narrow. "Friendly, you say? The press seems to think otherwise. There are rumors of a secret engagement floating around. Are you engaged, son?"

I let out a weary sigh, fixing my gaze on his. "What I do in my spare time is none of your business."

"So you are engaged?"

"I am not."

He studies me for a moment, and I can tell he's not entirely convinced. "Seems like your PA couldn't hide all the papers and magazines from me. Keep your personal and professional lives separate, Sean. This could jeopardize the reputation of the company."

I temper my anger and force myself to remain calm and collected. "Tell me this is not what this meeting is about. Is this some ridiculous chess move where you're trying to make me appear compromised? Any personal relationship I may or may not have with Jess Summers has no bearing on my job and has nothing to do with my proposal to bring her on as an employee. I suggested we bring her on because she's smart, capable, and willing to do what it takes to ensure that Westerlyn and its staff are running smoothly."

He waves his hand casually, as if my words hold no significance. "She's willing to do what it takes? According to this article, you dropped three million dollars on a damn drawing, son. Please, for the love of sanity, tell me you haven't let her wrap you around her fingers."

For fuck's sake.

So much for keeping things under wraps.

I take a deep breath, preparing to address the concern that's etched on his face. "She has proven multiple times already that she's willing to compromise and work *with* us—and that's a hell of a lot more than we've had in the past."

Before my father can respond, board members start to filter into the room.

My father simply looks at me, his expression unreadable.

Daniela Sanborne is the first to sit, and I can tell by the way she looks between me and my father that she senses the tension. I'm on high alert.

When my father clears his throat, they direct their gazes to him.

"I appreciate you all taking the time together," he begins. "I'm aware this is last minute, but I feel there's something important that we need to discuss. As you all are aware, it has been three weeks since we acquired half of Westerlyn Hotels, but there's still one major hurdle that has not been conquered."

Before my father can continue, Daniela speaks up, addressing him, "Wait, are you telling me that you gathered us all here—once again—to discuss the sale of a property that's already been bought by us?"

I turn to look at her, schooling my expression so she doesn't notice the surprise. As far back as I can remember, she's always backed my father's decisions, which makes her question bold and surprising.

"*Half*-bought," he corrects her. "And yes, that is still what we're discussing. The ramp-up phase shouldn't take longer than fourteen days. It has been long enough, and we need to act. Obviously, Miss Summers is not willing to sell, that means we have no choice but to take drastic action."

"She has one more week to decide," I say firmly.

"Nonsense. If she wanted to sell to us, she would have. Rumor has it that Rutherford is interested in her shares. Word on the street is she's considering selling to him."

Well, it was inevitable. Engagement rumors weren't the only whispers that made their way to my father. "That's complete BS."

"Son, remove your blinders. You don't know what's happening out here. Obviously, she's playing you to gain insider info. We need to act, and *fast*."

"And what exactly is that action?" I ask. "What exactly do you think we should do if she decides not to sell to us?"

My father gives a half-hearted shrug. "Oh, there's plenty. We can talk to our lawyers and consider legal action. After all, she was the one who insisted you write up that ridiculous contract agreeing to certain terms. Our lawyers are some of the best in the city, I doubt she has the capital to match. I'm certain Drexler has a solution."

Drexler, as in Samuel Drexler, my father's favorite legal Pitbull of Stanford & Partners. A ruthless bastard, never lost a damn case.

I shake my head. "Except for the fact that she has been upholding her end of the deal, and she's been more than cooperative," I shoot back.

"Besides, she has a right to choose whether or not she wants to sell, and if she doesn't want to sell then that's that."

Daniela clears her throat, and our heads turn toward her. "I had the pleasure of meeting Ms. Jessica Summers at this year's charity event," she says, "and the opportunity was open to all of you had you attended…" Her gaze sweeps over all the members. "I believe she'd bring great value to our team."

Huh.

The unexpected commendation from Daniela is a welcome change of pace in the boardroom.

I glance at my father.

His brow is furrowed, and his lips are pursed tight when he stares at Daniela. "Blackwood has a reputation to maintain. If we give leeway to one person, others will expect the same."

"The public has a pretty strong sense of how we do business," Daniela argues. "That's not going to change overnight. If anything, this will show that we're flexible and willing to be team players. That's never a bad thing."

"If I may," one of the other board members speaks up. His name is Osgood Reginald, he's in his seventies, and though I don't know much about him, I do know that he tends to take my father's side no matter the situation. Which is probably why he's been around for so long. "A stubborn client has never deterred us before. We've always been able to get them to see our way…or at least *replace* them with somebody who does."

"Exactly, Osgood," my father says. "Sean, the sale needs to be done no matter what." He shrugs. "Promptly. If you don't, then we will need to evaluate your work and determine whether or not you have a future at this company."

If you *don't*. Not if you *can't*.

I want to laugh because it's so ridiculous.

I want to tell him what I really fucking think of this sorry excuse for a father. He must really be pissed at me if he's willing to threaten my job in front of the entire board. His only son. The one he was insistent on following in his footsteps. The one who he trained since childhood to join his business. The one he instilled with profound love for this place.

Is he really willing to forget all that and throw it away to maintain the control he so desperately wants and needs? I've never been a family man, but damn, I thought being blood would count for something.

The only thing that stops me from walking out of the room without a second thought is the fact that he could have presented the art magazine to the board, proving his point—especially following Daniela's challenge regarding his and the other board member's non-attendance. It seems there still is a shred of decency left in him, like my mother claimed there was.

"I've heard enough." Calmly, I sweep my gaze across the table. "I will not have my skills and worth ethic brought into question. You all know me. Everybody in this room knows what I can do, what I'm capable of. We have Westerlyn, we have them where we want them, and we have the means—and the partner—to take them to the next level. It shouldn't matter how much of the hotel we own because we're already calling the shots."

I pause for a moment, gauging the reactions of the people around me. I can see one or two small nods of approval, but not as many as I would like.

"I don't need to have my job threatened," I add, "and I'm not going to stand for it either."

Silence falls over the room, filling it with uncomfortable tension. I look at my father for his reaction.

"Sean, you have brought a substantial amount of business to Blackwood and have never been one to shy away from a challenge. Get her to sell. You have three days to get it done."

. . .

With Connor away on one of his business trips and the meeting dragging on longer than anticipated, I make my exit from Blackwood HQ and head straight to the airport for my next destination. In a few days, I'll catch a flight to join him. Today's trip gives me the time and space to reflect on what the hell just happened.

I don't like this. There's a deep gnawing feeling in the pit of my stomach, making it churn. I'm a decisive person, and I'm swift to act. When I know what I want and what needs to be done, there's nothing I won't do to make it happen.

However, this is different.

In this instance, there's no cut and dry way to do this because emotions are involved. Not just mine, but someone else's. Jess's.

She's excited to continue working together and the plans we discussed are still very much what I want to do. But I don't want to do it without her. Her job is secured by our agreement. But I know my father, and judging by the meeting we've just had, he won't shy away from sneakier ways to muscle her out of a job without outright firing her. He can make her life a living hell if he wants to. How understanding is she going to be when her plans are constantly turned down? How is she not going to be frustrated when she's constantly stonewalled, and my father speaks to her the way he's talking to me?

That part will never happen. Over my dead body.

26

JESS

 hree days later

"So, are you gonna sell?" Pauline asks in a quiet voice as she takes her break in my office.

Sean has been out of the office lately, sealing deals left and right, so I haven't crossed paths with him much in the past few days. But we're scheduled for an after-work rendezvous today.

"I've been thinking a lot about his offer." I lean back in my seat, using my straw to twirl the melting cubes in my iced coffee. I'm so used to Sean bringing in coffee that the one I purchased just doesn't hit the spot. "The pros outweigh the cons. Westerlyn can do great things, especially with Blackwood backing us."

"You know where I stand, but it's your decision, Jess. You know I'll support you no matter what."

"Honestly, I feel like selling to Blackwood is the way to go," I tell her. It feels wonderful to say it out loud, to finally have that decision and to no longer be wrestling with it. It's the right move, and one I feel I'm finally ready to make. "This is a once-in-a-lifetime opportunity. I have to take it."

"I'm glad for you, Jess," Pauline says, rising to envelop me in a warm embrace, pressing her chest against me. "I can see how good you two are together. You guys make a great team, and once the probation thing is over and you're officially working for Blackwood, your potential will be boundless."

Pauline holds up her nearly finished coffee in a toast. "Here's to making big life decisions and seeing where they take us."

"I'll drink to that."

We drink and finish our break before Pauline leaves to get back to work. I return to my duties as well, excited but nervous about my decision.

I can't wait to tell Sean.

I grab my phone.

ME:
Drinks at 7? You in?

SEAN:
Not tonight.

Not in the mood to go out.

Gotcha. How about I grab dinner on the way? Any cravings?

You, in bed, covered in whipped cream. Fresh berries. Caramel sauce on top.

Naughty! I was thinking pizza, but your idea sounds definitely sweeter.

A fter work, I swing by my beloved NYC pizza place to grab a pie (his playful suggestion was just a teasing appetizer). When I get home, he's not in yet, so I change into comfortable clothes, opting for a cozy pair of snuggly pants and a soft, oversized sweater.

While I wait for him, I spend time with Pippin.

He ruffles his feathers and nips at my finger a little harder than he normally does.

"I know, I know, buddy, I'm not Sean but your best new pal will be over soon," I tell him when I take him out of his cage, stroking his cute feathery head. Pippin has been thrilled at Sean's attention over the past weeks, and he's taken to chirping every time he comes to visit. Seems like he's the biggest fan of Sean. Well, not right off the bat, though. At first, Sean barely paid attention and Pippin outright turned his back on him. The first time he did it, I found it hilarious and couldn't stop laughing. Now, they're besties.

"Hey, can I tell you a secret?" I ask him. "I kinda like Sean, and I know he likes me too. Thinking about talking to him about putting a label on this thing and making it official—what do you think?"

Pippin chirps, completely disinterested in what I have to say as he hops around the back of the couch as he loves to do.

"I know it's complicated...but the way things are going, I'm really happy, and I want to keep seeing him. Hopefully once I sell, that whole pressure from the board will be off his plate, and we can focus on making those changes we talked about. But mostly, I want to see where this goes. It's been a long time since I've been in a relationship, and I'm so ready to give it another try."

I know he can't respond, but talking to Pippin always makes me feel better. I know on some level he understands me, and when I reach out for him, he hops onto my finger and bumps his head against my chin when I go to kiss his beak.

In the hall I can hear the faint ding of the elevator, signaling Sean's arrival.

My heart flutters in excitement.

I'm putting Pippin back in his cage when my front door opens. There's a heavy sigh from behind me, and before I can turn around, strong arms are circling my waist, and a hot mouth is on the back of my neck.

"Hello to you, too," I say, leaning into Sean's touch. "Rough few days?"

He makes a grunt of acknowledgment but that's it. His hands reach down to tug at my pants and, while I'm into it—and my clit is already doing somersaults of excitement—I'd like to know what put a damper on his mood at work.

Turning, I slide my arms around his shoulders, giving them a gentle rub.

"Wanna talk about it?" I ask.

Sean's head falls back so he can stare at the ceiling. "There's really nothing to talk about—well, not right now at least. I don't want to ruin our evening. It's the same bullshit I've been dealing with for a while." He looks back down at me and brushes my hair away from my face. "Nothing you need to worry about, baby. I've got it under control."

"I'm not saying you don't. I just know sometimes it's good to vent about these things."

"I already told you what I need."

He leans in for a kiss, and I happily accept. If he doesn't want to talk, I'm not going to force it. Besides, after not seeing him for a while, I'm also eager for some molten moments of bliss.

Right then my stomach decides to growl, and I pull away, giggling.

"Probably should eat something first," I say.

Sean nods. "Works for me."

At a loud squawk, he turns to Pippin, rumbling, "Hey there, little fluffball. I know. I missed you too." Pippin responds with an excited flutter of his yellow feathers, and chirps a melody that sounds like a parakeet's version of laughter. Clearly, he's delighted by Sean's attention and is reciprocating the affection. Little traitor.

While I set up the table and pour our drinks, they play. But as soon as I put some fresh-cut apples into his food tray, Pippin leaps from the excitement of playing with Sean to the sheer thrill of having a full belly.

In the meantime, we settle on the couch and dig into the pizza. Nothing beats a great slice after a hard day of work. It's even better when you get to share that time with someone you care about. After taking a few bites, Sean leans back, impatiently pulling on his tie before he undoes a few buttons. Sure, he always carries a broody aura, but it's rare for me to see him this distracted.

Whatever happened at work must have really gotten to him.

"So judging by how well things are going," he begins, "and how quickly the staff has been able to pick up the new policies, I think it's safe to say that this transition period is nearing its end," he says, pausing to finish his slice. "I'll be easing up my time at the hotel more and more and transitioning back to working at headquarters. It means that the decision is going to need to be made on whether or not you're selling."

It's the first time we've broached the subject in a while.

"About that..." I begin.

He interrupts me, gently squeezing my knee. "It's okay, you have a couple more days, I know. I'm not expecting any kind of answer right now. In fact, I don't even want to talk about work."

"You sure? You brought it up."

"I know. I changed my mind. I just want to finish eating, crawl into bed, and do really naughty things to you."

"You must have really missed me if that's all you've been thinking about doing tonight."

"Blame it on my neighbor for being the tastiest snack around, always game for whatever."

"I wouldn't go that far."

Sean picks up the soda to top off my glass. "How far would you go?"

"What fun is it if I tell you? Wouldn't it be better to show you?"

He doesn't even give me a chance to put my glass down before he shifts me farther down the couch, out of Pippin's line of sight, and kisses me, his hand cupping my cheek as he draws me closer. Heavens, he's in rare form today. Not that he isn't always enthusiastic and down for sex, but he's rarely so insatiable that he can't even wait for us to finish our meal. I manage to put the glass down without spilling it, and a second later, I find myself being pulled onto his lap.

I match his enthusiasm, my hands sliding into his partially open shirt in search of that muscled chest of his. There's tension in his body that I'm not used to feeling, but it melts away when I slide my tongue past his lips. He buries his hand in my hair, clutching me tight. It's like his mouth is hungry for mine, barely letting me breathe between kisses.

Time slips by while we lazily make out.

He's clearly not in any rush to jump right to the good stuff and neither am I.

Honestly, I could sit here for hours doing nothing but this. If kissing Sean is all tonight is going to entail, I'm here for it. But I know he has plans, especially when he finally gets his hands inside my pants—or me out of them, rather. His palms skim along my thighs before he gives them an appreciative squeeze. Drawing back, I smirk down at him before placing a few pecks along his jaw.

"What's the plan tonight?" I ask.

Sean hums, leaning his head back against the couch as he thinks. "You know the answer."

"I think I vaguely remember you saying something about whipped cream and other dessert toppings."

His eyes sparkle. "That I did."

"Sounds like a plan to me." I pause for a moment, doing a mental checklist on what I have in the kitchen. "Though you'll probably have to go get some from your place because I don't have any here."

"You need to get groceries more often."

"Why? Now that I have access to your fridge, there's always food."

Sean rolls his eyes, smiling as he squeezes my thighs one more time. "Fine. I'll go grab a few things. Why don't you change into something more comfortable?"

"And by that, you mean, *get naked*."

"Precisely."

Chuckling, I slide off his lap and take the time to polish off my soda as I get to my feet. Sean gets up, places a kiss on my temple, and gives my ass a quick pinch.

"Be right back," he says and winks at me.

I smile as I watch him go, acutely aware that the heat in my chest has everything to do with the feelings I have for this man.

Humming to myself, I clean up our dinner and head into the bedroom. While we talked about me getting naked, he doesn't know that I recently bought some sexy lingerie as a surprise. I go through my drawers, picking out a silk negligee. It hugs my body and highlights my hips while showing off my thighs, all of which I know Sean really appreciates, judging by the amount of attention he gives them.

Tomorrow when we go into work, I'll tell him that I'm ready to sell, and we don't need to wait for the full week until the contract officially ends. But tonight is all about distractions, and I'm more than ready to lose myself in his arms for the next few hours.

A fter about five minutes, I start to wonder what he's getting. It doesn't take that long to go to his kitchen and come back. At the ten-minute mark, I'm mildly confused. Where is he? He definitely should be back by now. Once it reaches fifteen minutes, I'm concerned.

Slipping on my white robe, I step into my slippers and go to find out where Sean is.

A quick peek in the hallway confirms no one is around so I make my way to his door. It's opened a crack, but before I can let myself in, I hear voices coming from inside.

"We're not talking about this right now," Sean is saying, his voice filled with an anger I haven't heard from him before. "I'm *handling* it." He's behind his fridge door, shuffling through the contents.

The voice I hear is coming through the speaker on his phone lying next to the fridge, and is clearly work related, so I make a move to step away so I don't interrupt.

"You've done a good job so far," an old male voice says. "But now is the time to finish her."

"I told you, let *me* handle Jess."

I freeze.

Hearing my name is like I've been doused with cold water. It's like I lose the ability to walk or do anything. My hearing suddenly becomes bionic. Every word comes out sharp and clear, almost as if the man on the other line *wants* me to hear.

"I have been listening to you," the old man's voice says, "and the only handling you're doing isn't in the office. You've had your fun, son, but your time is running out. It's time to get serious. It's never a good idea to mix business with pleasure."

"It's been working pretty well so far." Sean huffs. "You'll get what you're after, relax."

"I require action, not promises. Seal the deal *now*. You have until midnight."

Somehow, I finally gain control of my legs and hurry back to my apartment. My heart is racing but for an entirely different reason. A sinking feeling settles in my stomach as I wrap my arms around myself. Has this all been just a trick? Some kind of sick ploy?

I can't believe I made the same mistake again.

I can't believe I put my trust in another man.

Norman was right. He warned me, but did I listen? He told me to be careful, that men like Sean Blackwood didn't make emotional decisions.

He cautioned me not to let my heart sway my judgment when dealing with him. God, and I told him I knew better, that I could handle it.

Now look where it's led me.

Once my mind takes hold of that thought, it's like I can't stop the avalanche of emotions that follows. I find myself questioning every touch, every kiss, every sweet, tender moment we shared.

Were they even real? Does he feel anything for me at all?

I feel like an idiot. I should have listened to my initial instincts. I should never have broken my rule. There's a reason why I adopted it to begin with. And here I was, thinking this could be more, that there was something else between us. That he loved me.

Looks like it was just wishful thinking.

Ugh.

Dammit.

I have the sudden realization that he's going to be coming over any second. Sex is the last damn thing on my mind. Within seconds, I hear footsteps and the doorknob turn. But before he can open it, I do it for him, just enough for him to see me but not enough to allow him to come in.

"Hey, sorry about that," he says. "Turns out I also have to get groceries. But that's okay, you're sweet enough for me."

His smirk does nothing for me. If anything, it makes me angry. He just had this intense phone call talking about me with his father, and then thinks he can just come over and have sex? Absolutely not.

"Actually, I'm going to call it a night," I say, standing my ground, even as he tries to step forward. "I'm tired."

Sean frowns. "I know I was gone for a bit, but it wasn't that long."

"It was long enough. It's been a day, and I just want to get some sleep."

There's a moment of silence, and I can tell he's trying to gauge why there's a shift in tension. "Everything okay?" he asks.

I don't have the energy to get into it and argue with him. All I want is to be alone and gather my thoughts. There's a lot I need to rethink and sort out. And I can't do that with him here.

"I told you, I'm tired," I say, plastering on a smile. "Sorry. Long day."

There's another pause as Sean's eyes search mine. He leans against the doorframe, which brings his face close to mine. "Sure I can't change your mind?"

His eyes are mesmerizing. His lashes lower as his eyes land on my lips.

I pull away. "I'm sure. I'll see you in the morning."

"Tomorrow morning, I've got an on-site meeting in Providence. I won't be around until the early afternoon."

I take a purposeful step back and start to close the door. "Goodnight, Sean."

When I try to close the door, he stops it with his hand, his face full of concern. "Are you sure you're okay?" he repeats.

"I'm fine. Goodnight."

"Why, Jess? Please wait. What the hell happened? Did I do something wrong?"

"Goodnight."

"Tell me this isn't still about that ridiculous rule of yours, is it?"

Ouch. Jerk. The mocking sway in his voice is unmistakable—he believes we've breached "that ridiculous rule of mine" one too many times for me to shuffle it back out. Without giving him an answer, I close the door and lock it. Securely.

Letting out a slow breath, I rest my forehead against the wood, trying to hold back tears. I don't hear anything on the other side for a few seconds, but then Sean retreats to his apartment and I hear the door close behind him.

Do not cry. Do not cry.

Never again will I cry over a man.

27

SEAN

For a second I stand there, staring at Jess's closed door, wondering what the hell just happened. She seemed pretty into things a few minutes ago, which makes the cold shoulder even more confusing. I know I took a while, but I didn't think I was gone for that long. She's always been pretty chill in situations where there was a delay of sorts.

I go back to my apartment more than a little annoyed. But it's not Jess I'm annoyed with, it's my father and his shit timing. It's unnerving enough to deal with him during the day, but now he's bombarding my phone outside of work hours, and that really takes the cake.

I've known this man my whole life, and I'm intimately familiar with his personality by this point, but something about this situation seems to be making him even worse to deal with.

What's worse, at this point, my hands are tied.

A dull throb starts right between my eyes, and I pinch the bridge of my nose. Maybe it's a good thing I'm not spending the night at her place. With this impending headache I could use some aspirin and a few hours of sleep. Which is exactly what I do.

. . .

The next morning I'm awake long before my alarm goes off, and I'm feeling marginally better. At least physically. There's an emotion I can't quantify once I fully wake up, and it takes me a moment to realize what it is. Emptiness.

For days now (ever since Mr. Grant graced us with his presence), with a few exceptions, I've woken up with Jess next to me, whether in her bed or mine. And I guess without realizing, I've gotten used to it. Not having her next to me, I feel incomplete. It's as if a part of me is just MIA.

I pick up my phone and shoot her a quick text. It's early, she might still be home.

ME:

Quick breakfast?

While I wait for a response, I do my old morning routine which I haven't done in some time. It feels good to get back on the treadmill and feel the familiar burn in my muscles that a good workout provides. By the time I'm done, however, she hasn't texted me back. I'm not concerned and figure she hasn't checked her phone yet or is busy getting ready.

After showering and getting dressed, I knock on her door. There's no answer, and I don't hear movement or sound, save for the squawking of her bird. I knock again, a little harder this time.

Nothing.

I shoot her another text, but that's not answered either. I'm not going to wait around. I'll see her later once I'm back from Providence, Rhode Island, where I'm meeting up with Connor to inspect a hotel.

When the elevator doors open at the parking garage, I notice her car is gone. Which means she must have left already. She has a lot on her plate, that explains the silence. I'm not concerned, not too much—she's busy. She normally gets in early.

One thing *does* feel odd though. I haven't had to do this before: balancing a work relationship with a personal one.

I told my father that my entanglement with Jess hasn't been affecting my work, but I have to admit to myself that that's a full-blown lie. Of course it's been affecting my work, however, it's not in the negative way that he makes it out to be.

Jess and I make a good team, and I still don't see why that would be considered a problem. Sure, logistically I can see why this *would* be considered an issue. Emotions and business don't typically go hand in hand. At least not the business I'm used to conducting. In the past, I've tried to keep my relationships as far away from work as possible, given the number of hours my job consumes.

Navigating a new relationship and a working partnership at the same time, it's uncharted territory. I've been putting it off, but it's time Jess and I sit down and talk things out. Figure out where we see this going. Maybe once that's clear, I'll have a better idea of how to handle the business side of the equation.

When I land in Providence, Connor is already waiting for me. He arrived a couple of days earlier to coordinate everything between us and the current manager for the new plans I've got in mind. This place, recently added to our portfolio, holds potential, and I can't help but feel inspired by Jess's vision about revitalizing the guest experience by providing a unique spirit to create something exceptional.

As much as I enjoy handling transitions, it's nice to slowly return to this side of things. Once I'm back in my office on a regular basis, I intend to dedicate time to focus on all our other properties.

After we finalize the tour and agree on the implementations, Connor and I stop to grab coffee and "johnny cakes" (small, flat cornmeal pancakes with a slightly salty and sweet flavor) as early lunch at this apparently legendary local spot, a well-kept secret I'm considering partnering with to deliver their specialties to our newly acquired spot. I grab some for Jess too, curious to see how she'll like them.

Back in my private jet, I give Connor a brief rundown of the conversation I had with my father. The longer I talk, the wider Connor's eyes get. I've never seen him clench his jaw this hard.

"What the actual fuck?" he asks, looking up from his pancake—they're so good, we're having seconds. "Did he seriously threaten your job over one stupid sale?"

"Yeah, but it's not about the sale, obviously. He's been waiting for me to screw up, insisting on maintaining traditional methods. And since I don't, he has to invent a scenario. For fuck's sake."

"And your time ran out, what, last night? What are ya gonna do?"

"Wait until she's ready," I tell him.

I don't say anything else, only look up from my pancake to meet his gaze.

When I do, understanding passes across Connor's face.

He swallows down his bite. "Oh, so this is *serious* serious? Feck." Connor studies me carefully. "D'ya think it'll be that easy?"

"You said it yourself," I say. "She's a keeper. And that's what I'm going to do: I'm going to keep her."

Connor doesn't need to point out I'm repeating myself. Nodding, he puts his empty plate down, crosses his arms, and leans back, his legs planted wide. "That's a solid fuckin' move if there ever was one, but— Jesus Christ, *lad*."

"What?"

"You can say it, ya know? It's obvious that you love her."

He says it so casually that it startles me for a second. Which is probably a dumb thing to be startled by, all things considered. However, despite my internal acknowledgment of my feelings, the word "love" hadn't entered my mind until that moment. But now that he said it, it's so obvious that's what this is about.

I love Jess, and I don't want to go back to the way things were before.

I take a sip of my coffee, then finish it in one fell swoop. Connor looks at me with amusement, shaking his head.

"How have you not put that together?" he asks.

"I have," I say, "but I haven't heard it out loud yet."

"Well, there it is now. So what are ya goin' to do about it?"

Good question.

What am I going to do about it?

For starters, I need to make her see that that stupid rule of hers is doing more harm than good. She's trying to protect herself, and I can't blame her for that. I know what a number the shithead pulled on her, but there's something there between us, something special. It shouldn't be thrown away. If anything, what we've been through has proven how right we are for each other, how much we complement each other. I can see it every time she looks at me, but she's pushing what we have away— like she did last night.

"Easy. I'm not giving her up," I tell him. "I'm going to keep her."

Connor grins. "That's the stuff. Show her who's boss. Show her how much you feckin' love her."

"All right, back to business. Anything else that I need to know?"

Connor shakes his head. "Nope. All runnin' smoothly."

"Good." With a nod, I grab my laptop to dive back into the numbers I need to prep for the quarterly board meeting.

"Wait. What's the story now that you've ignored your dad's ultimatum? Will he actually kick you out?"

"Empty threats," I say. "He won't fire me."

"Yeah, probably all bark and no bite. You'll be grand."

. . .

R evitalized and determined, I hop on my motorcycle and head to the hotel, my mind racing with thoughts. Jess might think our relationship is a dead end, but that's far from the truth. It's the only explanation as to why she suddenly acted so distant last night and still hasn't texted or called me back. She must be starting to feel the same way I do and got cold feet.

That's why she basically kicked me out. There can't be any other reason.

In a few short weeks, Jess has weaved herself through my life and my thoughts. She's the first thing I think about when I wake up and the last thing on my mind as I fall asleep.

Like I told Connor, I'm not giving her up. Not on this partnership and certainly not on this relationship.

28

SEAN

𝒶t about two p.m., I arrive with my "johnny cakes" gift in hand, and walk past Sarah's empty desk. I assume she's either taking a break or making a coffee run. A sense of déjà vu washes over me as I spot Richard Rutherford. He's sitting on the visitor's couch, waiting. For a brief moment I wonder if he enjoyed the art piece looking exquisite in the lobby. Of course, I'd never actually inquire.

When he notices me approaching, he gets up.

"Mr. Blackwood," he says, standing tall, impeccably dressed as always. "Good to see you again."

He's holding a huge bouquet in his hand. Did he bring her flowers? I'm well acquainted with the costs of flowers and the extravagant requests of the one percent elite who frequently stay in our priciest hotels. The exquisite orchid bouquet he's holding is an opulent creation with a price tag in the thousands.

"Mr. Rutherford, how do you do?" I ask, shaking his outstretched hand. "You brought my fiancé flowers?"

"Well—" he starts, glancing down at my plain gray pancake box, somewhat greasy on the sides.

I'm not worried, nor jealous—why would I be? Clearly, he doesn't know anything about Jess if he thinks he can impress her by throwing money around. Still, I cannot wait to hear what he has to say. After all, she's my soon-to-be-wife, so what the hell is he doing here with flowers?

Before he has a chance to answer, Jess turns the corner. "What are *you* doing here?" She marches toward us, ignoring me, eyes on Rutherford. If looks could kill, Rutherford (and his bouquet) would be pushing up daisies.

"Hey, Jessie," Rutherford says brightly.

"Not now, sorry."

He puts on a fake smile. "Jessie, I'm still waiting for your final answer. You haven't answered my calls."

Join the waiting list, buddy.

"I'm not selling to you," she says coldly. "That was and *is* my final answer."

Just before she walks into her office, I step forward. "Baby, can I talk to you?"

She might as well have said "Don't you fucking baby me" with the glance she shoots my way, as if I'm the less-preferred choice, perhaps even the more questionable one, but then realizes I'm her fiancé—so she forces a happy smile, nods, and steps past me.

"Have a nice day, Mr. Rutherford," I tell him.

He gives me a curt nod before he steps to the trash can by the guest sofa and drops the bouquet inside. It lands with a rustling, heavy *thud.* Then he walks off, empty-handed.

So much for *Jessie.*

Blackwood: 2, Rutherford: Still Trying to Catch Up.

Looks like we've got ourselves a worthy comeback.

I close the door behind us, following her citrus scent.

"I brought you something from Providence," I tell her. "You'll never guess what it is."

She ignores me.

I put the box of griddle cakes down on her desk and walk to the window where she's standing, looking out. I don't step closer than absolutely necessary.

"How the hell are you doing?" I ask.

"*Great.*"

All right. "Care to tell me why it feels like you're about to bite my head off?"

Jess sighs heavily and turns to face me. I'm met with a smooth mask of indifference, which is actually frightening, because I've never known Jess to school her emotions, unless it's Rutherford-related. She has always been open and honest, and I'm not used to this closed-off version of her. "You really don't know?"

"I don't," I admit.

"Really?" she asks, an ironic smile playing on her lips. "You think I'm stupid?"

"No, I know how capable you are."

"Is that so? Because it doesn't seem that way."

Am I missing something here? Her competence has never been called into question, at least not by me, and I don't understand why she's addressing me as if I'm unaware of what she's bringing to this establishment and her team.

"This is coming from a place that I've tried to silence for too long." Jess crosses her arms protectively over her chest. "When we first met, you came off as such a douche and I thought you had changed my opinion with your actions and sweet words. But it turns out my initial thoughts of you were correct."

"What are you talking about? Where's this coming from?"

"I heard you, Sean."

"Heard what?"

"Last night. I heard you on the phone with your father. You know, in the conversation where he told you to 'finish with me and be done with it.'"

As bewildered as I am by what she's saying, I'm surprised I didn't put two and two together, that I blamed her mood swing on her rule.

"You disappeared," she continues, "and I went to find you in your kitchen, and then I overheard my name. I don't appreciate being talked about behind my back."

"I thought we took care of this?" I counter. "I thought you had more faith in me and thought better of me. I already told you that I'm not in the habit of playing with my business associates to get what I want."

"But your father said—"

"*Fuck* what my father said." I huff. "You know I want you to sell your shares to me. It's not a secret. It's never been a fucking secret."

Jess vigorously rubs her face before running her fingers through her hair and tugging on her curls. "Fine. You're right, of course you are. It's not a secret why you're here. Maybe I shouldn't have been surprised." She lowers her hand and looks up at me. "Sorry, I can't keep doing this, Sean. All of this is becoming too complicated. I thought I could handle having a professional and romantic relationship with the same person, but it's just not possible. So I'm removing myself from the equation. From now on, we're strictly professional colleagues. Nothing more."

This is ridiculous.

This cannot be happening over a simple phone call.

"Just like that?" I ask. "You're going to break everything off and act like nothing happened?"

"I'm not saying 'act like nothing happened.' I'm saying I think we'll work better if we're just coworkers."

"Fucking coworkers." I chuckle. "Is that what you really want?" I ask in disbelief.

I notice the tears she's holding back.

"Jess. Look me in the eye," I say calmly, "and tell me this is really how you want things to be."

When she looks at me, I note the tension in her body. The tightening of her jaw, the way her fingers dig into her elbows, how her entire body is just shut down and closed off. That's what worries me more than what she's saying because I've never known Jess to be anything other than open to me.

"Yes. This is what I want." Her voice is hollow and emotionless.

I'm hearing what she's saying, but I still can't believe she's saying it. I want to argue. I want to tell her how ridiculous she's being, that she's throwing something like this—*us*—away for absolutely no reason.

She removes the fake engagement ring, and when I don't accept it, she places it next to the pancake box. "I'll have it returned to the jeweler in the morning."

"You're making a huge mistake," I say, unable to stop myself. "This isn't what I want, and I highly doubt it's what you want."

"I've made my decision," she reiterates.

"Good. I'm not going to argue with you. You want things to go back to how they were before? Fine. But don't use my phone call as an excuse. We both know damn well why you're doing this—it's because you're scared."

"Scared of *what*?"

"Of us."

"You know, Sean, just because you're smart doesn't mean you know me. Truly know me. We've only spent a month together. Don't stand there and presume you know my motives better than I do. You don't really know me and, as you proved last night, I don't really know you."

"I know you're smart. Courageous. Strong. Loyal. I know that you care about people, really honestly care about them. It's one of the things that drew me to you. I know that I—"

"Stop. It's not important, Sean. I don't want to know you anymore."

There's a moment of tense silence as we stand face to face, neither moving nor making any attempt to continue the conversation.

I know she's making a substantial mistake. If she really doesn't want us to be together, then she's going to have to do a lot of convincing, because I don't believe it for a second.

I'm not giving up.

I have to make her stay.

Just when I'm about to argue my strongest point, Norman's old fax machine starts ringing, rattling through a piece of paper.

Jess immediately moves to retrieve the fax, studying it. She's clutching it in her hand, reading it over and over. Then she holds it up to me. All color has drained from her face. "What is this?"

I walk over to take a look.

The fax is from Sanford & Partners.

In large handwritten letters on top of it, it says, "As discussed."

I quickly read through it.

Blackwood Inc.'s lawyer, Samuel Drexler, is invoking the force majeure clause, which allows for the immediate termination of the contract, citing concerns about Ms. Jessica Summers's management style and financial decisions, particularly budgeting, cost control related to group fees, and cancellation procedures.

My father's lawyer is arguing that her management style and decisions put the entire operation at risk.

For fuck's sake.

"I had no idea," I tell her.

"As discussed? Sean, it says 'as discussed.' Did you or did you not know of this?"

"It's not what it seems. It's my father's fucking handwriting. It's his doing. Also, he's the only human left on this planet who uses a damn fax machine. I had no idea he would take it to such extremes."

"So you've had this discussion. Why didn't you tell me? Warn me, at least? I trusted you, Sean. I trusted you." Jess quietly sniffles, and I watch her discreetly try to wipe a tear away. "We're done here."

"Wait. No."

Without looking at me again and without saying anything else, Jess grabs her purse and heads for the door. I want to reach out to try to catch her hand, tell her not to throw all that's between us away, but she's out of reach an instant later.

She leaves me standing in the middle of the room, coming to grips with the fact that my world has just imploded.

29

SEAN

*T*he unopened pancake box and the ring lying next to it mock me—along with the trash bin right underneath it—as I reach for my cell. I call my father's number to give him hell. Of course, his cell phone is turned off. True to his word, he refuses to use any modern technology unless he's forced to. His villa's landline goes unanswered. Jasmine tells me he's out of the office and reminds me that I'm scheduled to meet with him tomorrow, during the quarterly board meeting. Good. Before I end the call, I tell her to let me know if my father shows up, if not, I'll be in later today.

It was just *one* damn week. What the fuck was he thinking? That I'd happily nod and give my go-ahead to Drexler's scheme? Over my dead body.

The persistent rumors have certainly made an impact on my father. Maybe I should have been more effective in de-escalating the situation, explaining that Rutherford posed no threat. Yeah, right—like my father would have taken my word for it.

Once I pocket my cell, I head to my motorcycle. Full throttle, I drive to my next two meetings, clearing my head.

A few hours later, I've made up my mind.

I'm more convinced than ever that Jess and I are meant to be together. I'm not going to let her throw away what we have. I couldn't give a rat's ass if Blackwood owns all of Westerlyn or not.

My mind is preoccupied with something else.

Something more important than selling a bunch of rooms.

All that matters is Jess, and how truly special she is. How everything pales in comparison to the depth of beauty she carries in her heart. How I find myself unable to get enough of her.

It's addictive how she effortlessly lightens everything around her with her presence, her smile, her laughter, the bright energy she brings into my world with every step, reminding me to what truly matters in life. Pippin, her employees, people she holds dear. She ensures her guests leave the hotel uplifted, and ready to return next time. Despite the myriad challenges she's faced along her journey, her past hasn't brought her to her knees. Instead, it's fueled her determination to fight for what she believes in, standing like a force against Goliath.

There are a lot of things about her I'm unwilling to live without. It's unbelievable how easily she fit into my life without me realizing it, without me appreciating it until her presence was gone.

She may say she's done, but I'm not ready to throw in the towel.

We're in this together, and there's no way I'm letting go.

It's gotta be "we" or nothing.

The only reason why I'm not hounding her at her door and urging her to see reason is because pushing her is going to do more harm than good, because above everything else, what Jess is, is stubborn.

But so am I.

She'll see things my way. She'll realize that my father's threats don't matter. She'll agree there's more here and that we have to be together.

I need a strategy, not a "bull in a China shop" approach. If I charge in there recklessly, she'll show me the door faster than I can blink.

I glance at my watch, and it's half past five p.m.

. . .

Before heading home to face her with a plan of action, I make a pit stop at my office, as I do almost every evening.

Imagine my surprise as I step into the waiting area of my office to find Jasmine still present, greeting me with a crisp, "Mr. Blackwood, there's someone waiting in your office."

I frown, not knowing who the hell would be here to see me. "Who is it?"

"Oh, someone from the Westerlyn NYC property you'll be happy to see, I'm sure," she says with a smile, ready to leave for the day. "Anything else you need?"

"Have a nice evening, Jasmine."

"Thank you, you too, sir."

Heart racing, I open my door to find Jess standing by the windows. It's bizarre to find her in this space. I've kept my job at Blackwood and my job at the hotel separate. Having both worlds combine throws me for a loop.

"Hey, I was just about to go see you," I say, glad to see her, closing the door behind me.

Jess turns around and my heart sinks. I can tell by the look on her face that I'm not going to like where this conversation goes.

"I'm sorry to show up here," she says. "But this couldn't wait. You weren't at home, and your secretary said she expected you to arrive soon."

"Good, because I need to talk to you too, baby."

I cross the room toward her, but before I get a chance to say anything else, she cuts me off by thrusting an envelope into my hands.

I didn't even notice she was holding anything.

"Here," she says, letting go of it. "This is for you. I've signed and dated everything, even had it notarized."

"Signed what?"

"The papers for my half of the properties, the ones you drew up weeks ago. I looked them over with my lawyer, and everything is fine."

This isn't what I'm expecting or wanting. "You didn't have to do that. That's what I wanted to talk to you about—"

"Yes, yes, I do," she cuts me off. "I think it would be best for both of us if we finalize the sale. Which is why I'm leaving."

30

JESS

I can't stop shaking. I'm usually brave, but today broke me. This is the hardest decision I've ever had to make.

Once I made up my mind about selling to Sean, I knew I had to do it fast before I changed my mind.

This was never going to work.

To be honest, once the papers were gone over, and my lawyer watched me sign everything with trembling hands, I felt marginally better. However, there was another big step that had to be made.

"Leaving?" he asks. "No. What the hell are you talking about? You can't leave the hotel."

I've never been more conflicted in my entire life. How could I be so sure of something one minute and then completely unsure the next? It's frustrating and heartbreaking at the same time. I still can't get over what I overheard, the way Sean sounded, assuring his father he had it handled, coupled with that fax they sent, accusing me of mismanagement and practically forcing me out of the hotel I helped build.

Ironically, it was me who insisted on a contract. Story of my life. I trapped myself like a rat.

Now I'm paying for it.

In more ways than one.

Ugh.

Once more, ensnared by the charm of a CEO.

I know he says it's not what it seems, but it's so hard to believe him. So hard to get rid of that sinking feeling.

But not as hard as it is to cut him from my life.

I thought it would be easy. After all, I've been on my own for so long it should be easy to go back to that. But Sean has woven himself into my life and into my heart, and how can you extract someone who's become a part of you?

But as many times as I told myself it was physical, as many times as I tried to avoid falling in deep, despite my best efforts, I'm in love with him. Yes, I realized this early on, but I don't think I truly did comprehend the depth of my feelings until this moment, until now that I'm looking into his eyes.

It's so hard to walk away and leave him behind.

I don't even have the capacity to tell him that Jane Deets informed me that the adjacent building owner is open to hearing my offer, or that old Mr. Schuster at Schuster and Flint called to inform me that our bookings were about to skyrocket due to their newly acquired sister companies. These monthly conferences will even adhere to the new rates and cancellation policy. Mr. Schuster emphasized how our fair rates and policies over the years contributed significantly to their expansion—and this is his and Mr. Flint's way of expressing gratitude.

A huge victory (that almost made me cry), not just for me but for all the hard work my employees have put in over the years. A real "I freakin' told you so" moment that I don't even get to have.

Because I can't work at the hotel anymore.

It's undeniable that Blackwood Inc., with all its means and resources, would—sooner or later—undoubtedly find a way to push me out. While I pride myself on being a fighter, I don't want to live a life that's a constant downhill battle, filled with sleepless nights and daily arguments trying to prove myself, only to end up on the defeated front. I don't want to spend my days agonizing over the Westerlyn's future, or feeling the way I have in the past hours—miserable, unappreciated, and betrayed.

I want to smile again, to laugh, and to embrace each new day that life brings.

Most of all, I don't want regrets.

Never again.

Not with Sean.

Richard devastated me, but if Sean were to break my heart, I would never recover.

That's why I also can't live next door to him anymore. Hearing him come home, wishing for him to show up at my door, is too much. I need to find somewhere else to live. It'll be better in the long run if I do.

That's why I can't see him anymore.

That's why all this has to end.

Now.

With the financial means the sale will provide, I'll purchase a new place and a new hotel. One that won't be a shared venture, one that will be entirely mine. Big enough to bring in Pauline, Emma, and the rest of *my* staff.

"You're not leaving the hotel!" he exclaims, snapping me out of my thoughts.

I was not expecting his explosive response.

"I'm leaving the hotel, *and* I'm finding another apartment," I clarify. "I told you before that mixing relationships with work never ends well for me, and I was right. It's over."

He tosses the envelope onto his desk. "You're *not* right. It's not happening to us, and it won't. We're good together, Jess. You know we are. Not just with work but personally. Are you really going to stand there and tell me you don't have feelings for me?"

"Sean, please don't make this harder than it already is," I say and sidestep him, trying to move closer to the door in the process. "It's my decision to sell, and it's my decision to move. It'll be better for both of us in the long run."

"Running away is never the answer."

"It is when you need to protect yourself."

"From what? And who? Me?"

Yes, *you*. I want to say, but I don't.

As if he heard my thoughts, he says, "You don't need to protect yourself from me, Jess. You never have."

Of course I have.

I've had to protect myself from the beginning—or at least I should have. I thought I could keep our relationship separate from work. I thought I could handle this, *him*, but it's clear that I can't.

I never want to feel the devastation I felt when I overheard that phone call or read the fax.

This isn't just about him. This is about me and how I'm clearly not over what happened with my ex. I'm not gonna put Sean through my issues, and I'm not gonna let my trauma affect him.

It's clear that I still have a lot of things to work out, and it would make everything easier if we went back to the way things were before I knocked on his door for the first time.

When we didn't even know each other's names.

When we didn't know we existed.

"I need to protect myself from *myself*," I say. "It's not just about you, Sean. I have to do what's best for me."

The silence between us thickens, and we seem unable to look away from each other. His eyes look so sad, and I hate myself for thinking it, for noticing it.

My heart hurts, more than I think it's ever hurt before, which only strengthens my resolve.

"I need to go," I say, backing up toward the door. "Everything should be in that envelope. If you need something else, my lawyer's contact info is inside, and they will make sure it gets to me."

"Jess, no. Don't go. I haven't given up on all those plans we made. Please don't give up yet. You can still be a co-owner. I'd rather work together as equals than as your boss. I will protect you, if that's the last thing I do. There can be an 'us.' There needs to be an 'us.'"

I don't know what to say to that.

It sounds too good to be true, and I'm still too emotional. It could be so easy to give in. So easy to let myself be drawn in by him once more. But I'm a mess of emotions, and I've already made up my mind. His father would not rest. The board would not rest. Nothing good could possibly come out of this relentless turmoil.

"Thanks for everything," I tell him, reaching for the door as he takes a step toward me. "Goodbye, Sean."

I'm out the door and out of his office before he can say anything else. I can feel him following me, but he pauses in the waiting room. Either he doesn't want to continue the private conversation where somebody could hear, or he's unwilling to keep following me, I'm not sure. It doesn't matter.

I don't think I breathe properly until I fully leave the building. Once I step out onto the sidewalk, I take a deep cleansing breath and slowly exhale.

I'm confident I've made the right decision.

As difficult as it was to sign over my half of the hotels, I try to look on the bright side. So many of the things that have kept me up at night will no longer be on my plate. I can just focus on running the day-to-day and looking for a new place to live, at least for a little while.

And who knows? I'm sure I'll find something that means as much to me as WH does, or even more. At least I hope I will.

I'm trying to look on the bright side, but for the first time in my life, I can't.

It hurts too much right now.

Instead of going to Swayze's, I head back home.

I need to start packing. I still have unused moving boxes in my closet from the last move. While I waited for Sean in his office, I got in touch with Jane Deets, and while it may take some time to find a place I truly love, once I do, I'm going to need to be ready to move at a moment's notice.

On the drive, I call Pauline. She tells me I did the right thing—as far as selling the hotel is concerned, not breaking off things with Sean. She emphasizes that Sean isn't Richard. It's not the response I was hoping for. How I wish I could talk to Norman. But by now he's basking on a warm, sunny beach with his wife, savoring life to the fullest. Good for him. At least someone made a timely escape.

Once I'm home, I kick out of my heels and fall face-first on the couch with a noise of frustration. In his cage, Pippin flaps his wings and chirps, as if to remind me of his presence, and the fact that I didn't say my usual "Hello."

"Everything's a mess, Pippin," I tell him, turning in his direction. "Your mom is going through a crisis here, give her a second."

After unlatching Pippin's cage, I lie back on the couch with him hopping along my belly. I gently pet him, allowing the feeling of his soft feathers to calm me down like they always do.

I don't know how long I lie there, but eventually, I hear the faint sound of the elevator doors opening and Sean's footsteps draw closer.

My heart hiccups.

For half a second, I imagine him coming to my door like he's done so many times before. Just strolling in with a wink as he undoes his tie.

I picture us together again, our mouths unable to separate, our hands desperately moving over the other's body.

I can hear him pause, and I stop breathing. I sense Pippin's excitement, recognizing his buddy's steps.

But then there's the sound of the key in his front door, and he enters his apartment.

I let out a shaky breath.

Pippin looks terribly sad, the poor little guy. I shower the cutie pie with pets, kisses, and affection until he starts to feel better.

Mind still a horrible mess, I take a deep breath and sit up. As difficult as this is and as much as I need to figure out, lying here moping isn't going to help. With shaky hands, I pop Pippin on my shoulder and head to the kitchen to make myself a cup of calming tea.

31

JESS

"We're going to have to move, buddy," I tell Pippin, putting a teabag in my cup. I grab an apple and start cutting it into smaller pieces. "We'll upgrade to a spacious spot, and you'll get a deluxe, multi-level bird haven. And some friends." I need to talk to Rose from the pet shelter. "So you don't miss him too much."

He ignores me in favor of preening his feathers.

Deep down, I don't want to move, and of course I don't want to cut things off with Sean. But the urge to protect myself is greater than my desire to stay. After taking a sip of my tea, I turn some music on my phone and set about packing things in the living room that I'm not going to need for the time being.

It's bittersweet to say the least. I love my apartment, and I love this building. No matter how much I try to look on the bright side, sadness creeps in. I think about all the fun girls' nights I've had with Pauline, or the lazy Sundays where I stretch out on the couch with Pippin on my shoulder as I read.

Carefully, I pack away my books and the little nick-nacks I have on my shelves. Only a few minutes later do I realize how stuffy and warm it's gotten. I scoop Pippin up and put him back into his cage so I can open the balcony doors. He squawks in annoyance, but I ignore him and open the double doors, letting a breeze whip through. It's past eight p.m. and still light out, the temperature in the beautiful mid-seventies. How I love spring. It's a wonderful time to enjoy the outdoors.

Knock! Knock!

I jump in surprise. I've been so lost in thought, I didn't hear footsteps to my front door. It's not him. I wouldn't have missed *him*. Thinking it might be a neighbor asking me to turn the music down, I quickly shut "I Will Survive" off and cross the room, with an apology on the tip of my tongue.

The diplomatic smile I plastered on my face is gone in an instant.

It's Sean standing there, a raging storm in his expression.

"Sean? What—?"

He pushes past me, closes the door, and tosses his jacket to the side as I stumble back and accidentally plop down onto the armchair behind me. "Jess, if you thought I was going to let you throw away what we have, you clearly don't know me very well."

I barely register what he says. His steps are sure and purposeful as he approaches me.

"Sean, what are you—?"

"I didn't get the chance to present my most compelling argument. That's why I'm here, and you're going to listen."

"Sean." He's facing me, sleeves rolled up, both his tattooed arms resting on the armrests and trapping me in place so I can't run away.

"This thing between us isn't over," he rumbles darkly. "I don't want it to be, and I know you don't want it to be either. What we have is special, and it has been since the beginning. We might have been able to fool ourselves once upon a time that it wasn't, but you and I both know that's a load of bullshit. We know we're special, Jess. You know that and I know that."

I stand up, forcing him to back away. "Sean, please. Not right now."

He stands tall, his eyes a thundercloud of emotions. "Is it still about the phone call? The ridiculous fax? Because it's not what it sounded or looked like, and I cannot believe you're going to throw away something special over BS like that."

"Maybe BS to you! But no, Sean. It's not just about that, it's everything up until this point. You say there's more here, and I'm not denying that."

His shoulders drop. "Then what's the problem?"

"It's too damn complicated."

"Then let me make it easy for you."

He cups the back of my neck and pulls me forward into a kiss.

At first, I anticipate a forceful kiss, but to my surprise, it's gentle—soft, tender, and absolutely wonderful, filled with so much warmth I want to cry. I want to kiss him back so badly, but I can't. "Please don't make this harder than it already is."

"And you think it's easy for me?" he rumbles against my lips. "Jess, I love you. I'm in love with you. So fucking much."

My stomach clenches and my heart skips a beat when the words come out of his mouth.

That's *not* what I was expecting him to say.

"What?"

He cups my cheeks. "I love you. More than anything. More than life. More than I could ever put into words. And I know you love me too, baby."

Deep down, I know it's what I was hoping for, but didn't dare let myself think that it was a real possibility. Yet even though it makes me elated to hear him say those three words, it only increases the terror.

Shaking my head, I say, "Even more of a reason to keep our personal and professional lives separate. Love and business don't mix, Sean."

"They seemed to mix pretty fucking well over the last month. We're great together, Jess. We're dynamite. And if you're worried about Blackwood, don't be." He strokes my cheeks softly. "I want you to trust me.

There's a board meeting scheduled for tomorrow, and I'm determined to set things right, if that's the last thing I do. In fact..."

He opens the envelope I gave him earlier and pulls out the paperwork. To my amazement, he rips the packet in half, tossing the papers onto the floor. He does the same to the fax.

I stand there in shock.

"See? You're not pulling away that easy," he rumbles.

My mind is so blown that I don't hear the tell-tale squeak of Pippin's cage until it's too late. Sean notices it first, glancing past me and pointing. I spin around just in time to see a flutter of wings move past the balcony doors. The little guy somehow managed to open the door himself.

"Pippin, no!" I rush over with Sean right behind me.

I'm fully prepared just to see Pippin fluttering over the ledge with his clipped wings and down to the street below, but to my relief, he's perched on the railing. For half a second, I watch his wings flap up, managing to gain some air and land on the molding of the pillar between our balconies.

"Shit!" Sean says, alarmed.

"I have to get him down. He can't fly properly, and I don't want him to fall."

Quickly, I move toward the ledge, but then I feel a firm hand on my shoulder. Sean has stepped out onto the balcony with me, and he's glancing up at where Pippin is stuck.

"Let *me* get him. He's really high up, and I'm taller."

"You're going to have to climb onto the railing."

He side-eyes me. "I'm aware."

I remember our conversation and how he said he isn't a fan of heights.

Before I can protest and tell him that I can do it, he's already stepping up, clutching the pillar for support. Now my fear is doubled, for

Pippin and for Sean being so precarious. He tests his footing, and when he thinks he's got it, he starts to reach up toward the bird.

Pippin is spooked and instinctually starts to flap.

Oh no, oh no.

Sean's body wobbles, and my heart stops as it looks like he's about to fall. And then, it happens—he starts to slip!

My pulse pounds in my ears, anxiety gripping me.

Sean!

No!

At the last second, he manages to catch himself and wraps his hand around Pippin's tiny body, grabbing him before he can try and flutter away. I don't think I breathe properly until he secures his hold and extends his hand toward me.

He cradles Pippin. Relief washes over me as I take him into my hands.

"Thank you, Sean. You're a lifesaver," I say, grateful beyond belief. He grins, and everything is perfect. I rush inside and put Pippin in his cage.

Just as I secure the cage door, I see it happening from the corner of my eye.

Sean loses his footing.

"No!" I scream, but it's too late. Time slows to a crawl as I watch how he plummets, and my heart leaps into my throat. Without thinking, I rush onto the balcony, and my hands grip the cold metal.

My body breaks out in alarm.

I peer over the railing, my eyes fixated downward, a surge of horror coursing through me. "Sean!"

My focus is singular: him, falling.

My heart is hammering in my chest so fast and loud I can't think.

All emotion clutches in my throat.

No.

No.

Noooooo!

As I reel from the shock, a vivid vision overtakes me. The fluorescent lights flicker overhead as I burst into the emergency room. The sight of Sean lying there, pale and still, sends chilly panic through me. He's in a bad condition. Critical. Guilt and fear twist in my stomach. This should have never happened. Why oh why didn't I ensure Pippin's door was securely closed? A loud beep resonates through the room. The monitor is flatlining.

My heart stops. *Please, dear God, please.*

Tears blur my sight and I want to stumble back, but instead I blink, and the vision fades. Reality crashes back in.

Leaning farther over, I find Sean grasping onto the metal fixture at the balcony's edge. "Sean!" My hand reaches out, grasping for his, but as hard as I try, I can't pull him to safety.

He's hanging there, swaying.

Oh, Sean! In a sudden movement, he propels himself to the side, his feet fumbling for a surface that doesn't exist. Desperately, I clutch onto his hands for dear life. Somehow, he finds footing on the unseen brick formation below. With a determined resolve, he steadies himself, readjusts his stance, and then skillfully maneuvers himself back up and over the railing.

ThankyouGodthankyouGodthankyouGod.

And holy fuck.

Back in the living room, I close the doors tight behind us.

Then I launch myself into his arms, tears rolling down my cheeks, my body shaking. Not only is my body shaking, but all my limbs, and organs (and, believe it or not, my hair too). Every single cell in my body feels like it's doing the jitterbug, and there's no sign of slowing down.

"Whoa, whoa, I'm okay," he assures me, hugging me tight. His heart beats rapidly against mine, a clear aftermath of the adrenaline rush. "We're all right, we're both okay."

Sean looks at Pippin. "No escapes in the future, you hear, Pippin?" he scolds him (softly).

"Squawk."

I wrap my arms around him even tighter and squeeze. "Oh, my God." I sob into his neck. "Sean, I saw you fall to the ground. I swear!"

"But I didn't. And Pippin didn't get away. It was a close call, but phew, everything's fine." He holds me close until I relax, stroking my head and shoulders, then draws back and pushes the hair away from my face as his lips turn up in an amused smirk. "I guess that means you must really love me, huh?"

I can't even joke at this point.

"I'm so sorry," I whisper, my eyes locked on his. "You're a hero, you know that? Risking yourself for a tiny creature. You risked everything for Pippin, and I—"

"It's okay." He smiles weakly, interrupting me. "Told you I still had to deliver my most compelling argument."

I'm still not ready for his jokes.

"I'd do it again for you and that little bird," he says, "or for anyone attempting to escape your apartment."

"Sean, *stop*, you don't understand. I was so scared! Horrified!"

He studies me with those shining, dark-green eyes. He tips up my chin. "Because you can't live without me. Because I'm the best thing that's ever happened to you. Because I'm the man of your dreams. Because I'm the best—and only—man there is for you. You can't deny it. You love me. You love your Spider-Man." He winks and more tears spill from my cheeks. "Tell me you do."

"I do, Spider-Man, I do! That was so epic!" Tension leaves my body. "Just kiss me already."

I don't need to tell him twice. He brings me close and seals his lips over mine.

The doubts I've been replaying in my mind, the fear and the uncertainty suddenly mean so little. In those agonizingly slow minutes where I thought I might lose him, it brought everything clear into focus. He loves me. He outright told me that he's in love with me, and I'm undeniably in love with him.

I'm head over heels for my own Peter Parker.

He's not just better, he's a bit scarier too. And grumpier.

And the best thing that ever happened to me.

Who would have thought? Sean Peter Blackwood. My next-door neighbor. My Mr. Grumpy King. My kissing friendly fake fiancé. My forbidden Mr. CEO. He's my superhero, willing to swoop in and risk everything, only to make me happy. He literally stepped out on a ledge for me, without a second thought, and showed me how much he cared, how much I can trust him.

Even though it's still terrifying, even though I'm still scared beyond reason, not only because of what just happened, but because of what's to come, because of *us*—I know that being without him would be a million times worse.

That moment of fear was enough to put things in perspective. Drawing back, I try to catch my breath while he continues to pepper my lips with beautiful, tender kisses.

"How are...we going to do...this?" I ask between kisses, my breathing quickening.

"Every way we can." He nods, rumbling against my lips. "But probably me on top first."

I draw back. "No. Not that. I mean, this relationship. Working together."

Grinning, he says, "I know. We'll figure it out, baby. Who gives a fuck? Right now, there's something more important on my mind."

Those strong arms of his sweep me off my feet in a hurry, and he rushes me to the bedroom. It's like we have no more time to waste. Eagerly, I slide a hand in his hair and kiss him, reveling in the firm press of his lips. The lips I thought I wouldn't ever get to feel again.

There are still questions that need answering, "logistics" that need to be discussed. But we can do that later. We don't need to have all the answers right now.

Right now, all we need is each other.

In the bedroom, he lays me on the bed, his fingers deftly moving down the buttons of my blouse as he quickly undoes them. I reach to do the same to him, giving his shirt far less care than he gave mine. I yank and pull until the buttons come free, one of which flies off. Suddenly, there are far too many layers between us. I need to feel his skin. I need his heat to touch me, fill me, remind me that what's happening is real.

His mouth finds all the right places, nipping and sucking at my neck as his hands work my pants down over my hips.

"Goddamn pants. From now on, only skirts."

"Well...you're not my boss anymore, you can't tell me what to do," I tease, breaking off into a moan when his teeth graze my throat.

"I'm the boss, here, and everywhere else." His hand slips into my panties and I forget everything I've ever learned when his fingers brush over my clit. "That clear, baby?"

"Clear," I totally agree.

We tear at the rest of the clothing that separates us, throwing things left and right. The moment he slides my damp panties down my legs with his teeth, I squirm. I've never felt such urgency before, and I know in my heart, it's always going to be like this. I'm always going to want him, and he's always going to look at me like I'm the most gorgeous woman he's ever seen.

His eyes bore into mine. "Spread your legs."

He doesn't even finish his line before I do so instinctively. "K."

When his naked skin finally touches mine, I shudder beneath him. One of his arms slips around my waist, and he lifts me just high enough to line himself up. His cock is long, impatient, ragingly angry.

Finally, finally he thrusts into me.

Gasping in pleasure, my hands grip his shoulders, and I moan his name. "Sean..."

"I missed fucking you, baby," he growls, thrusting.

"Sean...Sean...Sean..."

My mind is stuck on a loop with the same word, unable to access anything else from my vocabulary.

Each thrust inside me sends waves of pleasure into my body.

Our movements are rough and uncontrolled, both of us too eager and overwhelmed to take things slow. I can't believe I was going to give him up. I can't believe I was going to run. I'd been so wrapped up in my past that I almost let this amazing man get away. How could I have doubted that he really cared about me? How could I have doubted myself?

"Jess, baby," Sean rumbles, panting, his hot breath ghosting across my ear. "You're mine. Forever."

"I know, Sean."

Buried to the hilt, he grinds into me, not withdrawing for even a fraction of a second, like he can't bear to have any kind of space between us.

It's hours later when we finish, sweaty and panting. Even then, his arms are still around me, holding me close even when he rolls onto his back. I'm sprawled across his chest, gasping for breath while he pushes my hair out of my face. My mouth finds his in a sweet kiss, and as he draws me in, he wraps me up in the warmest embrace.

"I love you," I say, the rest of my anxiety melting away. "I love you so much, Sean."

"I know, baby. I can tell."

He's so smug.

I look up at him.

His eyes find mine, and he laughs. "I love you too, baby." He softly places my head back onto his chest. "I love you. You better believe it, I love you."

I smile.

"Hear that?" he rumbles.

Thump-thump. Thump-thump. Thump-thump.

I nod, yes.

"This heart beats just for you. Furiously. Passionately. Unconditionally." He strokes my cheek. "There's no getting away. As long as this heart beats, I will continue to love you."

"For the rest of our lives?"

"No. For fucking eternity."

32

SEAN

The next day

Seated comfortably in my spacious office with a commanding view of the New York City skyline, my mind keeps drifting again and again. I gently shake off these distractions, reminding myself to focus on preparing for the upcoming board meeting.

It's our quarterly review—and I'm bracing for my father to repackage the expired ultimatum. I've steeled myself for a confrontation and for what might turn into a heated showdown.

Over the past few days, I've been reviewing our earnings. The numbers from the Westerlyn properties show no dip in earnings or revenue. That's good news, as changing owners or management generally leads to some kind of shakeup during the acquisition phase. We haven't touched the out-of-state properties, which could account for the steady numbers, but the most important is the New York branch, and it's in the green as well. Further proof that Jess's leadership is solid and that the deal we made with her was a smart move. I hope once my father sees the figures in black and white, he and the board will realize the same thing.

Weeks ago, I would never have put the word "hope" in any kind of notation involving my father. I learned at a young age that hoping he will see things my way is useless and a waste of time. Maybe Jess's silver-lining thinking has gotten to me more than I realize.

Knock-knock. Knock-knock.

I'm pulled out of my thoughts.

"Come in!" I call, rotating my chair to face the door. Jasmine is busy prepping the board room, or else she would have announced the visitor.

Connor strolls in, wearing his typical air of "here comes trouble," and I welcome the distraction from my spiraling thoughts.

"Hey, how's it goin'?" he asks. "Finally got the contract back from the place in New Orleans we were lookin' at. Just need ya to sign off."

I motion for him to come in and hold my hand out for the tablet as he approaches. He passes it to me and collapses on the seat across from me. "Is that the last big client you have on the hook for the rest of the month?" I ask, scrawling my signature as I talk.

"Yeah, for now. I've a couple of prospects, but nothin' on the docket."

"Okay, good. I don't want you to pursue those prospects just yet."

Connor raises his eyebrow. "And why's that then?"

I hand the tablet back to him. "I've got some ideas I'm going to be presenting to the board on what our trajectory should be moving forward. And if everything goes according to plan, it's going to cause a bit of a shakeup."

"And by 'a bit', ya mean a massive one?"

"Exactly."

"Okay, well, ya can't just drop a bomb like that and walk away. Ya have to give me a bit more."

"It's something I've been thinking about for a while." Working with Jess on the transition was eye-opening and has made me consider a lot of the practices we have as a company. Not that I wasn't considering them before, but it's made the necessary changes more apparent. Yes, it's great to buy these places and gather them under the Blackwood banner. It's our brand, it's what we do. "There's a significant amount of untapped potential in the properties we currently own and in the locations we tend to overlook during acquisitions."

"Ah, right. And that's why we've been goin' all-in on Providence?"

"Yeah. We need to focus on the experience, at what guests take away from our properties when they leave. One of the reasons why I bought Westerlyn and what drew me to them was the familiarity, the comfort, and the homey aspect of the property. I believe we can find a way to blend these aspects to offer an experience that preserves the property's welcoming charm while offering modern comforts and amenities."

Connor sits silently for a minute, mulling over what I've said. After a few seconds of silence he says, "Jaysus, I never thought I'd hear ya say somethin' like that."

"What does that mean?"

Connor puts his hands up in surrender at my sharp tone. "Hey, I'm all for it. I think you're bang on, and there's a lot of untapped potential in the properties we could be examinin'. But sure, we both know yer dad won't go for it."

"He's not going to have a choice."

Regardless of what happens during the meeting, there are only two outcomes for me. Either I convince the board that it's time for a change, or I don't. And I have a pretty good idea of what I'm going to do if it's the second option.

Connor must see the resolve on my face, because he sits up. "I'm ragin' I can't be there to see yer dad's eyes drop out of his head."

. . .

Connor leaves a minute later, and I gather my things to head to the conference room. It's already set when I get there, and Jasmine pours me a coffee before she leaves. I'm early. But so is my father, who's definitely more punctual than he normally would be. He's calm and overbearing, a combination that is never a good sign. But for once, it doesn't bother me and any frustration or rage that I would normally feel toward him is absent.

Well maybe not gone per se, but it's definitely not taking center stage. He doesn't even wait for me to sit down before he starts up.

"I hope you're prepared, son. This is going to be a long meeting, and there are a lot of things we need to discuss that happened during the last couple of weeks."

I let his words flow right over me, keeping my attention on the tablet in my hands with my figures and notes. "I agree. We do have a lot to discuss."

There's silence, and when I glance up, I can tell he's confused but trying to mask it. He's not used to me saying that he's right, and my response clearly wasn't what he was expecting. His eyebrows draw together as he studies me carefully. My expression is neutral to match my feelings. It's gone on long enough, and despite how much he wants to get a reaction out of me, I have none left to give.

"Tsk-tsk-tsk, I never thought I would live to see the day where my son would finally agree with me," he says. "But before the others arrive, we should discuss this cold shoulder you've been giving me as of late. No matter what our father-son relationship is, it shouldn't affect our work."

"That would imply that we have a father-son relationship. We don't."

For the first time in my life, I notice a genuine reaction from my father. Quite frankly, it looks like he's been slapped in the face. He looks thoroughly insulted, and even huffs like a child when he crosses his arms and leans back in his seat.

"After all I've done for you? *This* is what I get?"

"What have you done for me?"

After everything that's been going on, the years of fighting and frustration, I'm ready to be done with it. In order to move on, part of me needs to know what's going on in his head, because I've never been able to get a clear picture of the labyrinthian insanity that is my father's psyche.

He doesn't answer me right away. At first, I think he's stunned, or at the very least, not expecting me to demand examples. Then, after a few long seconds of silence, it dawns on me that he's not stunned. He can't find any examples, at least not one that doesn't sound made up on the spot. I let him stew in silence, not breaking eye contact as I study him.

All I can hear is the ticking of the clock on the wall.

I don't think I've ever felt the distance between us more than I do in this moment.

"I gave you your position in this company," he suddenly says, back straight and hands folded on the table. His voice doesn't quite have the gravitas that it usually does. "I have defended you to the board as much as I can. It was *me* who convinced them to keep you on, even when it was more than clear that your vision for Blackwood simply doesn't align with ours."

"I think you mean that my vision doesn't align with yours," I say calmly.

"No, I meant what I said."

"I've never needed defending from you or anyone else. Not because I've mis-stepped, but because I stand by my statements and decisions." He knows I'm a damn good manager, and I'm a damn good employee. I don't need to say it out loud.

"I will never understand why you keep fighting me like this, son."

"Maybe I wouldn't if you hadn't made it clear that you didn't want one."

Something shifts in his face, and for the first time in forever, I don't see my boss staring across from me. I see my father.

"Is that what you think?" he asks.

"You haven't shown me otherwise."

I hear footsteps in the hall, and I glance at the door in time to notice Daniela walking in.

My father's eyes are still on me. I can tell Daniela senses the tension, however, she doesn't comment. All the board members are used to walking into tension when my father and I are sitting alone in a room together. It's quite commonplace. Daniela takes a seat to my right.

One by one, the rest of the board members file in, and soon, all seats fill.

Before my father even has a chance to open his mouth, I start the meeting.

"Since we're all here," I say, getting to my feet and motioning toward the screen on the wall where my graphs are already loaded, "let's start going over the numbers for this quarter."

"Hold on there. Let's not get ahead of ourselves." My father interrupts, audibly clearing his throat so that everyone is forced to look in his direction. "There's still a major discussion that needs to be had."

I'm spared from responding by Daniela, who lets out an exasperated sigh. "I swear, Douglas," she says in a terse tone, "if you're going to bring up that Westerlyn chain again, I'm walking out of here."

You can hear a pin drop. Not only because of Daniela's forcefulness, but because she called my father by his first name, which she typically doesn't in an official setting.

Even my father looks taken aback.

"As long as I'm the head of the board of directors," he huffs, "I have the say on what we do and do not talk about."

"If that's the way you want it, then fine, let's address it," I say as I meet his glare with a steady look of my own. "I thought my record would speak for itself, but apparently that's not the case. Need I remind you, that before I took over as CEO, Blackwood profits were dipping? We've reported profits across the board consistently for the last five years and continue to grow under my supervision. We could go even further if I was allowed to make decisions on our future."

"Those decisions fall to *me*, the head of the board of directors," my father reminds me, his voice carrying a steely resolve.

"Then maybe we need a new head of the board," Daniela says.

My father's eyebrows fly up. He clenches his jaw as he leans on the table, fixing Daniela with a hard glare, then me. I'm surprised as he is but try not to show it. "This is *my* company, and as long as *I* sit in this seat, *I* will be making the decisions."

"There's something you're forgetting. This isn't a dictatorship, it's a democracy," I remind him. "You may have final say, but it's up to the board as a whole to decide. So let them decide."

"Sean, do you really want to do this, right now? Do you want to embarrass yourself?"

"Let's do it right now."

Regardless of the outcome, I know I won't humiliate myself by speaking up. I'm going to liberate myself, because if I don't have their support, what the hell am I still doing here?

"Fine," my father says, standing up straight and gesturing to the silent people around us. "Let's put it to a vote then."

Daniela addresses the board, saying, "All those in favor of Douglas Blackwood stepping down as head of board of directors, please raise your hand."

The smug look on my father's face fades fairly quickly.

Daniela's hand is the first to go up and, one by one, the others follow suit. Some look at me when they do, others stare at the table and avoid eye contact with my father altogether. His confidence is gone by the time the last hand goes up. Nearly every member of the board has voted against him. Only those closest to my father held back. It doesn't matter. Majority rules.

"Well, that settles that then," Daniela says.

My father doesn't respond. His eyes sweep across the room several times before they meet mine. "You can't do this to me," he says. "I started this company. I own this company. You can't just vote me out!" There's anger in his voice, but there's another emotion that I didn't anticipate.

He's scared.

My father, who's always been the epitome of a stern, authoritative figure, is actually scared. Seeing that fear in his eyes does something to me. While it doesn't excuse anything, I realize that the reason why he's been fighting me so hard, is because he's terrified. Of what, I don't know. It could be a number of things. Uncertainty, change, or perhaps even his own vulnerability.

"Apparently the board can," I say. "As you've said many times before, I'm not on the board."

"...which raises the question," Daniela interjects, looking at me, "of whether you could potentially contribute your expertise in the future."

My father is breathing heavily, doing everything he can to keep his composure. "You can't cast me aside!" he snaps, looking at Daniela and the rest of the board.

"Then back off," I snap back. "Stop ignoring my advice. You know I have good ideas and you know I have what it takes to implement some positive changes around here. Changes that will be to everyone's benefit. If you don't want to be voted off the board, then let me do what I've been training to do my whole life."

There's a beat of silence, and I know when my father's shoulders slump that he realizes he doesn't have a choice. Composing himself, he takes a deep breath and reins in his emotions.

For once, he looks old, older than his sixty-seven years.

"If the board agrees to let my son Sean have a seat in my place," he says, "then I will acquiesce."

"We agree," Daniela speaks up. "I think I speak for the others when I say allowing Mr. Sean Blackwood on the board as head would be in the best interest of Blackwood Inc. as a whole."

My father doesn't bat an eye this time.

He just stands there motionless, then gives a curt nod.

The room hushes momentarily as his nod signifies a rare agreement.

A few moments later, my father finally breaks the silence. "In the interest of the company, I agree. Let's move forward with this decision." He looks at me. "My son, Sean Peter Blackwood, now holds the position of head of the board of directors," he announces, and sits back down.

He wouldn't be my father if he didn't know how to gracefully accept defeat.

It feels like a weight is lifted off my chest. I take a steady breath and cast my gaze across the table. Daniela smiles softly and gives a nod of acknowledgment. The others who voted in my favor are waiting expectantly, eyes on me.

I present my reports and updates on our properties, trying to act like it's business as usual, even though it's anything but.

In my report, I point out the numbers we can expect for the next quarters, a testament to the invaluable contributions of Ms. Summers, the current—and remaining—co-owner and Director of Hotel Operations at Westerlyn Hotels. In order to clear her name fully, I emphasize that these achievements wouldn't have been possible without her expertise. I highlight our plans to acquire the adjacent skyrise, a development made possible through her connections (a juicy tidbit she dropped this morning, for which I plan to thank her thoroughly all night long). Furthermore, I take the opportunity to highlight the partnerships she has cultivated over the past years, resulting in a substantial financial gain that is poised for exponential growth in the coming months. I stress the importance of retaining dedicated team members like her who turn down offers not only from Richard Rutherford but from several major competitors, reflecting their commitment and loyalty to Blackwood's cause.

"And for the foreseeable future, our bookings have soared to heights even I couldn't have predicted." I don't hold back as I reveal the staggering numbers, making it clear that bookings have gone through the roof.

The room registers surprise, and a few subtle gasps and acknowledging murmurs fill the air.

Sometimes, numbers have the last word.

I close with the suggestion to allocate a significant portion of our resources to improvements for our existing properties rather than solely focusing on property acquisitions. The initial reaction is overwhelmingly positive, with everyone applauding—except my father. He just gives me a subtle nod, then gets up and leaves.

Countless ideas and thoughts continue to run through my mind, and I'm trying to keep them in check. There will be plenty of time to think about and implement the changes I want. I'm sure it's not always going to be smooth sailing by any means, but it's a step in the right direction.

33

SEAN

Two months later

It's funny how things sometimes work out. Before Jess, finding a silver lining seemed like a foreign concept, but now, it's become my compass in life. Optimism was never my go-to, but finding those glimmers in the darkness—well, it turns out, it's like having your own weapon against life's storms. For one, I'm finally having a say in the future of Blackwood.

Since I gained my new position, it's astonishing how different things are.

Connor has been training to take over my position as CEO. As much as I enjoy the position, I feel my future lies with directing the board and being free to work on personal goals.

Jess didn't end up moving out. In fact, the other neighbor couple on our floor, Lottie and Antoine, moved to Paris, France, so I bought their place, which means we now own the whole floor. We're in the process of remodeling the space into one large apartment, complete with two offices, a gym, and plenty of space for a family.

Which we're definitely going to have.

Jess is running the Westerlyn properties and crushing it. We've begun renovations to upgrade the amenities, starting with a few of the items we discussed and new ones—such as renovating the rooftop terrace, adding cozy reading nooks, upgrading the in-room entertainment systems, offering specialty pancakes in the mornings, fresh-baked cookies in the afternoon, and introducing a weekly "home-cooked favorites" night in our restaurants.

Our mornings have fallen into a comfortable routine. Usually, the alarm goes off, and I get up first to get a quick workout in. I know it's time for Jess to wake when Pippin and Pippa start rustling in their new parakeet palace and launching into a duet of squawks.

Putting the coffee on, I make sure Jess is up before hitting the shower.

Sometimes, she joins me.

Which is how this morning is going. I'm under the warm spray of the shower when I hear the bathroom door squeak and the shower cabin open. Smirking, I feel her arms wrap around me, and she places kisses between my shoulder blades.

"Good morning," I rumble.

"Mmmm, morning, handsome."

I turn around and get her under the water with me, pulling her into a deep kiss. She moans and melts into my arms. Life really can't get any better. I think about where we were before and how far we've come, and I can't wait to see what's in store for us next. Jess runs her hand down between us, cupping my dick.

"Someone's frisky this morning," I groan, pressing her against the wall.

"Hard not to be when you're all soapy and dressed like *that*."

I grab her and lift her up. Her legs fit easily around my waist, and I take her without hesitation. No matter how many times I'm inside her, it's never enough. I'm never going to get tired of it.

"Just like...*that, Sean.*" She moans my name, her hair plastered to her face as the shower rains down on us. I think about our first meeting, the infamous pink towel incident, and how I caught that first glimpse of the body that continues to drive me crazy. If I had only known how good she was for me, I would have made her mine right then and there.

By the time we finish, her mouth is attached to mine, even as I reach over to turn the water off.

"We're going to be late if you don't stop," she reminds me, while she's still nipping at my lips despite her own words.

"We're the bosses," I grumble. "We can go in whenever we want."

"Normally, yes, I'd agree," she reluctantly draws away, "but I have to hit the office today to school Pauline."

"All right. Go take care of your responsibilities." I reach for our towels. "And hurry up."

"Ugh, fiiiiine." Jess sighs dramatically as she accepts her towel and wraps it around herself.

"I know. The sheer dread of being a responsible adult."

I head over to the closet where I have my few suits hanging. Most of our stuff is in storage right now in preparation for the construction, except the bigger pieces of furniture and my treadmill. Our essentials are in a suite at the hotel, where we're going to be staying in the meantime. Jess is going to bring Pippin and Pippa with her today in their pet carrier, and the movers are going to collect the rest of the stuff once we head out.

I can hear Jess humming as she gets ready, and when I look over to see her getting dressed, I'm hit with such a wave of emotion that my heart races. Jess catches me staring and smiles.

"What?" she asks. "Why are you staring at me?"

"Marry me."

We haven't really talked about it much, other than to say we want to down the line. For me, that's too far away. I want her to be my wife as soon as possible. After all, why wait, when we know *this is it*—for the both of us?

Her eyes are wide. "Now?" she asks.

Chuckling, I toss my suit jacket onto the bed and cross the room to take her hands. "Not right *now*, but soon." I give her a smile. "Tomorrow," I tease.

She laughs. "We haven't been together very long."

"So? We're engaged, after all."

"Fake-engaged."

"True, but it's a fun kind of fake. We're rocking it."

Jess breathes out, and then she leans against the wall. "I don't know, hmm, hmm," she teases. "This is so sudden. And...you don't even have a ring."

True to her word, Jess had returned the fake engagement ring, which led to me receiving a call from a friendly sales lady and an offer of in-store credit. I respected Jess's decision. Having a fake ring on her hand that reminded her of Richard wasn't in my best interest.

"I didn't take you for the traditional type," I say.

"Diamonds are a girl's best friend, Mr. Blackwood," she hums.

I chuckle. "Oh, are they?"

I know she's messing with me, mainly because she can't even keep a straight face as she talks. It makes me grin, and I tickle her sides, sending her into a fit of laughter. She tries to bat my hands away, but I pull her into a tight hug, kiss and release her.

Next, I get down on my knee, pulling a little dark-blue box out of my pants pocket, and give her a wink.

Within two seconds flat, she is frozen solid.

Then she blinks.

And blinks again.

Instantly, tears well up in her eyes.

I open the ring box and her eyes grow wider. It's not the modest type of engagement ring she picked previously. This one is uniquely crafted. The centerpiece, a sparkling diamond, is encircled by a delicate arrangement of vibrant stones. There won't be a shred of doubt that someone has claimed this woman. Me.

She gasps and puts both her hands over her mouth. "No way...no way, Sean...oh my goodness..."

"Baby. Woman of my dreams. My one and only love. My beautiful Lockout Queen. My crazy Balcony Spider-Woman. Will you marry me?"

She starts nodding. "Yes!...Yes!" She breaks into sobs, tears cascading down her cheeks. "Of course I'll marry you!"

She falls into my hug.

I scoop her up and spin her around before covering her mouth in a million kisses.

I 'm in high spirits as I cruise into work. All the pieces have fallen into place, and it's amazing how well Jess and I are doing, balancing our work and personal lives. I'm not saying that it's been a walk in the park from the get-go. Given what Jess went through, her heartbreak cut deeper than any financial loss. She had trusted the wrong person, and it had cost her more than money—it had shattered her faith in men. But I'm patient, ready to spend the rest of my life making up for the pain that a deceitful shithead caused. I vow that she'll never have to endure such a loss of trust and finances again.

A fter I drop her off at the hotel, I head to Blackwood HQ.
Jasmine isn't at her desk when I arrive. Which is why I'm blindsided when I go into my office, and my father is standing by the windows. For the most part, he's backed off since our rather dramatic

showdown in front of the board, now occupying the role of a regular board member. Yet seeing him like this without warning instantly puts me on the defensive.

"Good morning," I greet. "Do I want to know what you're doing here so early?" I sit at my desk and start my computer.

He doesn't answer immediately, which is unusual. After several seconds of tense silence, he begins to speak, still facing the skyline, "I'm stepping down."

That's definitely *not* what I was expecting to hear from him. "I'm sorry, I think I misheard you."

He turns around to look at me, and I don't see his usual hard expression. He's tired, and now more than ever, I'm struck with how much he looks his age. "You didn't mishear. I'm resigning."

"Why?"

He crosses the room but doesn't sit. "Sean, I'm well aware I have overstayed my welcome. I tried so hard to keep things from changing. I guess I'm too old to learn new things. All this technology and growth is going over my head, and I'm already being left in the dust. It's best for us as father and son, and for the company, if I retire."

I sit with his words, trying to process what I'm hearing. I figured that was his problem but to hear him admit it out loud is another thing entirely. I take a deep breath and lean back in my seat.

"It's really not that difficult to learn," I tell him. "You don't have to give up your spot just because you feel you're being left behind."

He raises an eyebrow. "I thought you'd be thrilled to get rid of me."

I breathe out a heavy sigh.

His gaze meets mine, and we remain there, looking into each other's eyes.

"Please sit." I gesture to one of the chairs.

He takes a seat across from me.

As he settles onto the chair, I find myself searching for the right words.

I get up and take my seat next to him.

I'm not even sure why I ask—the question is out of my mouth before I can stop it. "Why didn't you save Mom?"

Heavy silence settles in the room.

Dad shakes his head, weariness etched on his face. "Don't you think I tried? Son, I tried *everything*. She was so damn stubborn. I lie awake every night, replaying it all in my mind, questioning what I could have done differently. Mary, she would not listen. Not a word when I urged her to quit her job, to take it easy, or at least give up that darn charity idea of hers. I even threatened that I would never attend if she didn't stop. Nobody could have convinced her. She didn't want to hear more doctors saying the same damn thing. She knew. She didn't want to upend her life."

I sense the unspoken pain in my father's eyes.

"Dad, I didn't mean—"

He cuts me off gently, his voice strained yet calm. "It's all right, son. You needed to ask. I've asked myself the same question a million times. But sometimes, no matter how much you try, you can't save someone from their own choices." He glances away, his jaw clenching. "I loved her, you know," he continues, his voice softer. "More than words can say. But...I simply couldn't sway her."

I nod, the ache in my chest echoing the pain in his eyes.

"I want you to stay, Dad." His gaze returns to me, an expression of disbelief lingering on his features. "I'll be thrilled not to be questioned at every turn. If you aren't questioning my every proposition and actually listening to what I'm suggesting, then of course I don't have a problem with you still being on the board."

"I don't do well with the unknown, Sean."

"Life is about the unknown, Dad. If I can do it, then you can do it."

He gives me a curious look. "What are you talking about?"

"Jess and I are getting married."

I wasn't planning on telling him, mostly because I didn't care if he knew or not. However, if change is really making him this worried, I need him to see that it's not all bad.

He stares at me with wide eyes. "Is she pregnant?"

I'm not upset at his question. It's a common assumption people might make. "No, she's not. Not yet, but hopefully, one day she will be."

"That's...wow, all right." His shoulders drop. "Son, I'm sorry, if I had known... I wasn't aware it was that serious."

"Well, it is."

"I should have caught on when you vouched for her in the boardroom, a move you didn't have to make, given your new position. I must say, I'm proud of you." His expression softens into a gentle smile. "She must be a special lady."

"She is," I say, a smile tugging at my own lips in response. Witnessing my father's smile—I never thought I'd see that day again. My fingers are itching to grab my phone and capture the moment, but somehow I sense it won't be the last. "I don't know what the future holds for us, but I'm willing to take the leap. I know I don't want to stand still."

"Congratulations." He takes a deep breath. "If things are going to change, I might as well embrace it."

"Change isn't so bad. Sometimes, the curveballs turn out to be your biggest wins. Who knows? It might just go down as the pinnacle of your success."

He rolls his eyes at my sarcasm, yet there's no malice behind it this time.

Then, after a few seconds, he says, "You know what? You may be onto something, my boy."

Getting to his feet, he pats my shoulder, gives me a nod, and heads for the door. Once he gets there, there's a moment of hesitation before he turns around.

"It's not that I didn't want a son," he tells me. "It's that when your mother died, I didn't know how to be a parent. She did all that, and it came naturally to her. So I focused on work, because *that* I knew and could control. If you and Jess have kids, don't let this place," he gestures around himself, "come first."

With that, he leaves the room.

I sit there in silence, realizing that was the first time in my entire life he's ever given me fatherly advice.

EPILOGUE: JESS

Several months later

Knock! Knock!

I wake up to the sound on the suite door.

With a groan, I reach for Sean, only to remember that he's not sleeping next to me. He's in the other suite one floor up because it's bad luck to see the bride before the wedding.

Oh, my God, the wedding.

My wedding.

I'm getting married.

I glance over and smile at the garment bag hanging from the closet, where my wedding dress is waiting for later.

The knock comes louder, and I sit up, rubbing sleep from my eyes. I'm so used to Pippin and Pippa waking me up, and at first, I wonder why they didn't, then I remember they're back at the apartment. Yes, my Pippin finally found his match, and Pippa's a charming little beauty, who's got him wrapped around her little claw. In fact, she's turning our surly guy into a real Casanova. Looks like even the toughest nuts crack eventually!

Speaking of toughest nuts: Sean had crews working around the clock to finish the expansion in time for our wedding. Apparently, when you're as rich as he is, money isn't an object. He was determined for our wedding night to be the first night in our new home—and it looks like that's exactly where we'll be starting our married life.

Knock! Knock! Knock! Knock!

When I finally open the door, Pauline bursts in.

She's dressed in comfortable clothes and flip-flops, showing off the pedicure we got together yesterday, along with the bridesmaids. "What in the name—? Were you still in bed?" Her expression mirrors that of someone who's stumbled upon a bear in its den, mid-hibernation. "You gotta start getting ready *now*. We have spa appointments, then we have to hit the salon. Up, up, let's go!"

My stomach rolls, and a wave of nausea hits me. The next thing I know, I'm running into the bathroom, dry heaving into the toilet. Pauline is at my side in an instant, rubbing my back.

"It's okay, you're okay. It'll pass."

"I hate this. I don't know if its nerves or morning sickness."

"Probably both."

I found out I was pregnant earlier this week. At first, with the tiredness and sickness, I thought it was just pre-wedding jitters. Picture my shock when I visited my doctor, and she dropped the bombshell: "These are no pre-wedding jitters. This is no flu. And sorry, darling, it's definitely not your home-made pancakes triggering an allergic reaction. Wanna take another wild guess?" Well, turns out, drumroll please, I've got a teeny, tiny roommate on the way. Surprise, surprise! Talk about flipping the script!

I decided to hold off telling Sean until tonight.

That's if I can get through the ceremony without running to the bathroom.

"All right, Maid of Honor to the rescue," Pauline declares after I rinse my mouth out in the sink. She comes back into the bathroom with a package of Saltines and a can of ginger ale. "Have both of these, take a hot shower, and you'll be right as rain."

"...and disgustingly cheerful?" I inquire, accepting the items.

"Yes, yes, and that," she confirms.

"I'd be lost without you," I admit, swallowing.

"Believe me, I'm acutely aware. Now, off to the shower with you!"

I cannot believe how much my life has changed in the last ten months. It's almost been a year since Sean and I met, yet everything is different. Sean is running the board of directors, Connor is now the CEO, and I've promoted Pauline to General Manager. It was a sensible and logical choice. Pauline has the necessary qualifications, experience, and a good understanding of the hotel's operations and can manage the property during my maternity leave. Best of all, nobody knows the staff's needs better than her. Happy crew, joyful hotel—that's the ticket to success. The plan involves hiring a new housekeeping manager to facilitate a smooth transition and maintain the hotel's efficiency. Upon my return, she can continue to provide valuable support in effectively managing the property. I trust her implicitly and know she's going to do great.

After showering and putting on some comfy clothes, I feel a lot better. "All right, what's first on the to-do list of the day?" I ask as we take the back route out to her car.

"The girls are going to meet us at the spa for mimosas and massages. Obviously, just fruit juice for you, but the girls will be too buzzed to notice you're not drinking," Pauline explains smoothly, clearly thinking she's concocted the best plan ever. "Then it's brunch before going to the salon. You've got your hair and makeup at 2:30 p.m. Then back here to slip you into that stunning dress."

"I'm glad it'll still fit. Imagine if we pushed the wedding off to the summer like I originally wanted to? I'd definitely have a bump."

"It's a good thing your man is so impatient to marry you."

I can't help smiling. Sean proves time and time again what an amazing partner he is. I know he loves me and has my back through thick and thin. I know he will always be there for me, just like I will always be there for him.

My phone buzzes as Pauline pulls out of the parking lot, and I smile when I see Sean's name. We've been texting nonstop since we last saw each other, not used to being apart for this long.

> SEAN:
> I can't wait to get you alone tonight, Mrs. Blackwood.

> ME, TEASINGLY:
> Who said I'm taking your last name?

> It has a nice ring to it. Jess Blackwood.

> Hmm, I could rock that. I love you. Catch you at the altar!

> I'll be the one in the snazzy suit.

They always say that your wedding day goes fast. They're right. Massages and mimosas (and orange juice, the pregnant lady's staple) fly by. It feels good to be pampered and waited on, especially after working so hard for so long. All I can think about is marrying Sean and the fantastic honeymoon he has planned. Neither of us has had a vacation in eons, so Sean decided we'd go all out and use up all the vacation time we have.

Three weeks on a sunny Caribbean beach, here I come. As the hairdresser fixes my curls into an elegant updo, I breathe slowly through my nose and wait for the morning sickness to fade. Before I know it, I'm back in the suite and Pauline is helping me into my dress. She's already wearing hers, a baby-pink off-the-shoulder bridesmaid's dress she'd helped me pick out.

The gown is a little tighter than it was when I last tried it on. Mostly in the boob area. Sean will be happy about that.

"Breathe, Jess," Pauline reminds me. "Deep breaths."

"I can't believe I'm getting married."

Pauline smiles and pulls me into one of her signature motherly hugs. "You deserve this. Sean's got you beaming like never before, and believe me—I never thought I'd see your joyfulness topped."

"Right? It's a shocker! I don't think I've ever been this happy." I squeeze her back, feeling the warmth of her support. "Thank you for everything, Pauline."

"Hey, you promoted me and that's thanks enough."

I laugh, pushing her playfully.

She finishes zipping me into my dress, and the photographer arrives to take photos. Time ticks by, and I count down to when I'm going to see Sean.

Holy moly.

He looks so damn handsome in his tux.

Walking down the aisle, all I can see is him as I draw closer. With a grin spreading across my face, I mouth "Hey there, Mr. Snazzy Pants! Didn't think you'd actually show up." His smile widens, his eyes only for me, and when I finally reach him, he gives me a subtle wink and extends his hand. I gladly take it.

Sean leans in and whispers, "Well, had to make an appearance. Couldn't let this dapper suit go to waste. But looks like you're the real showstopper in that sparkly dress, Mrs. Blackwood."

"Glad you recognized me," I quip.

"Only because you're not hiding behind one of your yogurt masks."

"I'm saving the yogurt for the honeymoon."

He grins. "Sounds like things are going to get *creamy*. I'll be licking... my lips all honeymoon long."

"Maybe we'll need to stock up on strawberries...for dipping."

"Baby. Count me *in*."

With us giggling the whole time, I honestly do not remember what the justice of the peace says. We had a rehearsal the other day, but this is entirely different. It's like my entire focus is narrowed on Sean and nothing and no one else. He's giving me that look that makes me swoon, the one that makes me feel like I'm the only woman in the world. And when we're pronounced husband and wife, he sweeps me up into a kiss that sends everyone into cheers.

In the ballroom, he leads me through our first dance. It's only then that we have a moment to actually breathe.

"Seriously. The world hasn't laid eyes on a more stunning bride," he says softly, his cheek pressed to my temple as we slow dance.

"You clean up well, Blackwood," I tease. "Might have to keep a tux around for personal use."

He chuckles. "I can make that happen."

I feel a little dizzy and sway. Thankfully, he's holding me tight enough that he keeps me up. Though, he gives me a concerned look as he draws back slightly.

"You all right there, baby?" he asks.

"I'm fine," I assure him with a smile.

"You sure? I know you haven't been feeling well. We don't need to do the full dance if you want to sit."

I have the sudden urge to tell him right then, right there.

He looks so concerned, and I know he's going to keep worrying for the rest of the night. I take my hand out of his and slide both arms around his neck while his wrap around my waist.

"About that," I begin. "I went to the doctor on Monday."

"Yes?"

"She said I can expect to feel this way for a while. But it should clear up around the second trimester."

It takes a second for him to register what I'm saying. Sean's eyebrows are knitted together in confusion, but then it dawns on him, and his eyes widen.

He stops.

Our first dance is completely forgotten.

"Oh, my God. Jess...are you—?"

I smile back and nod. "I am. Nine weeks along."

"Hell yeah! *Hell yeah!*"

Sean scoops me up and spins me around, laughing in excitement.

Guests start clapping and cameras are flashing all around the space. They have no idea what's happening. This special news is just for my new husband, who kisses me deeply.

Smiling, I kiss him back.

"I love you so much," Sean says, stroking my cheek. "Both of you. I bet it's a boy."

"I love you too, but how do you know?"

"My Spidey sense is telling me it's a boy." He punctures his declaration with a confident nod.

"Oh, yeah? I'm pretty sure it's a girl."

"Yeah? How's that?"

"I can just tell."

"Ha! Well, we'll see about that."

"Trust me. Women have a sixth sense about these things. And she's going to be really special."

He wraps his arms around me tight. "That's for sure. Whether it's a he or a she, our little one is going to be the most extraordinary kiddo around!"

EPILOGUE AFTER THE EPILOGUE: SEAN

I sigh heavily and sit down at my desk. It's been a long day, and all I want to do is go home and be with Jess.

My phone rings and I answer it immediately.

"What's wrong?" I ask.

I've started answering all my calls from Jess that way, convinced she's going to go into labor the one time I'm not around.

Jess chuckles. "Relax, nothing. I was just wondering where you were."

"Just finished talking with Connor."

"Thank God. Come home, babe. I'm hungry."

"Ah, so that's why you're really calling. You want me to bring you food."

"And I miss you. But mostly food."

"The usual?"

"Yes, please."

I hang up and place a quick call to our favorite Mexican place, Montaña. Funnily enough, ever since she entered her second trimester,

Jess has had an intense craving for avocado. Considering her original disdain for them, I tease her about it constantly. She blames our baby.

Our baby.

We're having a baby.

I still can't wrap my head around it. Over a year ago, I was answering the door for my crazy neighbor who wanted to climb over my balcony. The neighbor I caught au naturel, who couldn't keep her hands off me, but later had to because she didn't date CEOs.

The neighbor that almost drove me insane.

The neighbor who once played the role of my fake fiancée (even if it was just for a few unforgettable weeks), and is now the perfect wife to me.

Turns out, this same neighbor is expecting our first child.

We decided to be surprised when we informed the doctor to withhold the gender information. We're both dying to know, sure, but there's something exhilarating about letting the anticipation build and not finding out until the moment arrives—especially given our opposing predictions. I'm still banking on blue, she's all in for pink.

When I get home, Jess is stretched out across the couch, fast asleep. Her soft breaths fill the dimly lit room, with delicate shadows dancing around her. She can nap anytime and anywhere.

I put the food in the kitchen before going back to her side, welcomed by our feathered friends.

"Squawk."

"Squawk."

Slowly and quietly, I move closer to her, to the front of the couch where her head is. Leaning down from behind her, I press a gentle peck on her forehead, our faces in opposite directions—ready for an upside-down kiss, well, almost, anyway. I proceed to lean down and kiss her freckled nose, and that's when I feel her stir. Leaning down farther, I plant a tender kiss onto her mouth.

Jess smiles, her eyes fluttering open, and her face lights up with recognition. "Hi, my Spider-Man," she whispers with a loving tone. "I love when you do that." She gives me a dreamy smile and her eyes sparkle with affection.

"It's my favorite pastime," I rumble from behind, looking down at her.

"Did I doze off again?" Her voice is hoarse from sleep.

Smiling, I nod, rubbing her nose with mine. "Yup. Totally passed out." I reach out and smooth her wild hair away from her face.

"Did you bring food?"

"Absolutely! Spider-Man to the rescue! Clear the streets, citizens! Watch out, villains! First order of business: satisfy a growling tummy."

She reaches up to my neck and pulls my head down. "You're my hero in and out of the suit."

"Oho. My Spidey-senses are tingling."

The moment she presses her lips to mine, love overtakes me. Our kiss is tender, deep, filled with affection. I can feel her smile against my lips.

When I slowly pull back, it's confirmed—Jess is indeed smiling, but that smile quickly fades as she reaches out to grab my arm.

Suddenly, she lets out a cry.

"What? What's wrong?" I stand and move around the couch, pulling the blanket off her. I can see a wet stain on her sweatpants, and that's when I know it's go-time. "Holy shit, your water broke. You're having contractions."

"Yup, pretty sure that's what's going on," she pants. "I think our little girl is finally ready."

"Come on, let's get you to the hospital."

I help her off the couch, and she pauses for a moment to lean against me. At first, I think it's to catch her breath, but then I realize she's shaking and crying.

"It's okay, baby. It'll be okay. We'll get you to the doctor, and they'll give you something for the pain. I've got this under control. Lean on me."

"I'm not crying over that," she says, pulling back. "I love you so much."

I bring her into a tender hug. This woman has a way of melting my heart. She's my love. She's my world. She's my *everything*. "I love you too, baby."

Just as the words leave my lips, another contraction grips her, nearly knocking her back onto the couch.

"Hospital, hospital now!" she exclaims, clutching her belly.

"Let's go!" With my arm around her waist, I lead my wife out of the apartment. "Ready to meet the little man?" I tease, trying to keep her smiling.

It works. She smiles and says back, "More than ready... Sean?"

"Yeah, baby?"

"I think you're spot on, especially with a kick like that. It's going to be a little man. And he's going to be one heck of a special guy."

"Absolutely," I say, "it's time for Peter to swing into the world."

The End

Thank you for reading my novel. If you enjoyed "The CEO Enemy", you will LOVE "A Bossy Roommate," the next book in my *Next Door to a Billionaire* series. All books in the series are standalones.

I've included a sneak peek on the following pages, so sit back, relax, and enjoy a little taste of what's to come.

THE NEXT BOOK IN THE SERIES: A BOSSY ROOMMATE

That one-night stand with my boss? Total mistake.
That's not all—we're roomies too.

Thanks to a mind-boggling mix-up in moving days, I'm stuck living with none other than NYC's most eligible bachelor, billionaire Carter Bancroft—inscrutable, icy, and utterly demanding.
The female staff all fall head over heels for his larger-than-life presence.
But I'm immune: I've sworn off men after having been dumped at the altar.
But living with my boss from hell comes with a catch—a hefty one, at that.
His nosy aunt is dropping by for a visit, expecting to meet his loving wife.
Me.
One weekend. One secret mission. One bed.
Fast forward to me atop the washing machine (whirring beneath me), him caging me in, unleashing a torrent of dirty talk, and suddenly, the room is steamier than a sauna.

I should have screamed "cut!" right then. Instead, I screamed his name. But who can resist toe-curling nights that blur the line between what's fake and what's oh-so real?

Not this girl.

Honestly, I couldn't have concocted a more disastrous turn of events if I tried.

Epic fail ever after, anyone?

"A Bossy Roommate" is available on Amazon.

REAL FAKE HUSBAND EXCERPT

He called me "Goody-Goody."
He called me "Nosy-Josie."
He called me other things while he pulled my pigtails.
Now, his grandmother left us a surprise inheritance.
The catch?
We have to get married and live in her small NYC apartment.
For a month.
With just one bed.

Callum

My gran's apartment is pitch dark when I arrive.

I never remember her home being dark, even when I was a kid and we lived on the other side of Queens. She always kept the light on in the kitchen. I place my bags and helmet by the door, and the first thing I do is turn on the light above the stove.

The soft glow brings immediate comfort. Even though I know she's dead, I can feel her presence. Not because I believe in ghosts, but because good memories well up in my head.

Now that I can see, I let my gaze wander through the rest of the apartment. It's cozy. Beautifully quiet as always. Several vases and a collection of figurines, knick-knacks, and other decorative objects add a touch of her personality. The flowery dark-purple wallpaper holds a frame of my favorite photos of Gran, with her small body in the middle, between me and my childhood buddy, Theo. When the pic was taken, we were already much taller than her, and I recall we had to crouch down. Our heads are touching, and we're all smiling from ear to ear.

Everything is exactly how I remember it.

With one major difference.

The scent.

Taking a deep breath, I run my hands through my hair and lean against the counter. Her home smells like it used to. Clean and tidy. Flowery, like rose candles and soap. Only the familiar scent of freshly baked swirled butter cookies is missing. Gran used to make them in an old-fashioned piping she inherited from her mom—who inherited it from hers—and I can still taste the crumbly, light texture melting in my mouth. They were the absolute best.

When I got the call about Gran, it was like a punch to the gut. She was the one who raised me after both my parents died. Even before then, she was the only person who understood me. She had infinite patience with me, I can see that looking back. Gran hadn't been happy when I'd moved to San Francisco after high school, but she'd supported me anyway. Shortly after I left, she moved out of the apartment where she raised me, saying it was too big. She needed something a little smaller, somewhere that wasn't filled with old memories.

Now I'm back, and she isn't here.

I'm still pissed I couldn't make it to the funeral in time. I was on the road, wrapping a few things up, and didn't get the call until a few days after her death. Between that and several flight delays and cancellations, by the time I made it to New York, it was too late.

My eyes sting, and I shrug it off. I refuse to think about that right now. *You need to be on your guard for the nightmare you're about to walk into,* I tell myself.

It's easy not to dwell on the grief, because "the little surprise" in her will has been consuming my thoughts ever since I found out.

What in the name of all things holy were you thinking, Gran, huh?

I know Gran always wanted me to settle down and get married, but I still don't understand why she was hell-bent on Josephine being the one. Josephine Graham. Little well-behaved "good as gold" Josie with her frizzy hair, long pigtails that begged to be pulled, scatterbrain and nosiness—Nosy Josie. That was her nickname. One I'm still secretly proud of, even all these years later.

I still can't fathom why she's going along with this. The grandmother of an old childhood classmate (one you obviously hate with every fiber of your being) dies and tells you that you'll gain an inheritance if you stay married to him for a month and you say *yes*?

She must be really bored—or really desperate.

Yeah, I'm banking on the desperate part. People will do anything for money.

Gran wanted us together, but I never thought she would go *this* far. But I'll settle my beef with her in the afterlife. You hear, Gran? Right now, I not only have to prepare to get married, but it has to be to the most annoying, chaotic, and nosy person on the planet.

After I hang my biker jacket on one of the hooks near the entrance and adjust my tie, I head into the kitchen. Opening the refrigerator, I realize I'm starving, until I remember there's nothing here. Shit. It's late, but New York City never sleeps. I'm sure someone is still open for delivery.

Before I can get out my phone, I hear keys rattling in the door. I head to the living room to find out who the hell would dare let themselves into my gran's—*my* apartment—wait, unless *she* has a key.

The door opens, and I stop in my tracks.

I stare at a beautiful woman.

It's not *her*.

She's wearing black pants and a polo shirt, which is clearly a uniform. Her shirt is the brightest pink. Like, almost blindingly bright. But as far as one can say of this color, it suits her. Her clothes hug her curvy frame. A few strands of her blonde hair have escaped the messy bun atop her head, and my fingers itch to reach out and tuck them behind her ear.

After dropping her bags next to mine in a heaping mess—irritatingly so—she shifts to face me, chocolate-brown eyes narrowed in what seems to be distrust.

"Callum." Her voice is tight.

Josie? *This* is Josie?

There's *no* fucking way this woman is the same goody two-shoes who rolled her eyes every time I spoke. My gaze lands on the name tag on her uniform.

"Josephine," I say, using her full name just as she used mine. "It's been a long time."

"Not long enough."

And there it is. The attitude I'm so familiar with. Yeah, it's her. Her looks may have changed, but *she* hasn't changed a bit.

"I didn't know you had a key," I say.

She twirls the keys around her finger. For other women, this would be an expression of nervousness. With Josephine, the gesture clearly has something provocative about it. "I used to help Mrs. Blanchie from time to time. She made a copy for me."

"So, you just let yourself in?" I arch an eyebrow in question. "You realize it's *my* place now, right?"

She glares. "Well, I didn't think you would be here...considering you didn't show up for the service."

Fucking low blow. "She was my grandmother. If I could've been there, I would've. Not that I need to explain myself to anyone." *Especially you.* I know I don't have to say it out loud.

Clearly, neither of us are thrilled about the arrangement, and even less so about having to spend any modicum of time together. Before she has a chance to respond to my quip, there's a knock on the door.

I push past her to answer it, glancing at my watch. It's 8.30 p.m. He's punctual to the minute.

Vance, the family lawyer from Sanford & Partners law firm, is standing in the hall with a bright smile and a folder clutched in his hands. When he called to ask me to meet him and Josie here, he sounded just as young as ever. Now, seeing him in person, he's definitely aged. His black hair is now gray, and his face is lined with wrinkles.

But his warm smile is still the same. "Hello, Mr. Ashford," he says in a thick Italian accent, "*buonasera.*"

"Hey, Vance. Come on in." I step aside and let him enter.

"I would say it's great to see you again, son, but given the circumstances…"

"It's all right. Vance, this is Josephine Graham. Josephine, our lawyer Vance Lombardi."

"We've already met," Josie says in that matter-of-fact tone of hers. "At the funeral."

Yeah. Right. I don't owe her an explanation, I remind myself.

Josephine gives Vance a polite smile. "Hello, Mr. Lombardi."

"Please, call me Vance. It's good to see you again," he says, extending his hand. She shakes it as he leads us both to the kitchen table. "This shouldn't take very long. Everything's already been drawn up, as per your grandmother's wishes. All I need are your signatures."

The three of us sit, with Josie and I facing each other, though it's evident she's trying to avoid eye contact.

"Let's go over everything," I suggest. "Just so we can make sure we're all on the same page."

"Of course." Vance opens the folder and shuffles a few papers around. "In her will, Mrs. Blanche Ashford named you both as the inheritors of the sum of her estate, which includes this apartment, her storage locker in Queens, and a total of approximately 1.5 million dollars—"

"I'm sorry, *how* much?" Josie asks, her eyes wide.

There it is. Initially, Vance spoke of a "hefty amount." I'm also surprised, but have a much better poker face. I knew Gran was well-off. She always told me not to make a fuss when I took care of her bills and hired a maid to clean for her. But I never realized the extent of her finances. That being said, $750,000 won't change my life. Then again, I'm not here for the money. I'm here because I can't say no to Gran's last wish. It's what she wanted, and I would never forgive myself for ignoring it.

Judging by the look on Josephine's face and the fact that she's willing to go through with this arrangement, she needs the money way more than I do.

"One-point-five million dollars," Vance repeats. "As you know, I was instructed not to disclose the amount until both parties were present."

"Go on, Vance," I order.

"I know I spoke to you both separately, but it's crucial that we're all on the same page and there are no misunderstandings. The sum is to be split equally between Callum Ashford and Josephine Graham upon the completion of one month of marriage. The marriage must be conducted by Mr. Vance Lombardi of Sanford & Partners. Both parties must remain married and living together in Mrs. Blanche Ashford's Twenty-third Street apartment for the entire thirty days. Neither party is allowed to renovate or change the furniture due to the value of the apartment. Only after the month is complete will both parties receive their half of the inheritance and the keys to the storage locker."

"Wait," Josie interrupts, drumming her fingers on the table. "We're not allowed to renovate or change the furniture? We can't even move furniture around or buy new things?"

"That was Mrs. Ashford's wish, yes." Vance gives a nod. "I trust you will respect her wishes."

"Of course. No problem, but it's rather...odd."

Crazy is the word she's looking for. This whole thing is batshit crazy. Although, when I think about it a bit, the furniture and renovation thing is weird, but not surprising. Dear old Gran was an eccentric and loved her antiques.

"Seems clear enough," I say, finally looking at Josephine.

She's staring at me, and her mind seems to be racing a million miles a second. She nods.

Vance draws out a single sheet of paper from a manila folder, and a pen from the front pocket of his suit jacket. He clicks it and holds it out. "Everything is taken care of. I just need you two to sign on the bottom line, and you'll officially be married."

I take the pen first, scribbling my signature with practiced ease before pushing the page toward Josephine. I hold out the pen for her.

Her eyes meet mine, and she seems to ponder.

What? Has she changed her mind? If she's still the Nosy Josie I know, then she's weighed the pros and cons a hundred times over. Why is she hesitating now?

When she reaches for it, our fingers brush. It's only for a second—just the tiniest touch. But it's enough for me to feel a spark—*of something*—but not the good kind. My nerves come alive, and my focus narrows in on nothing but her. Did she feel it too? If she did, she doesn't show it. Annoying as ever. This month is going to be a nightmare, just like I thought it would be.

She snatches the pen from me and signs her name.

Done. She drops it and pushes the paper back to Vance.

"By the power vested in me by the state of New York, I now

pronounce you husband and wife," he says, gathering the paperwork. "Congratulations."

"What happens if either one of us doesn't go through with it?" she asks. "You know, moves out before the month is over?"

"Ah, right. Should either party violate Mrs. Blanche Ashford's last wish, the money goes to"—he flips through his papers—"Mr. Chad Turtlemaw."

"Who the hell is that?" I ask, slightly irritated.

"Mr. Turtlemaw runs a small YouTube channel about endangered algae and desires to create a heartfelt animated film about them, which requires him to own a custom eighty-two-foot cruising yacht, as well as a film production studio," Vance explains matter-of-factly.

What the...? I raise my eyebrow, dumbfounded. I've never even heard of this guy.

"Evidently," Vance continues without batting an eyelash, "your late grandmother was a huge fan of his work, and if you or Ms. Graham renege on the arrangement, there are explicit instructions to give the money—the full amount—to Mr. Turtlemaw."

That is the most ridiculous thing I've ever heard. A heartfelt *animated* film about algae? Okay, I'm all for saving the environment and shit, but how the fuck do you save the environment on a huge-ass luxury yacht? Eighty-two-foot! That's not a yacht, that's a fucking palace.

But honestly, it doesn't surprise me. I told you she was eccentric.

Vance doesn't stick around after that. He's gone about two minutes later—not before wishing us good luck and expressing his sincere hope to see us here again on the last day of this month, with the annulment papers ready—leaving me and Josephine behind to process what just happened.

"Congratulations, Mrs. Ashford," I can't resist teasing her. "Should we kiss now and seal the deal?"

"Hell will freeze over before I kiss you." A hand goes up to her hair as if to make sure I'm not pulling her pigtails. Then she rolls her eyes and grabs her bags. "And there's no way I'm taking your last name."

"Good. After this month is over, we can just move on and pretend like it never happened." I grab my bags as well.

"Fine by me." She shrugs indignantly.

"Fine."

We step toward the hallway, and there's a moment of awkward shuffling. We each try to go first. She ends up pushing past me, accidentally grazing my chest slightly, muttering under her breath, and I let her go because I'm a goddamn gentleman. Also, I get to see her swaying hips while she walks.

A second later, she stops abruptly. "You have *got* to be kidding me."

"What's the problem?"

Slowly, she turns to look at me. "There's only one bedroom."

Sure enough, there are two doors at the end of the hall, and one leads to the bedroom. The other is the bathroom. Ahh, I forgot about that. I look over her head into the room and see the neatly made queen-sized bed with a stitched rose floral comforter and an ornate mahogany headboard. Recalling Gran's instructions about not changing or moving furniture, I can't help but chuckle with amusement.

"Well, shit," I say, smirking at Josephine. "I guess we're sharing a bed, Mrs. Ashford."

End of the excerpt.

Real Fake Husband is a scorching hot enemies-to lovers, forced proximity, fake marriage of convenience romance. It is a complete stand-alone. Definitely for adult readers only. "Real Fake Husband" is available on Amazon.

ALSO BY JOLIE DAY

Next Door to a Billionaire Series

Ever fantasized about living next door to a sinful billionaire? Well, it's time to pack your bags. Get ready for forced proximity, heart-pounding (and oh-so-dirty) midnight encounters, some classic "stern boss" banter, and nights hotter than a New York summer. *All novels can be read as single books.*

The CEO Enemy

Guess who moved in next door?

NYC's most eligible bachelor.

And my welcome gift? A "keep out" sign.

(Jess and Sean)

A Bossy Roommate

Ever accidentally land in bed with NYC's hottest billionaire bachelor? Yeah, guilty. Now he's my boss, roommate and—surprise!—my pretend husband for the weekend.

(Eden and Carter)

Faking It in NYC Series

A steamy hot pretend-relationship series. Grumpy, moody, and licking-lips hot

CEOs meet the sassy, sunshiny goddess. Do you love the fake relationship trope? Yes? Then you'll love this romance series. *All novels can be read as single books.*

One Bossy Date

From fake date to fake fiancée to fake pregnancy. All in one night. Who's the guy? My grumpy boss.

(Zoe and Anders)

Real Fake Husband

He's my childhood bully. I didn't plan to see him again, let alone marry him. But his grandmother had other plans: She left us a significant inheritance. The catch? We have to tie the knot and live in her tiny NYC apartment. For a month. With just one bed.

(Josie and Callum)

Kiss a Billionaire Series

In this steamy-hot series, alpha billionaires working in the same company will catch your eye and drive you wild. Just some good old fashioned romance, comedy goodness, and sexy fun. *All novels can be read as single books.*

Crushing on my Billionaire Best Friend

She's my best friend. Of course, I'd never think about touching Laney. Not today. Not tomorrow. Not ever. Then she moves into my penthouse.

(Laney and Oliver)

Faking It with the Billionaire Next Door

He's my next-door neighbor. My mortal enemy. Cocky. Infuriatingly hot. The biggest jerk I've ever met. Imagine my jaw drop when he asks me to be his fake fiancée. Imagine his jaw drop when I agree.

(Rose and Miles)

Charming My Broody Billionaire Boss

He's the devil himself: Damon Copeland (he practically carries a pitchfork). He's the top dog at my father's company and my brother's best friend. Oh, and someone I *accidentally* slept with.

(Aria and Damon)

Assistant to the Billionaire CEO

I was madly in love with my brother's best friend.

Until he broke my heart. Now he's my new boss: Ace Windsor. Tall. Difficult. Insanely gorgeous. And insanely strict. Never run in the hallway. Never loiter. Never be late. Luckily, I'm Miss Punctuality. Until I'm running late.

(Stella and Ace)

Blind Date with the Billionaire Doc

First, Dr. Jerk ghosted me.

Now, I'm pregnant, and he's the daddy.

Skip ahead 9 months, and surprise! Guess who's delivering our baby?

(Lizzie and Dillan)

CONNECT WITH JOLIE DAY

From a sexy bad-boy hero and laugh-out-loud moments to the happily-ever-after. If you stay up way too late reading sizzling hot romance novels, you've come to the right place.

Do you want to read about the knight in shining armor—specifically, the man in a business suit during the day and biker gear by night—willing to do anything to protect his woman?

Then Jolie Day's books are for you.

Ready for new releases?
Subscribers to Jolie Day's mailing list will be the first to know when a new book hits the shelves. You'll also enjoy delightful surprises and exclusive opportunities to read (or listen to) new releases before anybody else:
www.joliedayauthor.com/newsletter

Read More from Jolie Day on
Jolie Day's Website:
www.joliedayauthor.com

Printed in Great Britain
by Amazon